Fallen Flower

Robert Imrie

Authors Choice Press
San Jose New York Lincoln Shanghai

Fallen Flower

Authors Choice Press
an imprint of iUniverse.com, Inc.

For information address:
iUniverse.com, Inc.
5220 S 16th, Ste. 200
Lincoln, NE 68512
www.iuniverse.com

ISBN: 0-595-19321-8

Printed in the United States of America

For Reiko:
"She is my slender, small love."

The nail that sticks up shall be hammered down.
—Japanese proverb

1

The sign on the bar said *Mr. Dandy.* Two of the plastic letters had fallen off, so actually it just said *Mr. and,* eliciting a smile from Officer Sakagoshi. He was proud of his ability to read English.

"What is it?" Koike, his patrol partner, said.

Sakagoshi ignored him, dismounting his bicycle. He crouched down next to the sign looking for the absent letters. A flattened Coke can lay amid discarded gum, scraps of paper, and the letters "D" and "y". The outline of the missing letters remained on the sign.

"It's nothing," the elder partner said. "This crappy sign for *Mr. Dandy* is falling apart, that's all." He picked up the errant letters. "Go on ahead to the Kinugasa Corp warehouse. I'll put these over by the entrance. That pig Tanaka doesn't give a damn how his shop looks." Sakagoshi reached down to pick up the Coke can, then decided against it. Let Tanaka clean up his own mess. "Go ahead. I'll catch up with you."

"Understood." Koike peddled off on his one-speed Police Special with the mesh basket resting primly above the front fender.

A moan emanated from the front of the building. Sakagoshi turned sharply, in one motion removed the flashlight clipped to his uniform, and snapped it on. A second moan joined the first. He pointed the flashlight forward and headed towards the sounds. Two horny cats snarled at each other. Sakagoshi jumped back and almost hit his head on the store sign.

Sakagoshi continued on towards the front of the building and decided to take a peek inside the front window. He barely noticed the sound of glass grinding under his shoes. What he saw inside caused him to stop.

"Koike," Sakagoshi barked into his hand radio.

"Yes."

"Come here immediately."

"Understood."

Chairs inside the coffee shop were scattered around randomly. One had been deposited on a glass coffee table and jewels of glass covered the floor, winking in the moonlight.

The body lay in the center of the room. "A foreigner," Koike said to himself unnecessarily. He used the term *gaijin*, so unpopular with the foreign community. *Alien*.

She was just about the nicest shaped blond Sakagoshi had ever seen. The form-fitting white knit dress had cinched up to her navel, revealing long, *gaijin* legs, no panties. Koike came in the front door and stared.

Sakagoshi noticed his partner gazing at the body's pubis. "Call it in."

"Yes sir. Right away."

Sakagoshi flipped open his notepad. Victim: foreign, mid-to-late twenties—though with foreigners it was hard to tell. Visible injuries: a stab wound to the chest and a deep slash traveling from one ear, down under her jaw, and up to the other ear. A pool of blood had congealed in her cleavage, which Sakagoshi mused could never happen with his wife. She was as flat as a straw *tatami* floor mat.

Headquarters ordered the two to seal off the building and look for suspects. They went through the motions, but at 2:05 AM there were few people out; no one had seen or heard anything. Until the detectives from Headquarters and the Toyonaka-North Police Station arrived to take control there wasn't much for the two patrolmen to do except watch.

*

Assistant Inspector Kennichi Murakami of Toyonaka-North Precinct showed up 30 minutes later and stood beside one of the squad cars, hands in pockets to ward off the damp winter cold. No need to rush. Neither the detectives from HQ nor his new partner had arrived yet and the two patrolmen had properly sealed off the scene. Murakami's Casio Databank said it was 3:16 AM on a mid-January Monday. The subways wouldn't start for another two hours and street traffic would be negligible until at least 7:00. Plenty of time. He might even have time to go home and shave before heading off to the precinct at 8:00. He was still feeling the effect of too many farewell toasts at the retirement party last night for Detective Tamada. He was thankful that out here in the dark no one could see his red face, blurred with fatigue and *sake*, Japanese rice wine.

There were soon ten or so detectives on the scene, forced by protocol to stand around doing nothing. Though they all knew their jobs, until the senior officer from HQ arrived and gave the go-ahead, regulations required them to sit tight. Murakami could overhear bits of the conversation passing between them. *Who was she? Wish my girlfriend had tits like that. Mine does. In your dreams. Ha. Ha. Even her patch is blond. She probably asked for it.*

The sudden influx of diverse ethnic and racial groups into the most homogeneous nation on Earth had the average Japanese, including Murakami, worried about Japan's future. What would happen to cherished Japanese traditions? A few years ago an American had become Sumo's first foreign *Yokozuna*, or Grand Champion, just the sixty-forth wrestler, Japanese or not, in history. Horrified experts had called for a ban on foreign athletes in the ancient sport. Murakami liked to think of himself as an enlightened man but it still made him nervous to go to certain parks in Tokyo and see more foreigners than Japanese milling about. Now a *gaijin* murdered in his precinct? Foreign decadence was seeping through the cracks.

Perhaps his new American partner, Thor, would help him adjust, as Captain Kume had suggested, but Murakami wasn't so sure. For one thing, he didn't relish the idea of having to act impressed while the guy recited phrases from some Berlitz guidebook. Nor did he care for American-style law enforcement tactics: Shoot now and talk later. He had seen the Los Angeles Riots on CNN. The Rodney King tape. He saw how their cops worked, how they treated anyone without white skin. This INPAC (International Police Associations Council) exchange with the Minneapolis Police Department struck Murakami as just another silly effort by the government to present the facade of internationalization without tangible benefit, save the PR value. *See how sophisticated we are? We have American police working here!* What could *Dirty Harry* teach Japan, a country that did not allow 44 Magnums, about keeping the peace?

Movement on the crossing bridge above caught Murakami's eyes. He saw Detective Eric Thor passing under a street light, looking down at him. Looks just like his file picture, Murakami mused. He'd half expected him to have red hair and a flowing beard like the Thor of Norse mythology he'd read about in school. How long had he been standing there?

"You are Detective Thor?" he called up.

"That's me."

"Could you come down here, please?" Murakami hoped he hadn't sounded too assertive. Like most Japanese, he found greetings and requests the most baffling aspect of the English language. Academic English was rather simple—you researched the topic, gathered the facts, studied the necessary vocabulary and constructed a report out of English sentences like those taught repeatedly in primary and secondary school. The unpredictability of two-way, spoken communication always left Murakami unsure of the impression he had left on his listener. Americans were so unpredictable.

Murakami noticed that one of the officers guarding the perimeter had stopped Thor.

"No. No," the officer said, depleting his entire English vocabulary.

"Excuse me," Thor started. "I'm Detective Thor, on loan from—."

"No. Police, uh, police here. You go."

Murakami decided to sit back and watch.

Thor removed the ID card issued him by the National Police Agency and showed it to the officer.

"*Eh?*" the officer said, motioning for Thor to wait while he conferred with a higher-up. "Wait."

"*Sumimasen,*" Thor said, grabbing the officer's arm. "*Watakushi wa Minneapolis Police Department no Thor desu. INPAC de kimashita. Osaka fuke haizoku saremashita. Murakami keiji ni oai suru yakusoku desu.*" (*Excuse me. I'm Thor from the Minneapolis Police Department. Detective Murakami is expecting me.*)

Impressive, Murakami thought.

After examining Thor's ID, the officer reluctantly began scanning the area for someone to pass responsibility to.

"Detective Thor," Murakami said, in English. "Welcome to Japan." The flustered officer bowed and hurried away.

As Thor approached, Murakami resisted an impulse to rub his eyes. The American kept getting bigger and bigger, like some distorted image in a fun house.

"*Murakami-san,*" Thor said, in Japanese, bowing deeply, "I am pleased to meet you." This also in Japanese. "My name is Thor." He took out his business card and carefully presented it, two-handed, to his new partner, who reciprocated in kind.

"Your Japanese is wonderful, Detective Thor." In English.

"No, not at all," Thor said, in polite Japanese, "I can't say anything." Thor knew that style was as important as the words. Modesty was admired, no matter how false. Or so his teachers had told him. Besides, he wasn't going to let this guy show him up.

"Shall we speak in Japanese then?" Murakami said, this time in his native language. "As they say, 'when in Rome, do as the Romans do.'" He had intended it as humor, to ease the tension, but could not gauge Thor's reaction. His face wasn't giving anything away.

"Sure," Thor looked Murakami straight in the eyes for a few heartbeats, then down at his business card.

Murakami put Thor's height at 193 centimeters tall, 6 feet 4 inches if Murakami remembered his conversions correctly. The momentary disorientation came from his build. Thor was not tall and lanky like a basketball or volleyball player. He looked more like a heavyweight boxer, at least two hundred twenty pounds. His hair was blond, short, receding slightly, combed straight back like Michael Douglas in *Wall Street*. Thor was wearing a dark-blue, double-breasted suit, no overcoat. His shirt was white, the tie burgundy, and his shoes shiny. His eyes were brown, his jaw firm and straight and he was clean-shaven despite the hour. Except for a two-inch scar running up and away from his left eyebrow, he looked like a model out of a fashion magazine, Murakami thought. Or a 21st Century Viking explorer, perhaps.

Thor was still staring at Murakami's business card.

"Is something wrong?" Murakami asked.

Thor pointed at the title under Murakami's name. "Just wondered how I should address you," he said. "Us being partners and all. I studied all the Japanese police ranks before coming over, but no one seemed to know the proper way to address your own partner. You know. My books were full of bullshit role-plays, like asking a cop for directions, reporting a fire. Nothing about one policeman talking to another."

Murakami cocked his head slightly to the right but said nothing.

"Your card says *keibuho*," Thor said, "which means *Assistant Inspector*, right?"

"That's right."

"But I also know the word *keiji*, which translates as Detective."

"Also correct. Very good."

"So," Thor said, "Do I call you Assistant Inspector Murakami or Detective Murakami, or fucking Pokemon or what?" He smiled slightly.

Murakami took back the card, looking at it as though for the first time. The confidence in Thor's smile, the strength he was projecting, made him nervous somehow. "It doesn't really matter," Murakami said, finally. "Assistant Inspector is my official rank and other officers, especially subordinates, use that title. The average citizen, though, would call me Detective."

"What about your partner?"

"Pokemon would not be appropriate."

"Damn. But I was so sure."

Murakami looked at Thor's Minneapolis Police Department card. It read Detective Eric Thor.

"Weren't you informed of what your rank would be?"

"Here in Japan?" Thor shrugged. "No. I just assumed it would be the local equivalent."

"Oh." Murakami said. "According to what Captain Kume told all of us at morning assembly, you will be given the temporary rank of Assistant Inspector, the same as me, valid for one year from your date of arrival."

"Suits me," Thor offered his hand. "Nice to meet you, Assistant Inspector Murakami."

"Nice to meet you," Murakami said, hoping his new partner wouldn't crush his hand, "Osaka Prefectural Police Assistant Inspector Thor."

*

The woman inside the shop hadn't moved, nor had any of the uniformed cops. The view was too nice. Looking at the sprawling arms and legs that a short time before would have attracted a different kind of attention, Murakami tried to imagine the woman as she had been. What had she done in her free time? What kind of books had she read? Why had she come to Japan? Why had someone wanted to kill her? He looked over at Thor.

"What do you think?" Murakami asked the handsome American.

Thor looked at her face. "I think she's dead."

"Yes."

The senior Inspector eventually arrived and the men from forensics got to work, descending like locusts.

2

Thank God for caffeine-laced vitamin drinks.

Naturally, Detective Murakami would not complain about getting home just in time to shower, shave and change before leaping on the subway near his house to return to Toyonaka-North Police Station, where he had been working just hours before. Not outwardly. In the police, of course, there was the possibility of a serious crime occurring at any time. You just had to plan your sleep so that it didn't conflict with your work. That left at least five hours a day for rest, occasionally even at home. Murakami had arrived at 8:00 AM to find Thor already busy at work, his desk cluttered with files, personal effects here and there, as if he had had that desk for years. Murakami wondered sourly how this American could fly twelve hours, work through the night and look like an oversized Brad Pitt so early in the day.

"Good morning, Thor-san."

"Morning, Murakami-san. I hope I haven't broken some ancient Japanese custom by arriving here before you. I was up early anyway, and decided to bring in my stuff and see what my new precinct looks like."

"No, that's fine. I would have come earlier if I'd known, but I've got *kaze.*" The term was usually translated as "a cold" but could include anything from the flu to general fatigue.

"Ah," Thor said.

"Yeah, I, ah," Murakami said. "A retirement party, actually. I was sweating off some of the sake in the bath when I got the call last night."

"I see."

"May I say you look quite fit? Didn't you just arrive yesterday?"

"11:30 last night. Had to change planes in Seattle. Some maintenance problem. Got here 6 hours late."

"No jet lag?"

"You sound disappointed." Thor switched to English and gave Murakami another of those disconcerting smiles.

"No, I just assumed, well, that you would be more tired."

"I slept like a corpse the whole way after Seattle. The train ride downtown and then taxi ride were fun. I'd just checked in and unpacked last night and was about to try the exercise room when I got the call from your Captain Kume, telling me about the murder. Said I could wait till today to get started but I decided heck, might as well jump right in. He gave me the crime scene address and I jumped in a cab. When I got back after we met last night I was too pumped to sleep. Finally gave up and made my way here about an hour ago. If anything, I'm maybe too juiced. Too much coffee, I guess."

"Your jet lag may begin affecting you later today."

"Don't sound so hopeful."

"No, no, I don't mean that. I'm just," Murakami said. "I'm impressed by your resilience."

"Resilience?"

"Have I used the word in error?"

"No. I just don't think anyone in my precinct knows any words over four letters."

"Ah," Murakami said. "Now you are teasing me."

"Maybe just a tad."

"Tad?"

"Sorry. A little. I'm just teasing you a little."

"Ah."

*

The short, fat man sitting across the desk from Assistant Inspector Murakami did not know about the detective's headache. Nor, apparently, would he have cared in any case. He wanted the police to know how unhappy he was that someone had demolished his coffee shop.

"Destroyed," he shouted. "A total loss. It's getting so a man can't make a decent living."

"Mr. Tanaka, please," Detective Murakami said.

"And what are the great police of Toyonaka doing? Sitting around taking English lessons from this *gaijin.*" he made the reference to the lone foreigner in the room sound like a toilet fungus. "That's what you are doing, when you should be out finding the people who wrecked my place."

"And killed one of your employees," Murakami pointed out. "A Ms. Lisa Madison."

"Yeah, that, too."

"Mr. Tanaka," Thor said, in Japanese, from the next desk. "You must have insurance on the property, don't you?"

"Huh?" Tanaka looked around for ghosts.

"Do you have property insurance, Mr. Tanaka?" Thor repeated.

"I don't speak English," he said to Detective Murakami.

"I'm not speaking English, Mr. Tanaka," Thor said. "I'm speaking Japanese."

"Huh? What's he saying?"

"I think you can understand him, Mr. Tanaka," Murakami said.

Tanaka looked around for a sympathetic face. The other officers were deeply engrossed in other matters.

"Well," Tanaka said, "What *were* you monkeys doing? Visiting the local whorehouse? Not protecting hard-working citizens like me, were you! First, I get my shop trashed and now I got some smart-ass *gaijin* GI giving me a hard time."

"That is enough!" Murakami slapped his desk. All movement in the station ceased.

Tanaka's mouth dropped. Police did not usually treat him this way.

"Mr. Tanaka," Murakami said. "A woman was killed yesterday, about ten hours ago to be more precise. A woman working at your place of business. We intend to make every effort to apprehend those responsible but to do that we need your cooperation. Detective Thor, who is not a GI, is here to assist us on this case and you will show him the respect he deserves."

Tanaka gazed out the nearest window.

"Listen to me!" Murakami walked around in front of his desk and placed both hands on the armrests of Tanaka's chair. "I don't care how many tattoos you have on your fat body or whether you have cut off every one of your fingers and given them to some gangster boss," there were a few gasps. Japanese *yakuza* gangsters were the only Japanese who sported tattoos. Normal Japanese learned at an early age not to tangle with such people. "You will stop your pointless whining and disrespectful behavior and start answering our questions—*both* our questions—or I will personally go back to your shop and find enough code violations to shut you down permanently. Do you understand?"

Tanaka's face had turned a dark purple but he kept his mouth shut.

"Do you understand?"

Tanaka gave Murakami the expressive equivalent of spit. Murakami didn't blink.

"Yeah, yeah." Tanaka shook his head.

"Now," Murakami said, genially. "Were you at the shop last night?"

"C'mon, what difference does it make?" He said the words like a boy. "Didn't you see my shop? It'll cost me at least two, maybe three million yen to repair the damage and restock."

Thor wrote down "$30,000 for repairs" on his notepad. He said, "What about the insurance?"

"Yes, Mr. Tanaka, what about insurance?"

Tanaka scratched the back of his head. "What about it?"

"Won't your insurance cover the damage?"

"Yeah. So?"

"How much you covered for?"

"Enough."

"Enough?"

"Yeah."

"Enough to...what?" Thor said. "To repair the damage? To rebuild from scratch? To relocate? To what?"

"I don't know. Enough, that's all," Tanaka said. "I don't have to tell you that."

Thor looked to Murakami for confirmation.

"So you have insurance, Mr. Tanaka. I see." Murakami scribbled something on his pad. "Although we don't need that information now, I'm sure you'll tell your insurance company to share whatever information we need, should we need it in the future."

"Yeah, whatever." Tanaka pouted like a child ordered to bed early. "But it was you guys who let my shop get trashed, remember that. And let the girl get murdered."

"Mr. Tanaka," Murakami said, "as you well know, the only other places of business near yours are boutiques, all closed by 8:00 PM. The nearest apartment block is approximately three hundred yards away and there is very little road traffic at 2:00 AM, the time Ms. Madison was killed."

"So where *were* my friendly neighborhood beat cops?" Tanaka said.

"As a matter of fact, Officers Sakagoshi and Koike were apprehending some youths on motorcycles who had been buzzing the area. Friends of yours perhaps?"

"Yeah," Tanaka said in a low voice. "Maybe they are. And maybe I've got some other friends who would like to meet you."

Murakami made a point of yawning.

"Had Lisa worked for you a long time?" Thor asked.

"About a year, year and a half."

"Did she have the proper visa?" Murakami wanted to know.

"Sure."

"Then who was the sponsor of her visa? Your shop is too small to act as one."

"She was married to some Japanese guy and they had a kid, see? The kid is Japanese, so when they divorced, her visa was still good 'cause she's the mother. You know."

"Uh, huh." Murakami was taking careful notes. "You seem to know a lot about immigration matters for a bar coffee shop owner."

"Hey, that's what they told me at the ward office. You can check if you want. They told me everything was square." Tanaka's crossed left leg was tapping vigorously on the floor and started bumping against Murakami's desk as well. He noticed Thor staring at his open-heel slippers, so popular with gangsters in Japan, and decided to recross his legs the other way.

"And she worked for you for about two years, right?" Murakami asked.

"No, a year, year and a half. Like I said."

"Oh, excuse me. And she was divorced, you say?"

"Yes."

"And her child. Do you know its name?"

"Megan." He pronounced it in two parts, MAY GAHN.

"What did she do with Megan while she was at work? Do you know?"

"Shit, I don't know. I was Lisa's boss, not her fucking father."

"Do you know how old she was? The daughter?"

"Five? Six? I don't know. I never saw her."

"Are you married, Mr. Tanaka?" Murakami had stopped writing.

"What they hell has that got to do with anything? I thought you were all hot to know about Lisa."

"I was. Now I want to know about you."

"Yeah, I'm married."

"How long?"

He thought a moment. "Eleven years?"

"What about children?"

"Two. My boy, 8 and a girl, 6."

"How old are you, Mr. Tanaka?"

"Thirty seven."

"Do you have any other business interests, Mr. Tanaka? Besides the coffee shop?" Thor asked.

Tanaka pretended not to hear.

"Mr. Tanaka?"

"*What?*"

"Any other sources of income?" Thor's smile revealed rows of perfectly white teeth. And those big, round *gaijin* eyes. The women were OK, Tanaka thought, but foreign men looked so primitive, dangerous. "Love hotels?" Thor said, referring to that unique brand of Japanese hotel, with rooms rented by the hour to couples, married and unmarried, young and old. "Protection rackets? Blond prostitutes, perhaps?"

"Hey, I don't have to take this!" Tanaka jumped to his feet.

"Yes, you do," Murakami said. "Now sit down. The sooner you answer our questions, the sooner you can get out of here and the sooner we can find whoever did this. Now, please. My patience grows thin."

"All right, all right." The fingernail on Tanaka's left pinkie was a half-inch long. He used it to dig out a giant booger, which he dropped casually on the floor. "I have some rental apartments in Suminoe Ward."

"And?"

He shrugged. "And a hostess club in Kita Ward." Hostess clubs in that part of Osaka charged anywhere from $70 to $700 per person just for the right to sit down for an hour next to a beautiful hostess who served clients drinks, lit cigarettes and engaged in naughty banter. An owner of such an establishment was always rich, often connected to the yakuza, Japan's Mafia.

"That all?"

"Well, and a hotel in Namba," Tanaka said, glancing in Thor's direction. "A *business* hotel. Strictly high class. No foreigners allowed."

Thor smiled. "Do you get along with your wife?"

"What kind of stupid question is that? I get along with her like any other guy gets along with his wife. She cooks and takes care of the kids. I come and go as I please. How is this finding the guy who trashed my shop?"

"Right now we are mainly interested in finding the person who killed Ms. Madison, Mr. Tanaka. You are interested in helping us do that, aren't you?"

"Yeah, yeah."

"Mr. Tanaka," said Murakami, "what time did you leave the shop Sunday night?"

"I wasn't there yesterday. Like I said, I got other things to do."

"Where were you, exactly?"

The pause was a microsecond too long. "At my club in Kita. You can check. It's called *Don*."

"We will, Mr. Tanaka."

"How many employees do you have at *Mr. Dandy*?" Thor said. "You know. The one that got trashed last night?"

"Four. I got one girl working the daytime crowd and two at night," Tanaka said. "Well, one now."

"What is the name of the other woman on the nighttime shift?"

"Yuki-chan. Yuki Nishimura. But she wasn't there Sunday on account of there isn't much business on Sunday nights. She and Lisa took turns."

"Any samurai in your family?" Thor asked.

"Samurai?" The laugh caused Tanaka to spit on Murakami's desk. "Sorry." He left the phlegm where it had landed. "No, no samurai."

Murakami took out a small pack of tissues and wiped off his desk. "Do you have any sword or knife collections?"

"No. Got some pretty good porno tapes, though." Tanaka laughed at his wit. "Uncut Hitomi Kobayashi. Even some American ones. *Deep Throat. Debi Does Dallas.* All the classics! Want me to lend you some?"

"Uncensored adult videos are illegal, Mr. Tanaka," Murakami said.

"Gosh. I guess I'm in deep shit, aren't I?"

"You don't mind if we send someone over to your house to look around, do you?"

"Suit yourself." Tanaka stopped talking, comprehension creeping over his face. He looked from Murakami to Thor to Murakami. His eyes squinted tighter and his mouth turned down in his best Cagney frown. "Hey, what is this?"

"Mr. Tanaka?"

"Oh, come on! You don't think *I* had anything to do with this, do you?"

"Naw," Thor said. "I just want a peek at those porno videos of yours. Kind of lonely, being over in Japan by myself. You don't mind if I come along, do you?"

3

The woman who answered the door was 49 years old, but looked 10 years older.

"Mrs. Madison?" Thor said.

"Yes?"

"I'm Detective Thor, this is Detective Yamamoto. We're from the Osaka Prefectural Police."

Mrs. Madison looked blankly from one man to the other.

Thor took out his Minneapolis Police Department badge and Japanese police ID, pointing to his name. "We need to ask you some questions concerning your daughter's murder. May we come in?"

"Oh. Yes, of course. Please, come in."

Thor and Yamamoto stepped into the small one by six-foot *genkan* entranceway common to Japanese houses and apartments. Thor and his partner took off their shoes before stepping up into a narrow hallway. Yamamoto put on one of the several sets of slippers arranged to one side, so Thor followed suit. Following Mrs. Madison along the hallway, they passed a closed door on the left, two on the right. The hall eventually opened to a small kitchen. There was a small counter on the right, with a sink and a small 2-burner gas stove. A small refrigerator occupied a space at the end.

A small folding table sat in the middle. Beyond the kitchen were two small rooms, one of which appeared to be a bedroom. Thor felt like a giant in a children's toy house.

"Please, have a seat on the floor in the living room." Mrs. Madison gestured to the room on the right. They sat down on the floor and put their feet under a table covered in a quilt. Thor felt heat emanating from under the table as he sat.

"*Kotatsu desu ne.*" Yamamoto, his temporary partner, said. Japanese for centuries had warmed their legs during cold winters by sitting at heated tables called '*kotatsu*.' Early *kotatsu* where holes in the ground or floor into the center of which were placed burning coals. Tables were placed over the holes, *futon* quilts were placed on the tables, and slabs of wood were placed over the quilts. Families and guests dangled their legs in the pit—avoiding the burning coals—and pulled the quilts over their laps, sealing in the heat. High energy prices encouraged present day Japanese to avoid central heating. Modern *kotatsu* had traded burning coals for heating elements attached to the underside of the tables.

"Would you like some coffee?" Mrs. Madison said. "I've got some already made?"

"Thank you, that's very kind of you." Thor answered for Detective Yamamoto, who did not speak English.

Thor guessed that Mrs. Madison had once been as beautiful as her daughter, but more than age had dimmed her beauty. Her blond hair was a lifeless yellow, stringy and brittle looking. Her mouth was puckered and small, with deep wrinkles around the edges. As she brought their coffee, Thor noticed the index and middle fingers of her left hand were stained a yellowish-brown with tobacco and looked like the polished leather of an old chair. A cigarette dangled out of her mouth, freeing her hands to carry the tray. Her eyes squinted from the smoke.

The grief of her daughter's death did nothing to improve Mrs. Madison's appearance. Tears had freed the heavy dose of mascara around her eyes, sending it trickling down her rouged cheeks. Her face looked like the Wicked Witch of the West in *The Wizard of Oz,* melting, melting.

"I know this is hard for you, Mrs. Madison, but I need to ask you some questions about your daughter, her life here, the people she associated with."

"Shoot, that's all right," Madison said, dabbing away some of the mud on her cheeks. "I checked out of the hotel this morning so I could take care of my granddaughter here. Might as well get it over with."

"For the record, can you tell me your full name?" Thor said.

"Belinda Mary Madison, Tampa, Florida."

"Thank you. When did you arrive in Japan, Mrs. Madison?"

"Just a week ago today, January 6th. I didn't want to miss New Years in Tampa."

"When were you originally planning to leave?"

"Well, I got reservations for this Sunday, the 19th is it? But my ticket is open. I don't know if I'll be able to make arrangements for, uh," her voice wobbled. "For Lisa's body to be sent back home by them." She cleared her throat. "Do you know when the Japanese police will be finished with her...her body?"

"No, I'm sorry, I don't. But I can check on it for you."

"Much obliged."

Thor wrote something in his notepad. "Have you ever been to Japan before, Mrs. Madison?"

"Yes, every year since Lisa got married. Such a beautiful wedding it was." Mrs. Madison's face lit up momentarily. Tears began to trickle down her face again but her voice held firm. "Summers mostly, but a couple of times in the spring for the Cherry Blossom season." She looked confused. "Don't know if you need all that."

"That's fine, ma'am," Thor said. "I don't want to keep you longer than is necessary, so if you'll answer just a few more questions."

Inspector Yasushi Yamamoto watched as Detective Thor and the victim's mother spoke. Detective Murakami had had to attend to a prior case that morning. Captain Kume ordered Yamamoto to replace him, for today. He was a short man, Yamamoto, about 5 feet 5 inches tall, broad and powerful without being fat. He had short thick fingers.

Yamamoto had never been outside Japan, had been as far as Tokyo only once, on his honeymoon. He had very little experience with foreigners and was not totally comfortable with them. Japanese were predictable. Foreigners were not.

Yamamoto was watching the new American, but hadn't spoken with him yet. His Japanese was supposedly good. Could he eat sushi?

Lisa Madison's apartment was furnished as comfortably as any 2DK (two small rooms plus dining room and kitchen) apartment could be. With only five hundred forty square feet to work with there wasn't much allowance for creativity. The furniture was mostly second-hand, inherited from another foreigner heading back home before her. A table lamp stood on the floor next to the futon. To the left of the one window was a cheap plywood dresser and tubular closet for her dresses. The traditional *tatami* straw-mat living room had a huge 29-inch TV and 2 VCRs. A couple of cheap wood block prints hung on the wall. Next to the TV was an expensive oak desk, incongruous amid the rest of the clutter.

Yamamoto's attention was drawn to what was above the desk.

"Lisa," Mrs. Madison said, following the detective's gaze.

Over the desk was a three-foot poster of a drop-dead gorgeous blond, photographed sitting on an old 1950's soda fountain chair. She was wearing black and white saddle shoes, red bobby socks, a string of pearls and nothing else. She was holding a large flower, petals brushing suggestively against her bright red lips. The chair was tilted back slightly and her legs were strategically crossed just enough to hide the grand prize. One large breast rested comfortably atop the back of the chair.

"Excuse me?" Yamamoto said. It came out as *EKU SKYUUZ MI.*

"That's the victim, Lisa," the American, Thor said. Yamamoto hated himself for his inability to speak a foreign tongue.

"That was taken 6 years ago, just after she got here. She met some 'photographer'"—she drew quotation marks in the air—"in a bar, a Japanese guy, who said he was assembling art pictures for a calendar. The exposure," she said, "would lead to modeling contracts, TV, etc. Yeah, right."

"Was this photographer the man she later married?"

"You kidding? No, he was a total scum bag. The photographer, not her husband. No, she met him a few months later, her husband. Said she knew from the start it was a scam but went along for the ride, so to speak, to see what would happen. She had done some modeling locally in high school, you know."

"This was from the calendar?" Thor inadvertently poked one of Lisa's breasts.

"No. He took a few pictures at their first 'session' and made his move. Lisa told him to fuck off, pardon my French, and that was that. She went back the next day to get the negatives and held onto them. Who knows why? After she got married, Hiroshi, that's her husband—well, former husband—found them and had one made into this poster, as a kind of joke, one Valentine's Day. They both had a good laugh over it. That's where she got her nickname."

"Nickname?"

"Tsubaki-chan. She told me that was the Japanese name of the flower she's holding in that picture. It's a Camellia. Japanese call it *Tsubaki*. Hiro used to call her that sometimes."

"About her husband, Mrs. Madison. What was his full name?"

"Hiroshi Kimura, though I always called him Hiro. A sweet boy. Some kind of fashion show producer or something. Lisa said he puts together shows for all the great Japanese designers, Jun Ashida, Issey Miyake, Kenzo." She counted them off on her fingers.

"But they got divorced."

Mrs. Madison stopped counting on her fingers. "Well, yes."

"Do you have any idea what soured things?"

"I don't know as it soured, exactly. More like Hiro came to his senses."

Thor's eyebrows rose slightly. "What do you mean?"

She shrugged. "I'd say he just got to know her better. You can see that my daughter was a very pretty girl." Mrs. Madison looked appraisingly at the poster for a few seconds. "She knew what men liked, had the looks, and was eager to please. I don't mean just sex, though she wasn't too bashful about that either. She'd head out with her friends without even thinking about whether I'd already made dinner or not." Her voice wavered again. "I know how this must sound, the typical dumb blond bimbo, but I don't mean she was like that." Mrs. Madison frowned in concentration for a moment. "Lisa was a kind, caring girl who just wasn't blessed with a lot of smarts. And she under-stood that. I think that's why she was so, you know, easy going. Her men friends had a habit of not calling back after the first date and she never did have too many girl friends. I think Hiro tried very hard to teach her the finer points of life. But it was just too much for Lisa. They ended up arguing about little things all the time. Maybe she thought he was making fun of her and he was frustrated at her for not being able to share his excitement, I don't know. I just heard things second hand. And I'll tell you, he *does* know how to live!" She shrugged and dug out another cigarette. "That's how I see it anyway."

"He was the one who asked for a divorce?"

"Well, Lisa was peeved, of course. She had Megan to take care of. Actually, I think Megan stimulated her mind more than anything else ever did. Did you know she has a photographic memory? Megan, I mean. Like a sponge, that girl is. Quite precocious. Lisa asked me to send her books on child rearing and teaching smart youngsters. Lisa was a good mother. But being a single mother scared her, as it would anyone, I guess. I think she just felt too old for the singles life and was afraid of facing it again. But she knew it was inevitable and finally gave in."

Detective Yamamoto cleared his throat. "Excuse me for a moment, Mrs. Madison," Thor said, "while I confer with my colleague." He translated what Mrs. Madison had said. Murakami wouldn't be back from Momoyamadai till late afternoon.

"Excuse me, Detective Thor," Yamamoto said, in Japanese, happily surprised at the American's relative fluency. "Could you ask her a couple of questions for me?"

"Sure." What Thor actually said was *Ii desu yo,* trying to project both politeness and friendliness to his new colleague. "Just keep your words as simple as possible."

Yamamoto nodded. "I would like to know about the financial settlement. I have read that American women often demand big payments during divorce and, well," he smiled, embarrassed, "she was a *gaikokujin.*" Yamamoto used the polite form *gaikokujin,* meaning *foreign country person,* instead of *gaijin.* His superiors had been harping on everyone to be careful. "And, also, when was the divorce?"

Thor translated.

"They separated about 2 years ago and I think the divorce was finalized about a year later. Hiro pays...*paid*," Mrs. Madison corrected herself, "for this apartment and Megan's preschool and promised to pick up all schooling and tutoring costs for her through college."

"Nothing for your daughter?" Yamamoto asked through Thor.

"No. She insisted she could make it on her own."

Both detectives waited for her to go on. When she didn't, Detective Yamamoto had another question, which Thor conveyed. "Had she been seeing any men since the divorce?"

"I'm not sure, really. Well, she dated, of course, but I don't know if she had any steadies. We talked on the phone once a month or so, and she was pretty good with letters, but it's hard to keep track of someone's life from 10,000 miles away. I live in Tampa."

"Yes, of course. Do you remember any names, though? It might be important."

"Well, a few, but I don't know how up to date they are."

"Anything you can remember would be a great help, Mrs. Madison."

She took a drag of her cigarette and looked up at the ceiling. "I know she was seeing a fellow named Peter Randall at some point." The smoke was collecting on the low ceiling. "She mentioned him in one of her letters soon after she and Hiro split up."

"You wouldn't have an address for him, would you?"

"How could I?" Mrs. Madison looked over at the desk. "But I know she kept a big address book. She always joked to me that she was forgetting everyone's address in the States and couldn't understand anyone's address here. It might be in there." She pointed with her cigarette.

Detective Yamamoto had chosen that exact moment to walk over to the desk and shuffle through a pile of magazines and other paraphernalia. The address book was on the bottom, under a box of writing paper and envelopes and a recent issue of Cosmopolitan. He handed it to Thor, who found Randall, Peter T. listed as living at 3-2-11 Gohshikisoh, Makino, Osaka. The entry included two telephone numbers.

"Any other boyfriends that you know of?"

"A Guy someone. Halpern? Halyard? I don't know. She didn't see him much. Sounded like a real loser, if you ask me."

"Here. Here," the non-English-speaking Detective Yamamoto said, pointing eagerly at Guy Halpern's name in the address book. "This?"

Thor nodded. "Who else?"

"No one that I can think of," Mrs. Madison said. "No, wait! There was some kid who called here last week. A Japanese boy. I made a note." She rummaged in her purse, pulling out a scrap of paper. "Here it is! Minoru." She pronounced it MEE NORRR OOH "Yes. I forgot all about him."

"Minoru what?"

"I don't know." She flipped the paper over and showed it to Thor. "I only spoke to him that one time. I asked if he wanted to leave his number and he said Lisa already knew it. He just asked me to tell her Minoru called." Her eyes filled up again. "I never got around to telling her."

Thor let his eyes wander around the room as he gave Mrs. Madison time to collect herself.

"Had your daughter ever mentioned him before? In a letter or on the phone or since you got here?" Thor rifled through the pages of the address book. No Minoru under 'M'.

"I don't think so." She shook her head. "Damn! I'm just not sure."

"That's all right," Thor said. "Do you mind if we take the address book with us, Mrs. Madison?"

"No, go right ahead."

"Your daughter had been working at the coffee shop for about a year and a half, is that right?"

"Was it that long? She had another job right after the divorce for a short time so I suppose you could be right. When she quit that she got the job at Mr. Tanaka's shop." She took a long drag of her cigarette. "He was very good to her."

Thor did a double take. "Tanaka? The owner of the shop where Lisa worked?"

"Oh yes," Mrs. Madison said. "He was very understanding about Lisa's special situation, her being a single parent and all. I thought that was especially nice in Japan, which Lisa told me isn't usually too hot on working mothers."

Thor wondered if they were talking about the same man.

"Did you ever actually meet Mr. Tanaka, Mrs. Madison?"

"Well, no, but Lisa talked about him in a couple of letters. I mean, he sounded nice enough."

"Tanaka has met your granddaughter, then."

"I guess so," Mrs. Madison said. "Yeah, I am sure of it. Lisa mentioned something about him bringing over groceries one time when she was down with the flu and couldn't work a few days. He even brought her a fruit basket and flowers. Damn nice if you ask me."

Thor walked over to the sink in the small kitchen and opened up the window. "Where did she work before that, Mrs. Madison? Before the coffee shop?"

"At some English school. Royal English Academy, I think she called it."

"She taught English?"

"Yes."

"Do you have any idea why she quit?"

"Money, I guess. They didn't pay what they promised they were going to, or they shortened the hours, or something like that. Anyway, Lisa needed more money than they could pay. She did say she enjoyed the work, though. The teaching, I mean. She liked talking to the students. I think teaching made her feel smart. Just didn't pay the bills, that's all."

"How did she get the job at the coffee shop?"

"That I don't know."

"I see." Thor looked over at Detective Yamamoto and motioned with his head that they should be leaving. "Well, thank you for your time, Mrs. Madison. If we need to—"

"Detective Thor, can I ask you something?"

"Certainly, ma'am."

"Are you going to find the bastard who did this? And before you feed me the official bullshit, let's be honest, shall we? This is Japan and Lisa was not Japanese. Do you think the Japanese authorities really give a flying fuck about one little dead American?" Mrs. Madison began to weep again, shoulders bobbing, head down. Thor handed her his handkerchief.

What could he say? How hard *would* the Japanese work to find the killer of this sexy, non-Japanese blond, whom many would assume was just a whore anyway? He knew he might.

"We have just begun the investigation, Mrs. Madison. I assure you the Japanese police will treat the death of your daughter as they would any other." Thor hoped his earnest look was convincing. He hoped his words were true. He read up on current events in Japan. A couple of foreign women had disappeared the year before in Tokyo but the local police still had no suspects. Letters to the Editor of papers like the *Japan Times* gave the impression there wasn't much interest in finding any, mainly because the missing people were non-Japanese.

The telephone rang from the kitchen. Everyone just stared.

Thor cleared his throat after a couple of rings. "Perhaps you should answer it, Mrs. Madison."

"Yes, of course." She crossed to where the phone hung on the wall next to the refrigerator.

"Hello?…Yes?…I mean, no. Who is this?…Oh." Thor motioned for her to pause. "Just a moment."

"Who is it?"

"Some guy says he's from InterBank. You know, that big American bank. Something about Lisa's accounts."

"Let me talk to him." Thor took the phone. "Hello. This is Detective Thor from the Osaka Prefectural Police. Who is this, please?"

"Tab Jansen from InterBank, Shinsaibashi Branch, Officer Thor." The voice sounded like a DJ's. "There seems to be some misunderstanding."

"Who is it you would like to speak to, Mr. Jansen?"

"I'm afraid I'm a bit confused here. This *is* Lisa Madison's residence, isn't it?"

"Yes, it is."

"Is Lisa…Is Ms. Madison in some kind of trouble?"

"She's dead, Mr. Jansen."

There was silence on the other end.

"Mr. Jansen?"

"Is this some kind of joke?" His voice had lost some of its pizzazz. "An American working for the Japanese police?"

Thor explained his situation.

"Then who was that who answered the phone?" Jansen said.

"Her mother."

"Lisa's?"

"Yes."

"Oh." More silence.

"Did you have an appointment with Lisa Madison today, Mr. Jansen?"

"Well, no, not exactly. I've been on vacation in Hawaii and just got back last night. How did she die?"

"She was murdered."

"Where? At her apartment?"

"I'm afraid I can't say."

"You mean somebody killed her?"

"That's right. Now, Mr. Jansen, I'd like to know what business you had with Ms. Madison?"

"She's a customer of mine. Of InterBank's. I was gone for a couple of weeks and decided to check in." Then more quickly, "To see if everything was going all right with her account."

"Had she been having some problems with her account?"

"No, I just mean I was calling to check up on things. You know, kind of a maintenance check."

"Do you look after all your customers this carefully, Mr. Jansen?"

"As a matter of fact I do, Detective Thor. Well, at least my good ones."

"Was Ms. Madison a particularly good customer?"

"Listen, I don't mean to sound flippant, Detective Thor, but, for all I know this could be some giant joke some friends of Ms. Madison are playing. I don't know you, I can't see you, I've never heard of any American police officer in Japan, for all I know—"

"Don't you watch TV?"

"It's on Japanese TV?"

"Yes."

"I see. Well, like I said, I just got back."

"Ask one of your colleagues," Thor said. "Or I'd be glad to drop by your bank with my colleagues and interview you there if you prefer—"

"OK. OK. Look, I'm sorry. It's just such a shock. You can understand."

"Were you and Ms. Madison close?"

"Hey, she was my customer, all right? I was doing my job. Maybe you don't know, Detective, but in Japan companies keep in contact with good customers a lot more than in the States."

"Was Ms Madison, such a good customer?"

"To me she was. See, I handle all the foreign accounts at InterBank. Most of our clientele are Japanese, of course, but we do have a fair number of US and European expatriates. As you can probably imagine, foreigners don't usually keep as much money here as Japanese do—they tend to send it back home—but those that stay long term tend to build up sizable portfolios."

"What constitutes a good customer then?"

"Well, there's no special criteria. But if they're keeping five million yen, say $50,000 or so, in an account I handle, then I make sure they get the best service I can give them."

"Lisa had that much money?"

"I can't really talk—"

"Mr. Jansen," Thor said. "I haven't been here long enough to get all the ins and outs of Japanese jurisprudence, but I'm sure it wouldn't be that hard to get some kind of court order if need be."

"It's not like that. But here in Japan they are really sticky about rules, big, small or insignificant. *I* don't mind helping you out—us foreigners have to stick together, right?—I've just got to be discreet. Hold on a second." Thor heard the clacking of a computer keyboard. "Listen," Jansen said in a low voice. "How about you ask your questions and I just answer yes or no?"

"Twenty questions? Fine," Thor said. "Ready?"

"Shoot."

"OK. How much does Lisa have in her account?"

"I told you, I can't—"

"Right, right. OK, does she have more than, oh, $50,000 in her account?"

"What currency," the banker asked.

"What currencies do you have?"

"Thirteen. The US and other dollars, the euro, most of the European currencies, and a few Asian currencies."

"Well, how about in US dollars?"

More clacking. "In US dollars alone, no."

"Yen?"

"Yes."

"How mu—" Thor caught himself. "More than ten thousand dollars equivalent? In Yen?"

"Yes. Easily."

"Easily. All right. More than twenty thousand dollars?"

"Yeah."

"Forty thousand?"

"Just about. She's got 4.2 million yen. In her yen account. That's about $40,000 at today's exchange rates."

"How about all together? Including dollars and whatever else she's got in there...? Did she have anything besides Yen and US dollars?"

"Yes. She's quite a sophisticated investor."

"All right, then. Adding it all up, is she worth more than, say, one hundred thousand dollars US?"

"Give me a second." More clacking.

Thor covered the mouthpiece and spoke to Yamamoto in Japanese. "Looks like Lisa had quite a nest egg."

"Wonder who laid the golden egg?"

Jansen came back on the line. "At the close of business yesterday, Lisa Madison had deposits totaling roughly two hundred ten thousand."

"Dollars?"

"Roughly, yes. That's including six different currencies, and using today's exchange rate."

"Mr. Jansen," Thor said. "How hard would it be to trace the origin of those funds?"

"Well, back six months or less, pretty easy. Wired funds, anyway. I couldn't trace money deposited at an ATM, of course." Jansen sounded eager to help. "We've got access to *zengin*—that's the system all the banks use to wire money to each other—on my terminal and could print it out for you. Beyond that and I'd have to go through HQ in Tokyo and there'd be forms to fill out and it would take quite a while. You wouldn't want to do that."

"How long?"

"To access statements more than six months ago? Believe it or not, a couple of weeks."

"Just to access some files? What happened to Y2K and updating all your computers? Are you telling me a fancy American bank doesn't have immediate access to customer files?"

"Detective Thor, it's really hard to explain. Yes, we *are* an American bank; in fact we are the largest financial institution in the world. But our presence in Japan, while growing rapidly, is still tiny compared to the domestic banks. And being American owned is, if anything, a hindrance. We are constantly at the whim of the Ministry of Finance for everything from setting hours of operation to how much we can spend on giveaways to new account holders. The so-called Big Bang deregulation of a few years ago, which was supposed to invigorate the financial industry much as a similar plan did in the UK, has just led to more bankruptcies, and therefore, closer supervision by the government. The fact that we are doing as well as we are seems to invite even more scrutiny."

"This means you can't just do a quick lookup on your computer for me?"

"Everything I do on my computer now leaves an electronic signature, which can lead to my dismissal if it is determined that I have abused my authority and/or disclosed confidential client information. And it's not just the Japanese government I have to worry about. We have regular, unscheduled internal audits that are, if anything, stricter than those conducted by the government. Checking someone's account balance I can always attribute to finishing up old work. Accessing old records requires filling out forms, getting them signed here, routed up to headquarters in Tokyo, and 2 or 3 layers of approval there."

"But you said you could access statements less than 6 months old," Thor said.

"That's true, but the branch manager must still input a four-digit approval code."

"So get it."

"All right." Jansen sighed. "Look, you really are who you say you are?"

"I really am."

"Then how about a compromise? Give me your badge or ID number, or whatever it is that identifies you. Is there a hotel near you?"

"I think we passed one a few blocks ago. Why?"

"They'll have copy and fax machines. Copy your ID, showing your picture and ID number. Fax to me here. When I get it I'll fax the information to your precinct? Do you know your fax number there?"

"Hold a second." Thor covered the phone with his hand. "Yamamoto-san. Do you know the number of the fax nearest my desk?"

"There is only one on our floor." He wrote it down on the back of his business card. Thor read it to Jansen.

"I'll have it to you by the end of the day," Jansen said.

"And give me your number at the bank," Thor said.
Jansen gave it to him.
Thor hung up.

4

Mrs. Madison had excused herself to go to the toilet while Thor was on the phone. He heard a door open and expected to see her. What he saw instead was a miniature replica of Lisa Madison.

"*Konnichi wa.*" Thor wasn't sure whether to use Japanese or English with this blond-haired girl with vaguely almond, brown eyes. Her hair and mouth matched her mother's perfectly.

"Hi," Megan said in English, without a trace of the shyness most Japanese kids displayed.

"You must be Megan," Thor said.

"Yes."

"Your grandmother is in the bathroom, Megan." Thor noticed Yamamoto's face brighten considerably at her entrance. "She and I were having a little talk."

"Oh? Who are you?" Megan said.

"My name's Eric."

"Are you one of my mother's boy friends?"

"No," Thor said.

"Oh. Are you a basketball player?"

"I'm a policeman."

"Neat! Do you smoke cigars?"

Thor looked at her blankly.

"You know. Like on TV."

"Japanese detectives smoke cigars?"

"No, silly. Like Colombo. He always has one and he's always dropping ashes on people's rugs and things and they always get angry at him and he always finds the killer. You know."

Thor hadn't seen an episode of Colombo since high school. "You watch Colombo, do you?"

"Oh yeah. Mom and I watch that every week. It's on Channel 2."

Thor didn't know what to say.

"What's your name?" she said.

"Gosh, I'm sorry, Megan. My name is Eric, and this is..." Thor realized that he didn't know Detective Yamamoto's first name. Adults didn't use them in Japan.

"Yasushi." The Japanese detective pronounced it very slowly.

Thor said, "Did you just get back from school?" It was 1:00 PM.

"Yes."

"What grade are you in, Megan?"

"Um, well." Her face scrunched seriously. "*Yohchien.* You say kindergarten in English."

"I see," Thor said. "Then you must be about 35 years old, right?"

"No, silly," she giggled. "I'm five! Almost six!"

"Isn't she cute?" Yamamoto said, squatting down to Megan's level.

"*So desu neh,*" Thor said. *She sure is.*

Yamamoto produced a piece of plum candy from his pocket and showed it to Megan.

"Do you know what this is?" Yamamoto asked.

"Candy!"

"Aren't you a smart girl?" Yamamoto said, dutifully impressed. Then, as if struck with inspiration, "Do you like candy?"

"Dai suki!" I love it! She jumped up and down.

"Here you go." Yamamoto placed the candy in a hand barely larger than one of his thumbs.

"Arigatoh!" She thanked him and popped it into her tiny mouth.

"Aren't you a smart girl?" Yamamoto repeated, as Japanese so often did.

"Where's Mom?" Megan asked Thor, back in English.

Thor managed to keep reaction off his face. *Funny you should ask, Megan. Last time I saw her she was spilling her guts at some dive in Ryokuchikoen.*

"Megan, dear," Mrs. Madison was through with the bathroom. "Are you home from school already?"

"Yes."

Mrs. Madison glanced questioningly at Thor who shook his head. "Well can you be a dear and go to that vegetable stand next door for me and get a few things?" Thor noticed improvement in grammar and word selection when Mrs. Madison spoke with her granddaughter.

"OK."

"I need 1 onion, a tomato and 2 green peppers...Do you know what green peppers are?"

"Pihman. I know."

"If you say so. And one of those things that looks like lettuce."

"Do you think you can remember all that, dear?"

"Of *course* I can!" She was a bundle of energy.

"All right then. Here's 10,000 yen. That should be plenty. Just give this to the man at the store and wait for the change."

"I can buy hundreds of *pihman* with this, Grammy."

"Whatever. Just bring back the change, sweetie."

"OK." Megan carefully folded the bill and slid it in the front pocket of her sun dress. "I have to go now, Eric. Bye."

"Bye Megan. Nice talking to you."

"Me too!" She bounded out the door and down the stairs on legs that had known no sadness, no pain.

Mrs. Madison took hold of Thor's big right hand with both of hers. "Please find the man who did this, Detective Thor."

Thor looked out the window at the little girl on the street below and thought about Lieutenant Colombo always catching the killer. Whatever Lisa Madison had or hadn't been in life, no matter how much or little the Japanese police cared about catching *gaijin* killers, that innocent little girl did not deserve the agony awaiting her when she found out her mother wasn't coming home anymore.

"I will, Mrs. Madison," he said. "I promise you. I will." Whatever doubts he had had before were gone. He would find the killer of Lisa Madison.

5

"Royal English Academy," the voice said, in Japanese. "May I help you?"

"Yes," said Detective Yamamoto. "This is Osaka Prefectural Police Detective Yamamoto speaking. Is the head of your school a Japanese or foreigner?" Yamamoto could not, after all, speak English.

"Our director is Mr. Tamura."

"Fine, then could you put him on the line?"

"Just a moment, please."

The telephone played a muzak version of The Beatles' *When I Was 64* while Detective Yamamoto waited. Detective Yamamoto liked The Beatles.

"Hello. Tamura here."

"Yes, hello," Yamamoto said. "This is Detective Yamamoto of the Osaka Prefectural Police. I need some information about a former employee of yours."

"Yes?"

"Her name was Lisa Madison. Do you remember her."

"I'll have to get her file. Last name, Madison?"

"That's right." More muzak.

"Lisa Madison. Yes. She was a teacher here. Left a year ago last March."

"Can you tell me the circumstances under which she left your employment?"

"Well," Tamura said with a sigh, "she just left, like most *gaijin*. You know how it is. They come in for an interview, all dressed up and looking dedicated, you hire them, they stay a few months, and then they either start to date our students, get lazy, quit, go to a different school or head off to Thailand to smoke marijuana."

"Yes, yes, I understand," Yamamoto said, "but what I want to know is whether you were satisfied with Ms. Madison's work while she was in your employ. She wasn't fired then?"

"No, she was fine, I guess," Tamura said, surprised by the question. "They are all the same, aren't they? They sit down with the textbooks and our carefully planned lessons in front of them and just gab away. If it's a girl and she's good looking like Madison and the student is a businessman, he stares for forty-five minutes and goes home happy. Her record lists no student complaints, if that is what you mean."

"Could you tell me what her salary was?"

"Am I being investigated for something here? Because let me tell you, all of our teachers receive at least the minimum wage as stipulated by the government and we don't hire anyone without proper visas, and if you think—"

"No, no, Mr. Tamura. We are just looking for information on Ms. Madison."

"OK. Just so you know. We run a legitimate outfit here."

"Her salary, Mr. Tamura?"

"Starting salary for all our foreign teachers is 250,000 yen per month for 30 hours per week, 1-year guaranteed, renewable at our discretion. 2,750 yen per lesson for overtime."

"Did Ms. Madison work much overtime?"

"She didn't work *any* overtime. Says here in her file that she had a daughter to take care of."

"So she got just the 250,000 yen per month."

"Minus taxes. Yeah."

"What reason did she give for leaving?"

"Just a moment," Tamura said. "Yes, here it is. Says here she quit to return to the US."

Yamamoto looked up from his note pad. "She went back to the US?"

"I don't know. Lots of them say that, usually just to get out of their contract. Dying mothers, sick relatives, that kind of thing. All I know is that we had no trouble lining up a replacement, so we let her go without a fuss. Can I ask what this is about? Is she in some sort of trouble?"

"Ms. Madison is dead, Mr. Tamura," Yamamoto said. "Don't you read the papers?"

"That was Lisa-chan?" he asked. "I thought the face looked familiar."

*

The fax from InterBank came in around 4:00. A young police-woman brought it to Thor's desk. He looked up when she said, *"Fakusu desu." This fax came for you.* She was wearing a white blouse, blue vest, and a blue skirt that ended just above her knees. She was about four feet eleven and had a cute face. Thor wondered what she looked like without her uniform on.

He smiled and thanked her. *"Arigatoh."*

She nodded shyly and left, her slippers gliding along the linoleum floor.

Lisa Madison, as of December 31, had a $30,000 12-month US dollar CD maturing next month; $40,000 in US dollar cash savings, $40,000 in euros, $30,000's worth of British Pound Sterling, $30,000 in Australian dollars, and the rest in Japanese yen.

Thor dialed Jansen's number. "InterBank, Shinsaibashi Branch."

"Could I speak to Mr. Jansen."

"That's me. Detective Thor?"

"Yes."

"Did you get my fax?"

"I did, but I've got a couple of questions. Is now a good time to talk?"

"All right. What can I do for you?"

"This printout says Lisa has 1,200,000 in her Yen account."

"Wait a second, I've got the printout here." Papers shuffled. "Yes. That's right."

"You said on the phone earlier that she had 4.2 million yen."

"Yes, I remember saying that. Hold on, I'll call her account up on the screen." Clack clack clack. "No, she's got just 1.2 million yen."

"Why the discrepancy?"

"Let me check something else. All right, here it is. It says here that 3 million yen was withdrawn from an ATM today."

"When?"

"My terminal doesn't show that information. But it had to be between the time we spoke and the time I printed out the statement, which was about 3pm."

Thor said, "You mean her account is still active?"

"Not now, no. After you called this morning I filed a report requesting a temporary freeze on Ms. Madison's account pending official written notification of her death from the Osaka Prefectural Police."

"You did that right after we spoke."

"Well, a few minutes after. I filled out the form and gave it to my superior. I assume he put the freeze on soon after that. But he is the branch manager, after all, he does things when he wants to. I can ask, but I'm fairly sure he did the work right away."

"So, you mean that in—what?—in the twenty to thirty minutes after we spoke and before you froze Ms. Madison's account someone walked up and took $30,000 out of an ATM machine? I can't even get three *hundred* out of a machine at my bank in Minneapolis."

"That's what it looks like, yes."

"Don't you guys have any limits on how much people withdraw?"

"That's it, 3 million yen. That's the daily limit."

"Per *day*?"

"Detective Thor, Japan is very much a cash-based society. Checks are almost nonexistent here. Credit cards and debit cards are common, but people still like to use cash whenever possible."

"But 3 *million yen*?"

"People even pay for cars in cash sometimes. ATMs are practically everywhere. Violent crime is still pretty rare here so people don't worry about getting robbed. I had a customer come in last week and empty 15 million yen, about $150,000, right on my desk. Changed it all to US dollars."

"I see." Thor was drawing concentric circles around the numbers in the fax. "Then that means that someone had Lisa's ATM card."

"That's right."

"Were there duplicate cards or did Lisa have just the one?"

"I've already checked. Just the one."

Thor drew spokes in the circles. "What about the other currencies? Can they be drawn from some special kind of ATM?"

"No. Just Yen."

"All right, thanks."

"Detective Thor, I didn't know Lisa really well, but we spoke on the phone a lot and she came to the bank a few times. She was pretty popular here—as a person, not just because she had some much money deposited—and I'd like to help in any way I can. Just let me know."

"Thanks," Thor said, now making boxes around his circles. "I'll let you know if we need anything."

*

Thor put down his pencil and massaged his eyes. Theft was a possible motive. The killer had taken her ATM card, leaving the rest of the wallet's contents intact. The killer knew Lisa had a lot of money. Question: did the killer / thief know there was more in the account? Had this started as a simple robbery that escalated? Then why go to the trouble of trashing the coffee shop? Subterfuge? Was Lisa even the primary target or was her murder some elaborate scam? Could her death have been a warning from one of Tanaka's yakuza friends, perhaps? Or one of Lisa's friends?

He picked up Lisa Madison's address book and looked up the address and phone number of her ex-husband and found a listing for Cosmo Fashion International, Athens Building, Suite 103, 24th Fl, 2-23 1-Chome, Umeda, Osaka. Thor dialed the number listed. The receptionist answered on the first ring.

"*CF International desu.*"

"Yes, hello." Jet lag was beginning to catch up with him and he decided he had spoken enough Japanese for the day.

"Eh?"

"I'd like to speak to Mr. Kimura, please."

"*Dochirasama desu ka?*" *Who is this, please?*

"Excuse me," Thor said slowly, "do you speak English."

"Just a second, OK?"

The voice that came back on the line was rather deep for a Japanese and brimming with self-confidence. "Good afternoon. This is Hiro Kimura speaking? May I help you?"

"Hello, Mr. Kimura. This is Detective Eric Thor of the Osaka Prefectural Police."

"What?"

"I'm actually part of the Minneapolis Police Department, on loan with the Osaka Police."

"I see," Kimura said. "Well, what do you want?" Thor knew from experience how much difficulty even the most fluent Japanese had in mastering polite English, a problem made more difficult by the fact that most of their teachers were recent American college graduates more comfortable with *Austin Powers* idioms than *Harvard Business School* power English. The tone of Kimura's voice indicated simple curiosity even if the choice of words seemed to say, "Hey, buddy, what the hell do you want?"

"I'm sorry to bother you at work, Mr. Kimura, but I'm calling in connection with the death of your ex-wife, Lisa Madison."

"That's OK. I was expecting this. What can I do?"

"I'd like to talk to you. Can I drop by your office today? This afternoon, perhaps?"

"No, today is no good. I have a show in Kyoto until late."

"I see."

"Unless you can get here in about 20 minutes. I have to leave by 5:30, though."

Thor looked at his watch: 4:35. "I'll be right over." He hung up.

"You have made an appointment?" Murakami was standing behind Thor, still wearing his overcoat.

"Where'd you come from?"

"Court. I had to testify about some documents we found at the office of a president of a construction company. He's being prosecuted for bribing a Prefectural official."

"How'd it go."

Murakami shrugged. "He'll probably get off with a minor prison term, suspended for a few years, after which time everyone will have forgotten about him and he will live happily ever after."

"Fun."

"Yeah."

Thor told him about his appointment with Kimura. "Want to go?"

"Sure."

Thor filled his partner in on what he had learned about Madison's finances. He already had Yamamoto's notes from his call to the Royal English Academy.

"Say," Thor said, grabbing his briefcase. "I thought you wanted us to speak in Japanese."

"I'm Japanese, Detective Thor," Murakami said, as if that explained everything.

"Call me Eric." He pushed the elevator button, wondering what the hell his partner meant.

"Ah, now that would create a dilemma," Murakami said. "If I call you Eric, then you must call me Ken. But I don't want to be called Ken. Ken is an Americanism, a kind of cultural anthropomorphism Americans use to make Japanese seem less the little yellow race and more palatable to the great white masses."

Thor looked down at his partner.

"Or so my sociology professor used to say. On the other hand, calling me just Murakami would probably be awkward for you, since you Americans insist on attaching 'Mr. to a last name."

Thor continued to stare. "You sure know a lot of big words for a little yellow bastard."

"Now you are utilizing gentle invective to promote male bonding. I know this because I am a big fan of cop 'buddy' movies."

"You sound like a cross between Spock and Data."

"*Star Trek* and *Star Trek: The Next Generation.* Yes, I am fans of those programs as well."

"Japanese like big words. The bigger the word, the less susceptible it is to the vagaries of colloquialisms."

"Vagaries?"

"Plus I was a psychology major."

"How come you didn't talk like this yesterday?"

"I just met you. I was still shy."

"And now you are not."

"No, I am beginning to understand you more, to 'get a handle on you', shall we say?"

"You're a robot."

"Not at all," Murakami said seriously. "How's this? You call me Murakami-san and I'll call you Thor-san."

"Fine. Except I thought we were already doing that. But you still haven't answered my question," Thor said. He was beginning to like his bespectacled, slightly nerdy partner. "Why the sudden switch to English? What about the 'Do as the Roman's do...' speech last night?"

"As I told you, Thor-san, I am Japanese."

"So?"

"That means I am genetically programmed to say I hate speaking English, even if I don't."

"But you speak so well."

"Ah, I see that you, Thor-san, have been programmed in how to respond Japanese style. I say my English is terrible, you say it is not; I wave my hand and lower my head in mock modesty, you insist you are sincere; I finally accept the compliment, reluctantly. Very Japanese. You have prepared well."

"You're American, right?"

"Nope," Murakami said. "Japanese, born and bred."

"You didn't learn to speak English like that here in Japan."

"Oh sank yuu bery machi, Mihstah!" he said. Thor chuckled, and Murakami inwardly heaved a sigh of relief that his attempts at humor had been accepted. "Actually, I went to UC Berkeley for four years."

"You studied psychology at an American school?"

"Yes, and I am happy I did. The experience was very good for me in terms of learning more about how you Americans think."

"What are you, a spy?"

"No." Now it was Murakami's turn to laugh. "I just feel embarrassed sometimes at how little Japan and my people know about America. We study your history in school, watch your movies, and read about you in the papers, yet our politicians go overseas and look like overgrown children, even to us. Not just because so many of them are short," another laugh, "but because of the way they act. So stiff, so, what can I say, unworldly? And when I was in high school I thought, how can they be so clumsy when we Japanese study so much about foreign countries and almost everybody went to Hawaii or LA on their honeymoon. We practically owned the rest of the world in the 1980s and early 1990s, but nobody wanted us at their parties."

They had reached the subway platform and lined up for the next train, which the schedule said would arrive at 4:45. Thor looked at his watch just as he heard the blare of the subway horn. Four-forty-five. Right on time. Japanese subways were always on time. The trains were always on time. His Toyota Camry at home had never broken down. His SONY VCR could be set to tape every Monday Night Football game from now until the 23rd century. Yet he found himself agreeing with many of his partner's observations. Thor would never have confessed it publicly, but pictures of assembled world leaders *did* always look like several adults and a child. Not just because the Japanese were often a foot shorter than everyone else, but because they were so awkward, unable to engage in small talk. They looked like the class geek at a school party, better off in the corner of the room. These were the leaders of the world's second largest economy. When some Japanese Diet—their equivalent of Congress—member compared African-Americans to prostitutes or labeled the Nanking Massacre a Chinese fiction, the American media was quick to chastise the individual who made the comment but always stopped short of making an issue of how it was possible that Japanese politicians could make such outrageous comments and continue to stay in power. Japan's economic leverage insulated it's leaders from more serious rebuke.

"Let me tell you two things about us Japanese," Murakami said. "One, we hate heroes and two, we hate to criticize people."

"So Japanese don't mind political geeks."

"We love them. The average Japanese sees the Prime Minister bumbling around with US presidents and may be a little embarrassed, but deep down he is happy. His very foolishness means that he is no threat to become too powerful."

"And if it's OK for the PM to bumble around, then it's OK for everyone else?"

"Yes," Murakami nodded vigorously. "The average Japanese doesn't come out and conceptualize the thought, of course, but that is what we feel."

"You should have been a psychiatrist."

"I thought about it," Murakami said. "But I decided, believe it or not, that psychology is a bunch of bullshit. I could never quite convince myself that society was to blame for a criminal's acts or that serious sociopathic behavior could really be successfully treated."

"So you decided to become a cop."

"First I decided *not* to become a shrink. Then I started looking for a place where I could use my knowledge of human behavior in a more practical fashion. I don't believe in behavior modification, but I do believe in the predictability of human behavior. Police work seemed a natural. I do believe in removing criminals from society at large, whether they can be treated or not."

"Your English is getting better by the second."

"I haven't spoken much English since my college days, Thor-san. I was a bit rusty, and hung over, when we first met. And shy."

Two passengers got off at the next station and Thor and Murakami took their seats. A poster of Harrison Ford holding a cellular phone hung on the opposite wall.

"It's funny," Thor said "What you said about Japanese. I've thought some of those same things ever since I started studying Japanese history and the language in college, but kind of kept them to myself for fear of sounding politically incorrect."

"And perhaps," Murakami said, "also because, when we invest so much of our energy and interest in a project, we would rather not learn that what we are studying or pursuing has flaws, because then we would have to ask ourselves if we were right for studying or pursuing it in the first place. If you let yourself realize what a bunch of weirdoes we Japanese are, you might lose interest."

"In the US when I was in college, you had basically two choices when discussing Japan: Either the Japanese were a bunch of kimono-clad, shoe box-dwelling ants out to rule the world, or they were super-human, telepathic Zen geniuses, rightfully destined to rule the world following the inevitable decline of decadent Western civilization. The recession since the mid-1990s sure squashed those images."

"Japanese are no longer perceived of as nerds, just dweebs," Murakami said.

"Great word," Thor said. "But no, oddly enough the stock of Japan and the Japanese has risen since the slide. Do you remember Kristi Yamaguchi?"

"The figure skater? Yeah."

"I remember the year she won the Olympics nobody in the US seemed to care. She ended up with one minor endorsement deal— National Milk Council or something like that—but nothing major. This was at the height of Japan's seeming economic dominance. 'Buy American' ad campaigns were all the rage. Richard Gephardt was smashing Japanese TVs on the Capital Hill steps. Politicians and business leaders were falling over themselves to paint Japan as the next Soviet Union. Apart from liking Akira Kurosawa movies, it was politically incorrect to say anything nice about Japan. You must have felt it when you were studying at Berkley."

"Yes, but, well, I just assumed it was residual animosity from World War two combined with jealousy."

"It was more than jealousy. Americans thought you were out to rule the world."

"You keep using the past tense," Murakami said. "Americans no longer fear the Japanese?"

"It's more than that. Japanese are human-looking now. Or maybe it's American-looking. You have that *Om Shinrikyo* religious sect that gassed the subways. Mazda and Nissan got taken over by foreign companies. The Firestone tire quality debacle."

"Americans are laughing at us."

"No, Americans see you as human now. We have religious and anti-government nuts like David Karesh and Timothy McVeigh, you have Asahara Shoko. We have failing companies, you have failing companies. Americans can now see Japanese as humans, not automatons."

"And therefore less threatening."

"Less threatening and more intriguing. We always bought your cars and cameras. Now Americans are into Pokemon, Kitty-chan, *anime*, and the Iron Chef. Now we are importing your culture, not just manufactured goods."

"And this is a good thing? Importing Kitty-chan?"

"Maybe not the Kitty-chan, but the more comfortable we are culturally, the better it has to be for long-term relations."

"What about you?" Thor said. What did you tell your parents when you decided to study in the US? That took some smooth talking I'll bet."

"I sat my father down one night and told him I wanted another view of the world."

"Just like that."

"Surprisingly, he said OK. We had not discussed the US that often while I was growing up. My grandfather sometimes recalled the droning of the B-29's on bombing raids and friends of his who had died in the war. But my Dad was so busy being a typical *salaryman* / businessman that I was usually asleep when he got home."

"He didn't care one way or the other?"

"That's the weird thing," Both stared at an attractive young woman walking by in a tight, black knit dress. She carried a mink stole. Thor smiled at her and she looked the other way.

"You scared her away," Murakami said.

"She was overcome by my manliness."

The subway pulled into the station. "I had prepared my speech for a couple days and was all set for a big fight and didn't let him get a word in for about 5 minutes. When I was done, he just said that he knew nothing about the outside world, had never been abroad, and had no interest in going abroad. It was just the way he was, he said. But he had always hoped I would be different. He wanted me to see other countries and to see Japan from the outside so that I could come back and make it a better place."

"Sounds like quite a man."

"The older I get, the more I realize he is."

6

The Athens Building was the tallest structure in Umeda, the most expensive commercial district in Osaka. Three trains and six subways all had major hubs there. Hundreds of thousands of commuters passed through each day to and from work, fair prey to the large department stores and hundreds of small shops and restaurants lining Midosuji Street waiting to relieve them of their money.

The weather was windy and cold—typical for mid-January. Inside or out, the dampness crept into your bones and froze your marrow. This provided incentive for shoppers to spend extra time wandering the aisles of the centrally heated stores.

Thor and Murakami entered the ground floor of the Athens Building with hundreds of others. There were four sets of elevators, four elevators to a set. They passed the section marked *Floors 1-20* and stopped at the *Floors 21-42* section. Thor looked at his watch. It was 4:56. Not quitting time yet but the throngs of people crowding into each and every elevator made him feel like he was on the Midosuji Subway during morning rush hour.

They stepped into the closest car. Murakami said, "Twenty four, please," to the beautiful white-gloved, white capped elevator operator.

Everyone else called out their destination, the operator responding to each one with the same "I see" in the most stratospherically polite level of multi-layered Japanese.

"Twenty-forth floor," she said as they reached the 24th floor, bowing as they left the elevator.

"I wonder how many times she bows in one day," Thor said.

Murakami smiled and looked for Suite 103. They followed the doors down the hallway and stopped before a set of mahogany doors with the initials CFI engraved on each door. They opened one of the doors and stepped into a large office with dozens of desks separated by chest-high, movable partitions. Each person was busy with his or her own task. One man appeared to be drawing a floor plan. A woman was pinning some photographs to a corkboard. A stunning young woman with long jet-black hair, wearing a blue uniform and white blouse walked up to the counter and addressed Detective Murakami.

"Welcome," she said.

"We are here to see Mr. Kimura," Murakami said. "We have an appointment."

"Come this way, please," she said, taking them to a fifteen by nine foot meeting room typical of most Japanese offices. There was a medium size sofa with leather upholstery facing two matching chairs, a glass coffee table in between.

"Would you like coffee or tea?"

"I'll have coffee," Murakami said.

"Green tea, please," Thor said.

"You like Japanese tea, Thor-san?"

"I drink it because I heard it has less caffeine than coffee. Caffeine keeps me awake."

"Actually, green tea has more."

"Oops."

She was back a few moments later with their drinks and some Japanese sweets. Thor noticed that the skin of her face and hands were absent imperfections—no pimples, no pock marks, no scars—impossibly smooth. He wanted to reach out and stroke it.

Kimura came bounding in with the energy of the successful entrepreneur. He wore a gray double-breasted suit with a striped maroon and turquoise tie. He did not look old enough to be president of a Japanese company. With his shoulder-length, pony-tailed hair, wide shoulders and long purposeful stride, he looked more like a model than a businessman, but athletic and tall for a Japanese. He turned with a grace that told Thor he was quick on his feet. Thor wondered what sports he had played in college.

"You must be Detective Thor," he said.

"And this is Detective Murakami," Thor said. The two Japanese exchanged greetings in Japanese. Thor noticed that the level of politeness Kimura chose was adequate, though not as gracious as Thor had seen other Japanese use in similar situations.

Kimura took a package of cigarettes from his pocket, shook one free and lit it. He blew a stream of smoke out of the side of his mouth, snapped shut the tiny lighter, sighed, and said, "Who killed my wife?"

"We don't know," Murakami. "Yet."

"How can I help?"

"First of all, by answering some routine questions, if you don't mind."

"No problem." Kimura took a long drag on his cigarette. "But like I said, I don't have much time. I'm out of here at 5:30."

Thor looked at his watch. Five-ten. "How long were you married, Mr. Kimura?"

Kimura did not stop to calculate. "Four years."

"You remember that so exactly?" Murakami spoke in English so as not to interrupt the flow.

"It was the happiest period of my life," Kimura said.

"It was?" Thor said. His face was expressionless but inside he was wondering if jet lag had affected his mind.

"Yes. Come to think of it," Kimura said. "this Sunday would have been our anniversary."

"Then if you don't mind my asking," Thor said, "why did you get divorced?"

Kimura shrugged. "She didn't want me anymore."

"*She* didn't want *you* anymore?"

"That's right."

"May I ask why?"

"I don't know," Kimura said. "I wish I did. Lisa was a beautiful woman, loving wife, and excellent mother. I could not have asked for more."

Murakami cleared his throat. "Why don't we start at the beginning."

"OK. What do you want to know?"

"Where did you and Lisa first meet?"

"In Kita-ku." He turned to Thor. "That's in downtown Osaka. She was working at a club there."

"As a hostess?" Murakami asked.

"Yes." Kimura smiled without warmth.

"When was this?"

"About 6 months before we got married."

"Uh, huh."

"I was being entertained by one of my clients. He took me to a club I hadn't been to before."

"Was this club called *Don*." Murakami was thinking of Tanaka's club.

"No. *Shiki*. Near the US Consulate. Lisa was one of the women assigned to our table. We had already been to a couple of other clubs and I was pretty drunk. By the time we got to *Shiki* I could barely stand up. Lisa was refilling my whisky glass and I spilled it all over her. I felt like a fool and asked her to send me a bill for the cleaning but she said not to worry about it. I went back on my own about a week later to apologize again and ended up staying until closing time. I asked her out to dinner. She accepted. That was the beginning."

"What kind of woman was Lisa, Mr. Kimura?"

"Well, as I said, she was beautiful, loving." Kimura looked out the window. "Lisa was the most wonderful woman I've ever known in my life. You meet a lot of attractive women, especially at clubs, who have gorgeous faces and bodies, but little else. They know how to put on makeup or spend money. Lisa wasn't that way. She was alive. If anything, her beauty was a mask, hiding an intelligent, vibrant woman with a real lust for life. She wanted to try everything at last once."

"This may sound like an odd question, but did you have any pet names for Lisa?" Thor asked.

"Pet names?"

"Nicknames?"

"Well, I sometimes called her *Tsubaki-chan*. Why do you ask?"

"I saw the, um, poster at her apartment of her holding the flower. Mrs. Madison mentioned it."

"She showed me the negatives soon after we met. I made it into a poster one Valentines Day, as a sort of a prank. She was still working as a hostess and I made some joke suggesting that she use that name at her club instead of her real name."

"What for?" Thor said.

"Hostesses often choose aliases for use during their working hours," Murakami said. "Mostly to maintain their anonymity."

"That's right," Kimura said. "And many will choose a foreign sounding name because they think it makes them sexier. I joked to Lisa that, since she was foreign, it might be fun to adopt a Japanese name. I don't think she ever really did. It was just for fun."

"Getting back to your marriage and divorce, Mr. Kimura," Thor said. "I'm still trying to get a handle on what broke you two up."

"I don't know."

"Not a clue?" Murakami switched to Japanese. "I don't mean to be rude, Mr. Kimura, but you must understand how strange your story sounds to us. The picture you described is of a harmonious marriage of the kind most people can only dream. Next thing you know, you and Lisa are divorced. Something must have caused it. An affair, perhaps? Money issues? Problems communicating?"

Kimura threw up his hands. "Megan was born. Have you met my daughter?"

"Yes. She's adorable. Are you saying her birth put strains on your marriage?"

"No, I am not," Kimura said. "You have met the bitch, I assume?"

"The bitch?"

"My ex-mother-in-law, Mrs. Madison."

"Yes, I met her."

"That fucking, fucking bitch," Kimura said. "She was against our marriage from the very start. Didn't want us dating, tried to talk Lisa out of marrying me. And now, here she is, wanting custody of my daughter. The nerve! *My* daughter. She seems to believe that she can just pack her up and ship her back to the US. I have nothing against the US, Detective Thor, but there is no way that monster is getting Megan out of Japan."

"Forgive me, but I got the impression that Mrs. Madison liked you," Thor said.

"Oh really?" Kimura laughed. "Really? Well she is quite the actress." He sipped some tea. "You want to know what happened to our marriage? Her mother."

"How's that?"

"Mrs. Madison hated Lisa her whole life. She was jealous of her looks, her intelligence. The stories Lisa told me were enough to make me sick. Didn't want her to take college-track classes in high school, said they wouldn't do her any good. Said she wasn't smart enough for a serious career. Her husband ran out on her when Lisa was still young. She's been trying to make sure Lisa does no better ever since."

"Mrs. Madison?" Murakami noticed Thor's scar wrinkle slightly as he raised his eyebrows. "The Mrs. Madison who is in Japan now?"

"You met her, right? She wears enough makeup for ten people but it can't cover up the tread marks. Her looks were disappearing as Lisa got hers and she couldn't stand it. Always trying to put her down, make her feel like a loser. It didn't help that Lisa was so smart."

"Smart?"

"Bright, intelligent. There wasn't anything Lisa was interested in that she couldn't do well. She had an almost photographic memory, Detective Thor, like Megan. It was hard for me to keep up with her."

"You wouldn't say she was...I don't mean to be rude...slow?"

"Slow? Is that what the bitch told you? She was a genius. She picked up Japanese reading *and writing* after she got here just by studying text books and watching TV. She could read the *Nikkei Economic News* and understand it better than me. She was responsible for whatever I am now. I was a flunky floor manager at Marudai Department Store when we met. It was her idea to start CFI."

"So you are saying that Mrs. Madison somehow poisoned Lisa's feelings towards you and persuaded her to leave."

"Well, after Megan was born things changed quite a bit. You can't be as active as Lisa and I were when you've got diapers to change and formula to make. No matter how much you love your child, it's still a strain. And about this time, her mother comes up with the idea of coming to Japan and living with us so she could take care of Megan. Lisa thought it might be good because of the freedom it would give us but I knew her mother didn't give a damn about her or Megan, so I said no. As smart as Lisa was, she still clung to this silly hope that their relationship would improve, that if her mother saw her new life here, that she would finally accept her. But I wanted to help, so I suggested we just get a baby-sitter. She wouldn't. Insisted on taking care of Megan herself."

"She stopped working." Murakami said.

"Yes. And that's when the problems started. At first I thought she was resentful of Megan, for taking all of her time, keeping her away from all the activities that we used to do. Too late I realized it wasn't Megan she was unhappy with, it was me."

"For not allowing her mother to come live with you?" Thor said.

"For not being there for her."

"She must have understood that you had to work?" Thor said.

"Japan has different customs from the US, Detective Thor. As my new business started to take off, I had to spend more and more nights out late. In Japan it is necessary to entertain your customers constantly, not just provide good products and services. Japanese like to do business with their friends; their friends are those who stop by for visits, for dinner and drinks, for golf. If I don't wine and dine my customers someone else will and then they won't be my customers anymore."

"I see," Thor said.

"Lisa was feeling stifled and trapped and I wasn't there for her anymore, couldn't be. Her mother started calling and telling her what a louse I was and how she shouldn't put up with my excuses. It started to affect her. We started fighting. Why couldn't I come home earlier? Why did I have to play so much golf on weekends? I hired a maid to help with housework, but it didn't help. Ultimately, it wasn't the extra work of having a child that got to her, but the fact that I was there so rarely to share the experience with her, especially after we had been so close before. She tried getting a hobby, studying flower arranging and tea ceremony with a neighbor, but it wasn't enough. When I got home at night, if she was still awake, she'd be all eager to talk about her day but I was often too tired. I'd want to sleep, she wanted to talk, we ended up fighting. After a while we just stopped talking. I came home one Friday night and saw her bags packed."

"The divorce was her idea, then."

"Yes."

"Do you know why she went to work in the *kissaten* coffee shop after your divorce?" Murakami said.

"No idea. A woman like Lisa, fluent in spoken Japanese, I'd have thought she would get work in some trading company or bank, part time until Megan was older. I even offered to fix her up at one of the fashion houses I do business with, but she didn't want any help. So first she teaches English to a bunch of bored house-wives and businessmen and then becomes a waitress at a coffee shop. At least English teachers get decent money. It just didn't make sense. I asked her once, when I went to see Megan."

"What did she say?"

"She said, 'I'm tired. I need a rest.'"

"That's all?"

"Yeah. This was while she was still teaching."

"I would think, if what you are telling me is true," Murakami said, "that she would have wanted more excitement in her life. After being shut up with a child for so long."

"Me, too."

"Then why did she take those particular jobs?"

"As I said, I really don't know."

"I am sorry to have to ask this, Mr. Kimura, but was Lisa seeing any other men? While you were still married?"

"No. How could she? We lived in an apartment and neighbors are very nosy about people coming and going. I'm sure she wasn't."

"And you?"

"You may find this hard to believe, Detective Thor, but no, I never slept with another woman while we were married. If you had met Lisa, you would understand why."

"After the divorce, did you ever think you might get back together again."

"I did at first."

"What changed your mind?"

"I don't know. I loved Lisa but as time passes so does the pain and the love that causes the pain. I thought she might get over it, or get desperate, ask for a second chance."

"But she never did."

"She never did."

"And during this time, how often did you see Megan?"

The subtle change in Kimura's expression caught Murakami's attention. "Did you see Megan during this time?"

"Well." Kimura got out another cigarette and lit up. "The first few months after the separation were pretty tense. And I guess I was sort of embarrassed. Divorces are not very common in Japan." Kimura said to Thor. "It took me a while to realize that, even if the marriage was over, I wanted to remain an active part in Megan's life."

"When did you see Megan again?"

"I guess it was 5 or 6 months after the divorce."

"Was there any disagreement over custody?"

"No." Kimura put out his cigarette half finished and lit another. "Well, yes. You have to understand that I was very upset by the divorce and the shame of having my wife leave me. I am, after all, Japanese. After we were living separately but before the divorce papers were final we had a fight and I told Lisa that she had no way of supporting Megan and that she would be better off with me."

"And?"

"She said no, of course. And I gave up."

Thor looked at his watch. Five-twenty.

"I have to ask this: Where were you from 11:00 PM Sunday night until 3:00 AM Monday morning."

"I was in Hiroshima all weekend from last Thursday doing some preparation for a show we are putting on next month. I got back Sunday night."

"Did you spend Sunday night at home?"

"No."

"Did anyone there see or talk with you during the hours in question."

Kimura was beginning to look uncomfortable. "I was with a colleague."

"One of your staff from the office here?"

A long pause. "Yes."

"Do you mind if we talk with him?"

"It's, ah, he is, well…" Kimura's cool demeanor was falling by the wayside. "It was a female colleague."

"You're divorced," Thor said. "I don't see anything to be shy about."

"I'd rather not involve her in this. You understand."

"Mr. Kimura, we have to establish where you were at the time of Ms. Madison's death."

"Well, you see, Detective Thor, she works here in the office and no one knows about our relationship. These things can be very embarrassing in Japan. Please."

"Mr. Kimura," Murakami said. "We will be discreet I promise you, but we must know her name and we must talk with her. I'm sure you understand."

"Yukiko Matsuda." The name came gushing out as if he couldn't hold his breath any more. "She will tell you she was with me." Kimura looked at his watch and started to stand. "I'm sorry, but I have to get going."

"Just a few more questions," Thor said. "When was the last time you saw Lisa, Mr. Kimura?"

"About 2 weeks ago."

"What was the occasion?"

"I went to see Megan. To bring her *otoshidama*."

"*Otoshidama*?" Thor said.

"New Years gift," Murakami explained to Thor. "Kind of like Christmas, only kids get cash instead of gifts, and it's on New Year's instead of Christmas. Mr. Kimura, how did you and Lisa get along on that occasion?"

"We were fine. After the first few months we had no trouble talking to each other."

"No fights? About custody, money, her mother?"

"No. I told you, I was just angry and ashamed at first. I knew it was more practical for Lisa to keep Megan. Now things are completely different. As soon as I heard that Lisa was dead I checked with the authorities on the matter. Megan has dual American and Japanese citizenship until she is 16 but under Japanese law the father always gets custody of children in cases like this, except in unusual circumstances."

"What about the constraints on your time that you mentioned?" Thor said.

"Constraints?" He didn't understand the word.

"You said before that you didn't have enough time to take care of Megan because you are always working so late. How will you deal with that now?"

"That won't be a problem now."

"Why is that?"

Kimura seemed to consider his answer for a moment before slumping back in his chair. "Because," he said, "I will be getting married in October."

"To Ms. Matsuda?"

The door opened and in walked the beautiful woman who had served them tea. "President. It's time you got going."

"Gentleman," he said, "I really must leave now."

Thor said. "Could you give us Ms. Matsuda's telephone number?"

The woman looked up, startled. "Better than that," Kimura said, "why don't you talk to her right now?" He waved the young woman into the room and motioned for her to close the door. "Detective Thor, Detective Murakami, I'd like you to meet my fiancée, Yukiko Matsuda."

The young woman removed two business cards, handing them in turn to Murakami, then Thor.

"I'm very pleased to meet you," she said to each, then excused herself and left.

"Just two more things, Mr. Kimura."

"I really have to go," Kimura said.

"This won't take long. "It's about Lisa's InterBank cash card. Do you have a duplicate copy of your own?"

"Why would I, Detective? We closed all joint accounts after the divorce."

Thor looked for a reaction in Kimura's face. Fear, surprise. He found none. "Yes, of course. One was missing, that's all. We just thought you might know about it."

"I have to leave, gentleman."

"Well, thanks for your time."

*

Captain Kume read Murakami's report first, then Thor's. He smiled as he saw how many pages the American had used. Thor had requested permission to write in *hiragana*, the Japanese phonetic alphabet students learned in elementary school. Thor could write fewer than one thousand of the more difficult *kanji* pictographs, not enough to read a children's book, much less write credible crime reports. The advanced grammar Thor employed contrasted with the childish impression the abundance of *hiragana* made.

The meeting took place in Captain Kume's office in Toyonaka-North at 8:00 am. Thor and Murakami were seated in front of Kume's desk like two truant students, knees together, backs straight. A uniformed police woman had brought in tea. Thor wondered if there were such as thing as decaffeinated green tea. Murakami clutched his cup with both hands. The room was cold despite the kerosene heater in the corner.

Captain Kume, leaning against his filing cabinet, looked up and said, "What have we got so far?"

Murakami spoke first. "There isn't very much yet, Captain. We have no witnesses, no murder weapon, no fingerprints. The victim was killed with a long sharp instrument, possibly a knife or pair of scissors. The absence of bruises and glass fragments lodged in her body indicates there was not a struggle."

"Which could mean she knew the killer."

"Or was just surprised at the attack. She died of a stab wound to the chest. The cut throat came later."

"Rape?" Kume asked.

"Coroner says no traces of semen, no bruises around the genitalia."

"Theft?"

"Perhaps," Thor spoke for the first time. He told Kume about the three million yen mysteriously withdrawn from Lisa's account, the missing ATM card.

"Anything missing from the shop?"

"Nothing, according to the owner."

"Then Madison was the intended target."

"Could be."

Kume looked at the American and wondered whether he played any Japanese games of skill, such as *Shogi* or *Go*, two games he enjoyed very much. "Then why the destruction of the shop?"

"A red herring?"

"Huh?"

Thor had translated the term literally, which had no meaning in Japanese. He explained.

"So you think the killer may have trashed the shop in order to make us think it was an act of random violence."

Murakami said, "Why not the other way around?"

"What do you mean?" Kume said.

"Maybe the intention was to destroy the shop all along and Madison's murder was just for show."

"And the money taken from her account?"

"Part of the cover up."

"Who would want to do that?"

"A loan shark? Some yakuza boss Tanaka had pissed off or is in hock to?"

"The fact that only Madison's InterBank card, and nothing else, was missing indicates the killer knew her," Kume said. "Pretty elaborate cover-up."

Murakami glanced down at his copy of Thor's report and noted absently the few mistakes in his writing. Too many strokes here, backwards there. Readable, all in all, and rather good. For a foreigner.

"An irate customer?" Kume said. "Boyfriend?"

"According to the owner of the *kissaten*, the victim was working alone that evening and there usually weren't many customers that late on a Sunday. It could have been a customer. Probably weren't many people around to watch or hear."

"It says in your reports she was divorced. What of the husband?"

"Her ex-husband says he was with his fiancée and hadn't seen Lisa for two weeks before the murder."

"Any way to corroborate his story?"

"We talked with Kimura at his office. After he left, we talked with his fiancée, a Miss Matsuda, and she backed him up, though they could have coordinated stories before hand. She says they went to Hiroshima to lay the groundwork for a fashion show and spent Sunday night at her place. We're still looking into that. She was pretty embarrassed by the whole thing."

"Boyfriends?"

"Her mother gave us a few names which we are checking. We also got an address book full of names and addresses. Nothing so far," Murakami said. "We thought about Tanaka, the owner of the *kissaten*, but he says he was at another club he owns during the time of the murder. We're checking into that, too."

"What about the mother?" Kume spoke to Thor as naturally as if they had worked together for years. Thor liked that. Not like some of the others in the precinct who were clearly suspicious of working with a *gaijin*.

"She came to Japan once a year to visit her daughter; sometimes in the summer, sometimes not," Thor said.

"It must be hard for her."

"She did her best to put on a brave face. Her granddaughter doesn't know yet," Thor said. He wondered how to proceed next. He knew that Japanese bosses liked to follow their own prepared agendas. Subordinates were supposed to wait, answer questions and follow orders, not interject their own ideas. "It's just…"

"Yes?" Kume's attention belonged to Thor.

"The description she gave of her daughter troubles me. She as much as said that Lisa was a dumb blond who liked a good time but could barely tie her own shoes. Her ex-husband said just the opposite; that she was intelligent, clever, and imaginative. It was like hearing about two different people."

"People can put on different faces for different people," Kume said.

"I suppose. It just seemed funny coming from her own mother."

"She was jealous of her daughter's beauty, perhaps?"

"Yeah. Or maybe just lying."

"For what reason?"

"I don't know." Thor shook his head. "And another thing. Kimura, her ex, made no secret of his dislike for Mrs. Madison, but she gave us the impression they got along great. Called him a 'sweet boy.'"

"Perhaps the change of culture brought out a side of Lisa Madison that had remained hidden in her home country." Kume straightened a pile of papers on his desk. "Not to say Japanese society is better or worse than that of the United States. Just that, as some people behave differently at work and at play, some people go through a kind of metamorphosis when they move to a society radically different from the one they grew up in. Perhaps the Lisa her mother knew was just as real as the one her ex-husband knew, just an earlier version. Or a different part of the whole."

"Maybe," Thor said. "But what about the mother and Kimura?"

Kume tilted his head slightly to the side in the Japanese equivalent of a shrug. "People are not always aware of the signals they transmit to others. Kimura may have his own reason for disliking Mrs. Madison that she, and we, are completely unaware of. For her part, perhaps the elder Madison is attracted to her ex-son-in-law in a, shall we say, less than maternal way?"

"Or perhaps one or both is keeping something back," Murakami said.

"That is possible, too," Kume said. "I would be interested to know if there are any other sides to Lisa Madison we haven't yet encountered."

7

Nishi-ku, which means Western District, was not a place many foreigners visited, or even knew about. Tokyo had its skyscrapers. Kobe its international ambience. Kyoto the Old World charm. But Osaka, Nishi-ku in particular, was a businessman's town. A roll-up-your-sleeves, cigarette-hanging-out-the-side-of-your-mouth-while-on-the-phone town of endless 2 to 10-man trading companies, lumber and raw material resellers, printers and Japanese sake distributors. Osaka may not have been the most glamorous of towns, but its residents loved to point out they earned every yen they made through business savvy, not by virtue of having been chosen as the capital as Tokyo had been. Osaka had its share of prominent international businesses too, like Matsushita Electric, owner of the Panasonic brand. But it was the little father-to-son-to-grandson companies that gave it so much spunk.

There was a little street connecting Midosuji and Yotsubashi Streets that was full of such enterprises. Nobody knew its name or if it even had one. In the middle of the block was the Hanshin Expressway overpass, a raised highway straight out of Fritz Lang's *Metropolis*, snaking its way through downtown Osaka. Overhead you had shiny cars speeding purposefully to and fro. Underneath were a few shops built into the beams and columns, but mostly just open arches peopled by Osaka's homeless.

On the west side of the overpass was *Tambaya*, a small restaurant run by Mr. and Mrs. Asanuma. Every morning Mr. Asanuma fired up the coal barbecue and grilled that day's catch of eel. Eel was all they served in their tiny 4-table restaurant, and you had to get there before noon if you wanted any. Across the street was *Tenmatsu*, specializing in tempura, cold beer and loud parties that were always finished by 9:00pm.

Fujino was even smaller. Two tables and a counter where breaded veal was served with a side of shredded cabbage. Old Mr. Kishi cooked, waited the tables since his wife died of cancer a few years before, washed the dishes and made enough money to take a trip to Hawaii every May during the Golden Week holiday. Americans might call him *a character*, maybe a *curmudgeon*, though Japanese would be too polite to do that, even among themselves. *Cute* was about as far as anyone would go. He talked your ear off if you let him, complaining about the declining work ethic of Japanese youngsters, the perennial cellar-dwelling Hanshin Tigers baseball team and the high price of beef. He worked until 9:00 PM seven nights a week and slept upstairs in the room he kept in the 2-story building his father had built just after the war.

Nobody wanted to get stuck talking to him but nobody wanted him dead, either. He was a nice old fart.

It's so sad! Everybody said the day he was killed.

Noise pollution was one nuisance the Japanese had not yet been able to eradicate. The government erected sound-absorbing fences alongside the highways and built a new airport in the middle of Osaka Bay so the planes wouldn't bother people. Neighbors were considerate for the most part. But marauding motorcycle gangs, known as *bohsohzoku,* were a menace that defied central planning. Many of them toiled by day in regular white or blue color jobs, stressed out by overbearing bosses. Some lived at home with rich overachieving parents. When most people were getting ready for bed, *bohsohzoku*, either in groups or solo, headed out on their missions of glory, showing the world what today's Ninja could do. Riding motorcycles customized for maximum decibel production, each night meant finding a new highway to cruise or a new neighborhood to terrorize with their engines screaming at ten thousand revolutions per minute. Police on their 90 cc Hondas and Suzukis were too slow to keep up with the 250-750 cc monsters and the squad cars couldn't navigate the side streets. Most Japanese, conditioned to the inevitability of typhoons and earthquakes, put up with the noise, hoping its perpetrators would just go away as soon as possible.

Tuesday night at about 11:00 PM, Mr. Kishi was done cleaning up for the day and anxious to get some sleep. The frosty Osaka winters were increasingly hard on his old bones but his restaurant customers complained if he kept the heat up too high. The cold gave him the chills and diarrhea but he braved it as best he could. As long as he could enjoy his nightly bath, a hot cup of *sake* and a good night's sleep he could make it through the day.

The *bohsohzoku* hadn't bothered this neighborhood much previously, preferring the greater numbers of victims the suburbs presented. When the noise terrorist started his march up the street on this evening, Kishi thought absently that he would zoom past once and be on his way. He didn't. Up and down he went, once, twice, three times. He did race away briefly, but apparently liked something he had seen, and returned.

Kishi couldn't tolerate it this night. He was tired, his joints hurt, he wanted to sleep and he wasn't going to take it anymore. By the time he found and donned the down parka his nephew had gotten for him last Father's Day and got down to the street, the biker had been buzzing the area for about five minutes. Yet Kishi was apparently the only person out of bed. He was practically the only person who lived in this mostly commercial area. The rider didn't see Mr. Kishi on the first pass and he certainly didn't hear him, so Kishi walked out into the street and shook his fist in anger. This seemed to encourage the rider, as he now had an attentive audience. He revved his engine even louder and took to darting within inches of Mr. Kishi before whooshing by on each succeeding pass. The old man kept yelling what a spineless fool the young man or woman was and decided to stand in the middle of the street until he got attention. He would not allow this transgression to continue.

The street was narrow; that was true. But there was plenty of room for a bike, a car, and even a small truck to drive around Mr. Kishi, had it been so inclined. But the old man presented a target just too inviting for this particular rider to pass up. In the light of the full moon, he looked like a gargoyle from one of the video games the driver loved to play so much. It wasn't anger that gave birth to the urge to run the old geezer down. Nobody was around, his bike was singing, the sky was clear and it was just something he had to do. So he did.

He had only gotten up to 40 mph before slamming into the old man, hitting him dead center. The impact lifted him off his seat and sent him soaring over the top of the bars, sailing thirty feet or so before landing on the street. Lucky for him he was wearing his helmet, gloves and leather riding suit. His left knee hurt where it had caught on the handle bars but the suit hadn't torn. Apart from a couple of bruises he was fine. The rider didn't know it, but Kishi The Curmudgeon was dead. The front fender of the bike was crumpled but serviceable. The young man bent it up and out of harms way. The front fork was undamaged and the engine started right up. A fine machine! The left side of the gas tank was scratched where the bike had scraped the street, which was a bummer. He had just paid about $5,000 for the two Guns 'n Roses logos. That fucking old man had just cost him $5,000, plus whatever it would take for a new fender. He decided he had some serious stress to burn off before calling it a night.

As he brushed himself off and boarded his trusty metal steed, one of the homeless denizens of the nearby overpass happened to be returning from his nightly rounds. The man was pulling a cart that looked like a giant, flat-bad rickshaw, piled high with flattened cardboard boxes he had picked out of the trash bins of various establishments. He would sell them tomorrow for a few yen. He watched the motorcycle speed off into the wild blue yonder, then headed for his spot under the bridge and went to bed.

*

There were over fifty uniformed officers around the restaurant when Detective Yamamoto arrived. As senior detective at the scene he was in charge, and obviously so. He was easy to pick out as the man in charge. Despite his small stature Yamamoto emitted a kind of power, a determination.

A search had already been made for witnesses, with little luck. This surprised no one. Hit-and-runs were always difficult to catch. In a business zone like Nishi-ku, late at night, it was almost impossible. Who was out that late? Yamamoto looked down at where the body had been found. Two killings in a couple of days. *What is becoming of my city?*

"Excuse me, sir," his new partner, Miyoshi said.

"Yes?"

"A witness, sir," Miyoshi said, excitement tingeing his young voice. "We may have a witness."

"Who?"

"One of the people under the bridge. He says he saw what happened."

"OK. Let's talk to him," Yamamoto said and headed for the bridge.

There were five or six men living under this particular bridge. Bridges were popular because they kept the rain off. Japan didn't have many homeless shelters, didn't allow people to stay down in subway stations overnight, had no abandoned buildings. Bridges *were* the only homeless shelters in Osaka. Most vagrants staked out their spots and guarded them jealously. Homes consisted of their carts, a blanket, some cardboard or a sheet of plywood, and sometimes a dog or two. Passers by often speculated whether the dogs were for companionship or nourishment. The streets were too full of people and cars in the day to allow for easy movement of the bulky carts, so most homeless just slept all day and scavenged late at night.

"This is him," Miyoshi said.

Yamamoto looked at the man. His age was hard to guess, even for a Japanese. He hadn't taken a bath in so long his skin was a brownish-gray. His had long hair and a scraggly beard. Most of his teeth were gone. He could have been anywhere from thirty to fifty years old. His pants were two sizes too big and the zipper was missing. His T-shirt said "Dick Boy 1" in English.

He looked like a nut but this man had come forward on his own to offer help in finding a killer. He might indeed be a crackpot, but he deserved his chance.

"Could I have your name, please?"

"Ando." His hands were shaking. Yamamoto suspected it was not from fear or the cold. He looked like he might blow away in a stiff breeze.

"Mr. Ando, I understand you saw something last night."

"I sure did," he said. "I saw it all."

"Everything?"

"Yes, sir. I saw the whole thing. You can ask me anything and I'll tell you." He nodded encouragingly. "Go ahead."

"Why don't you just start by telling us what you saw, Mr. Ando."

"I told you already. I saw him." Ando was getting testy.

"And what was that?"

"He was dead."

"Mr. Kishi, you mean?"

"Yeah, the dead guy. I saw it. He was bleeding all over the place. He was dead. And then a bunch of police came and took him away. But you can still see the blood on the street."

Yamamoto wondered if the man was drunk, retarded, crazy from years of malnutrition, or all of the above.

"Did you see the person who killed Mr. Kishi, Mr. Ando?"

"Well, it wasn't me." He guffawed.

"Thank you for your help, Mr. Ando," Yamamoto said, and turned to go.

"It was a motorcycle," Ando said.

Yamamoto didn't turn back immediately. "Are you saying you saw a motorcycle run Mr. Kishi down, or did you dream this in an alcoholic hallucination?"

"Sure I did." He swaggered slightly. Staggered, perhaps.

Detective Yamamoto turned back and looked his only potential witness squarely in the face. "Mr. Ando, we are extremely busy. A man has been killed and we are anxious to apprehend his killer. If you are playing with us I will be very angry. If you have any information on the killing spit it out now."

"It was a motorcycle, yeah." Ando didn't get to talk to many people. He wanted this to go on for a while, but could tell the detective was losing interest.

"What make was it?"

"I don't know."

"Did you see the driver?"

"Yeah."

"What did he look like?"

"I dunno."

"You just said—."

"I saw him, but I don't know what he looked like. It was dark. He had a helmet and dark clothes."

"It was a he, then? You're sure."

"I guess."

"What about his clothes."

"It was too dark, I told you." Ando was feeling defensive. "And besides, I wasn't really looking. When he drove by me I didn't know he'd killed anybody."

"Did you see the license plate?"

"No."

"Color?"

"Blue," Ando said. "Green, maybe."

"Do you know the model?"

"No."

"Engine size?"

"I don't know anything about motorcycles? Shit! I never even got a driver's license." Then his eyes lit up. "Leather!"

"What?"

"His clothes were made of leather. Yeah! I could see the street lights shining off them. Jacket and pants. That's it!"

"Could his clothes have been vinyl? Or nylon?" Yamamoto said.

The light went out of Ando's eyes. *"Damn!* I don't know."

Yamamoto looked around at the squalor. People spent days sleeping and nights wandering around. The boredom must be almost unbearable.

"And a rose," Ando said.

"A rose? The driver was carrying a rose?"

"On his bike. It was on the gas tank. Painted on. A red rose. The tank was blue."

"Are you sure?"

"Of course I am sure." Ando said. "I know what a rose looks like. Sticking out of a pistol."

"Let me check what we have here," Yamamoto said, getting out his notebook. "You saw a man on a motorcycle run down Mr. Kishi and drive away from the scene."

"Well, I didn't actually see him hit the guy. I just saw him get on his motorcycle and drive away."

"What time was this?"

"I don't got a watch."

"And you saw a picture of a rose sticking out of the end of a gun painted on the side of the gas tank, which was blue."

"Or green. Yeah, that's it."

"Well, thanks a lot, Mr. Ando," Yamamoto said. "You've been a great help."

"You bet I have! And don't you forget to tell the newspapers my name! I'm a genuine hero!"

8

Murakami was sitting at his desk watching the American detective fill out reports. What was Thor feeling? Far from home, a new job, new colleagues, new rules. His first case a dead woman from his own country. Did he believe this kind of thing happened every day in Japan? Murakami couldn't remember even reading about another murder of a foreign national in Osaka. Not a white foreigner, anyway. Was he feeling what Japanese felt when they went to a large American or European city? *Dangerous!* He must know that violent crime was as rare here as American cars. Did he fear for his own safety? Thor was as smartly dressed and unruffled today as he had been on Monday, showing no signs of either jet lag or culture shock. Just a man doing his job. Murakami wished he could bore inside that *gaijin* head and listen to what was going on.

"Excuse me, Thor-san," he said to the American. "I've told you my life story but just realized I don't know much about you."

"What are you, senile? I almost pontificated you to death on the nature of Japanese American relationships the other day."

"No, I'm thinking more of why you become a cop? How you came to be part of this exchange program? I hope you don't mind my asking?"

"Doesn't bother me." Thor locked his hands behind his head. He leaned his chair back, so that it was balanced on the back two legs.

Murakami mused that no one in the precinct had ever attempted such a feat, nor would they ever. He also noted sourly that he himself was to short to do so in any case.

"Well, you want the long or short version?" Murakami noticed that the American's eyebrows rarely moved when he talked, even when joking.

"It's up to you."

"I'm 32," Thor said. "I went to law school. My father was a lawyer, I thought I wanted to be one too. After graduation I worked a couple of years in criminal defense but found it degrading, keeping all those crooks out of jail. Made me feel dirty."

"So you decided to put them in jail instead."

"Something like that." Thor said. "There are still plenty of lawyers making sure the O.J. Simpsons of the world are afforded their constitutional right to a vigorous defense. Just not by me."

Murakami opened his mouth to speak but Thor broke him off. "No, hold it. That's not really why. Not all of it, anyway. Truth is, I *was* sick of being forced to help guilty people stay out of jail. But more than that, I got off watching the police go about their business. Being around them during trials, watching what they do, I began to envy them. Envied their ability to apprehend the people committing the crimes. Sure, it's up to the lawyers and courts to actually put them away. But I wanted the rush you get from chasing down and catching the bad guy. Like sacking a quarterback for a loss. Or snatching that fly ball before it clears the left field fence. Do you understand what I'm getting at?"

"I suppose so," Murakami said. "Though I fear that police work in Japan is more a job and less a passion than what you are describing."

"Oh, I'm not speaking for all cops in the US," Thor said. "Just me."

"Then what do adrenaline and testosterone rushes have to do with coming to Japan?"

"I minored in Japanese language as an undergrad at the University of Minnesota."

"Whatever for?" Murakami said.

"Don't sound so shocked. You've got to remember that when I was in college, Japan was still hot shit. I didn't know exactly how or why I'd need the language skills, but I figured it couldn't hurt to be a bi-lingual lawyer once you guys finally took over. Languages, for some odd reason, are not that difficult for me—I studied French in high school—I thought, 'What the hell?' When the INPAC exchange program was announced at our precinct. I applied and here I am."

"You must be proud to be selected to represent your country."

"I don't know about the represent my country part," Thor said, "but I was the only one among the Metro police who could speak Japanese. I think they just figured it would be cheaper than sending some other guy to Berlitz."

"I am sure luck had nothing to do with it," Murakami said.

Thor noticed a small piece of folded paper sitting on one corner of his desk, peaking out from under a folder. He read the note twice, tore it up and tossed it in the wastebasket. He looked around the room, watching other officers going about their business.

Kimura caught his eye. "Something?"

"No," Thor said. He turned his attention back to his report. "I've got to get back to this report."

∗

Wednesday morning and they had precious little to show for their work. The equivalent of thirty thousand dollars taken from an ATM machine with a missing cash card. A few names in the victim's address book. An ex-husband with a personality and views of the deceased quite different from those given by the victim's mother, and an iffy alibi on the night of the murder. Murakami hoped they could nail something down quickly.

Thor's telephone rang. "Detective Thor," he said in Japanese. "Yes. Could I have your name, please? Just a moment." He put the call on hold. "It's Kimura."

"Lisa's ex," Murakami said. "I'll take it." He punched the blinking light on his phone. "This is Murakami."

"Yes, Detective Murakami. I found something when I got home last night you might be interested in. A letter from Lisa."

"When was it sent?"

"Last week some time. She wrote the address in English, plus somebody spilled something on it—coffee or something—so it's pretty smudged. I'm guessing that gave the Post Office problems and led to the delay."

"What's it say?"

"Well, I'd rather you looked at it yourself. Can you drop by my apartment? I don't have any pressing work until this afternoon."

"Certainly. What's the address?" Kimura gave him directions. "We'll be right over," Murakami said, and hung up.

"Important?" Thor asked.

"Could be."

"Let's check it out."

*

Miyakojima was an area east of Umeda, encompassing four square blocks in what was once a run down slum full of flop houses for Osaka's day laborers. It's proximity to central Osaka eventually encouraged new construction and raised property values so much that most of the cheap apartment buildings had been bought and torn down by developers eager to cash in on the real estate boom of the 80s.

The condominiums in Miyakojima started at the yen equivalent of $1 million and went up from there. Money was not the limiting factor; connections were king. Foreigners were, of course, not allowed. And with the advent of tougher anti-gang laws a few years before, yakuza were out as well. Not everyone left Miyakojima during the real estate gold rush days, however. There were equal numbers of ancient Mom and Pop restaurants scattered among the new high-rise condominiums in zoning-free Japan. The shops resembled facades for a slum movie set, picturesque but temporary. The condos looked like transplants from upper Manhattan. One had a heliport on the roof.

The four buildings put up by Nakatomi Construction were known as Brownstone New Town. Each of the four condominiums had names intended to invoke the most expensive image possible, in keeping with the prices and clientele. British and French names were the preferred appellations. Ringing the complex were Wellington Garden, Bon Paris, and Charles. The large center building was Lexington Manor. Hiroshi Kimura lived in Lexington Manor.

The guard emerged from his office even before the two detectives had reached the building door. He was about 60 and wore a blue uniform, hat and gold shield with what looked like decorations for combat valor. A walkie-talkie hung from his belt. On his right shirtsleeve was an insignia containing the Nakatomi logo. He waited for the entrants to address him.

"We are here to see Mr. Kimura in 1002," Murakami said.

He stood his ground, looking over the two men. "May I ask your business?" he said.

"Police," Murakami said, showing the man his ID card. "I'm Detective Murakami and this is Detective Thor."

"I don't know about this," he said. "*Gaijin* police." He shook his head. "I should check with my boss."

"Detective Thor is fully accredited by the National Police Agency and has been assigned to work with me." Thor pulled out his ID, showing it to the guard.

"I don't know," the guard repeated, sucking breath through his teeth. Many in Japan, especially the older generation, had trouble understanding the whole concept of foreigners. It wasn't racism in the Western sense of the word—theirs wasn't the hatred of Southern whites against blacks, or even Hiroshima related A-Bomb anger. Japan had no history of voluntarily integrating any non-Japanese into their culture. They had been closed off for 350 years and then forced to adopt Western business, social and military strategies or be co-opted. The GIs after the war had been nice enough, but no one had asked them here and everyone was glad when they finally left. If only they would leave *all* of Japan, including Okinawa and bases on the main island of Honshu.

Stereotypes are tenacious in all countries, more so with populations as homogeneous as Japan's. Lisa Madison's boss, Tsuyoshi Tanaka, had recalled two of the most popular, and pernicious of Japanese syllogisms—*Americans speak English and all foreigners are American, therefore all foreigners speak only English* and *Foreigners Just Don't Belong*—when he had initially refused to acknowledge Thor's presence and ability to speak Japanese. For many elderly Japanese, the concept of foreigners occupying normal positions in Japanese society was anathema. For the elderly guard in Lexington Manor, the idea of an American police officer, in Japan, in *his* building, was not something he was prepared to deal with.

"I'll have to check."

"Now just a minute—." Murakami tried to stop him but he was back in his office on the phone, conferring with higher ups.

"I'm sorry," Murakami said to Thor.

"Forget it." Thor leaned closer to his partner and said, "When he gets back I'll tell him I have AIDS and that he contracted it by touching my ID."

"He probably believes that already."

"I could kiss him."

"Please, don't!" Murakami said. "You'll convince him the stereotypes are true."

They burst out laughing as the guard came back. He frowned at them. "Give me the telephone number of your station"

Murakami told him. Five minutes later the guard buzzed them into the elevator area.

Thor and Murakami got off at the 20th floor. Walking down the corridor, they found Kimura's door, and pushed the doorbell. There was a small camera mounted just above the button. Thor ran his hand through his hair. Murakami straightened his tie.

The door opened.

Kimura was wearing gray slacks and a white silk shirt, open at the collar. "Come in, gentleman." He headed back into the apartment. "I was just getting dressed. I have a late lunch meeting in Senri Chuo in about 2 hours."

The two detectives removed their shoes as they stepped into the apartment. Murakami did a quick survey of the living room: at least twenty-five *tatami* mats, about nine hundred square feet. Huge for Japan and bigger than many entire apartments. He found an old-style room for entertaining guests, and three other closed doors he assumed were bedrooms. The kitchen contained the latest hi-tech appliances, including a Whirlpool dishwasher, a luxury still uncommon because of its large space requirement. The verandah outside the living room was large enough for a table and chairs. Osaka Castle was visible off in the distance.

"Can I get you gentlemen tea?"

"Thank you," Murakami said.

"Please," Thor said.

Kimura set the glasses down on the *kotatsu*. Unlike the one in Lisa Madison's apartment, table guests at Kimura's *kotatsu* could dangle their feet in a pit custom built in the floor.

"I'll get the letter. You don't mind if I dress while you read the letter, do you?"

"Not at all."

Thor looked around the apartment, wondering how much per square inch it cost. Space, he knew, was the most precious commodity in Japan. He remembered an old Star Trek episode where a race of immortal humanoids had kidnapped Kirk, hoping to extract a virus from him that would pare down their own huge population. The female alien, Kirk's love interest that week, said that her people would kill one another for the chance just to be alone. Thor wondered how long it would be until Japan was that crowded. It seemed almost overrun now.

"Here it is," Kimura handed the letter to Murakami. "You read it and I'll go get dressed." Unbuttoning his shirt, he left the room again.

The envelope was a beige rectangle, with the flap at one end. Standard Japanese design. Lisa Madison had addressed it to 'Mr. Hiro Kimura, Apartment 1002, Lexington Manor, 1-12-3 Miyanosaka 530.' The postal code was right, but Kimura lived in Miyakojima, not Miyanosaka, which was twelve miles away. The ever diligent postal service had somehow tracked down the right address and penciled it in red letters across the top of the envelope.

Murakami pulled out the letter.

Lisa Madison wrote in a standard, concise hand. The letter was short and seemed to have been written in a hurry. It was dated January 9th, three days before she was killed. Today was January 15th. Lisa Madison had been dead three days. Murakami gave the letter to Thor. It said:

Dear Hiro,

I need to talk to you as soon as possible. I tried calling your office all day but they said you were in Hiroshima on business until Sunday or Monday. Did they tell you I called? Call me as soon as you receive this. It's very important!

If I'm not home call me at Yuki's or at Mr. Dandy. The number there is 06-104-4302. Call me!

Love,
Lisa

Thor read it twice before handing it back to Murakami. He was reading it when Kimura came back into the room.

Kimura had since put on an all-silk suit, silk shirt and tie. "What do you make of it?"

"I was going to ask you the same question," Murakami said.

"Well," Kimura shrugged. "It looks to me like she was scared about something and wanted to talk to me about it, wouldn't you agree? But even if it had arrived last Friday I still wouldn't have seen it until Monday at the earliest. What could I have done?"

Thor had taken the letter back and was looking over it again. "I am curious about one thing, Mr. Kimura. Why the 'Love Lisa' at the end? I thought you guys were divorced."

"That was her way," he said. "She signed all her letters 'Love, Lisa' unless they were bills."

"When did you leave for Hiroshima, Mr. Kimura?" Murakami said.

"Thursday morning, the 9th."

"What time?"

"Well, I'm not sure what time I left here exactly, but I do remember taking the 11:49 AM Hikari Super Bullet Train from Shin Osaka Station."

"What kind of business did you have in Hiroshima?"

"Like I said, we are doing a show there and I had things to take care of."

"What kind of things, exactly?" Thor asked.

Kimura turned sharply towards Thor. "What is this? I told you I was there on business. I was doing my job."

"Mr. Kimura," Murakami said, "I'm sure Detective Thor meant no rudeness. We have a murder and are trying to gather all available information. You understand."

Thor's neutral expression did not change as he waited for an answer to his question.

Kimura checked his suit for lint. "You want to know what I did in Hiroshima, right?"

"Yes, please."

"OK. First, I have to check out the banquet hall my staff has arranged to rent. Make sure the size is adequate, that sort of thing. And I make sure the time slot we have is fixed with the hotel. Sometimes they over-book. Then I contact the local contractors and show them the floor plans and answer questions they have on dimensions, materials, and so on. We are very careful in every aspect of the shows. Also, in this case, I have to meet with a caterer, since the guests all get coffee and cake at the end of the show."

"And you planned to be there the whole weekend?" Murakami asked.

"Well, through Saturday, anyway. And since we were already going to be there, I figured it would be nice to spend the weekend with my fiancée."

"What time did you and Ms. Matsuda return to Osaka?"

"About 10:00 PM Sunday night."

"The night Lisa was killed."

"Yes."

"Did you call your office upon your return?"

"At 10:00 PM?"

"I suppose not. Then what about your answering machine here? Were there any calls from Ms. Madison?"

"I told you. I didn't spend Sunday night here. I was with my fiancée. And Monday I went straight to the office. I didn't get back here till Monday night."

"And were there any messages from your ex-wife?" Thor said.

Kimura sighed. "Three. She said she was trying to get in touch with me at the office and to please call her."

"You don't check your answering machine while on the road?" Thor said.

"Not my personal one. Urgent messages are sent to my office phone," Kimura said. "Well, except for these."

"All right," Thor said. "How did Lisa sound?"

"I guess she sounded the way she always sounded. Yes, she asked me to call her, but she didn't say what it was about, she didn't say, 'Someone is about to kill me.' Remember, by the time I heard them I already knew she was dead, so I wasn't listening to particulars. After the first message I just erased the other two as soon as I knew they were from her. Didn't seem any point to listening to them."

"All right, Mr. Kimura," Murakami stood up. "We'd like to take this letter with us if you don't mind."

"Fine. Go ahead." He looked levelly at Murakami, then to Thor. "Are you seriously considering me as a suspect?"

"We are not accusing you of anything, Mr. Kimura. But there are some discrepancies in your story. You have to admit that."

"What time was Lisa killed?" Kimura said.

"About 1:00 Monday morning, according to the coroner."

Kimura sat up, slapping both hands on his thighs. "Then there you are. I have a witness."

"Your fiancée? Hardly the strongest of alibis."

"You don't believe her?"

"I didn't say that. But alibis can be rehearsed," Murakami said. "Or coerced."

"Coerced? You must be joking."

"As I said. We are withholding judgement for the time being."

"How about this then?" Kimura said. "Check with the superintendent of Yukiko's building. The tenants are all female. Every person entering must sign in before being allowed in. I'm not sure, but I believe they also have a video monitor. Their records will show I was there all night."

"We will," Murakami said. "But for now, I must ask you not to take any more overnight trips out of Osaka."

9

Star Motors was in a poor part of Osaka called Dohbutsuenmae. In a country where 95% of those polled considered themselves middle-class, poor to Japanese meant not having enough money to shop at department stores. No one asked you for handouts or grabbed your handbag in Japan. But there were people who had missed the escalator to success so many others had taken. In Japan, failures were pushed out on the streets and ignored. The homeless were not forgotten: they did not exist, had never existed, in the collective consciousness.

Dohbutsuenmae was Osaka's sewer, an eyesore invisible to those who did not live or work there. Businesses consisted mostly of vegetable markets, noodle shops and street vendors hawking everything from used trousers to little balls of fried dough with an octopus center called *takoyaki*.

Star Motors was in the heart of Dohbutsuenmae on the corner of Route 26 and Yamato Avenue, a 1-floor cinder block structure with two auto bays. Hiroyuki Ishida, Star Motors' president and owner, repaired and customized motorcycles. He did most of the work himself, but hired part-time employees when conditions warranted.

Star Motors was dark inside as Detectives Yamamoto and Miyoshi found Ishida crouched next to a large motorcycle, his hands and coveralls covered with grease. He had been putting a new clutch in a Harley-Davidson Sportster when the officers arrived He was beginning to wish he hadn't been such a Good Samaritan. It had taken three weeks for the Harley parts to arrive from the US and his customer had taken to calling every day to check on the progress. *No, Mr. Shoji, the clutch is not here yet. No, I can't take one off a Yamaha. Yes, Mr. Shoji, I'll get to work on it as soon as it arrives.* Foreign motorcycles were a pain but the owners were rich and didn't haggle over the rates he charged. Ishida didn't need this shit with the police but when he had heard the description on the news of the Guns 'N Roses logo he was pretty sure it was his work. He decided to give the police a call.

"You called about the hit-and-run," Yamamoto said after introducing himself.

"Yeah." Ishida stood up.

"You think you did the work on that bike?"

"Sounds like mine."

"Have you done many of this style logo, Mr. Ishida?"

"Used to," Ishida said. "Don't get much call for those anymore. Done maybe three or four in the past couple of years."

"Were any of the bikes you've done recently blue?"

"Well, that's the thing. I got none on a blue bike, at least not that style and not for quite a few years. But I did a complete paint job, including a Guns 'n Roses logo, on a bike about two weeks ago. The paint on the bike itself I got from the US. They call it Teal. Kind of a cross between blue and green." Ishida picked up a can and sprayed a swatch on an old newspaper.

"That could be why Ando kept wavering between green and blue, sir," Officer Miyoshi said to Yamamoto.

"You don't mind if I take this with me, do you?" Yamamoto asked, already folding the paper.

"Sure."

"Have this checked with the paint residue found at the crime scene. They may be able to match the brand. They'll at least know if it's the same color."

"Yes, sir," Miyoshi said. He began to turn, then stopped. "Should I take it now, Detective Yamamoto?" Miyoshi had been a detective less than a year and was very nervous with the older officers.

"No," Yamamoto was thinking of something else. "I'll drop you off at the lab on the way back."

"Yes, sir."

"Excuse me, Mr. Ishida," Yamamoto said. "You talked about roses and guns like they meant something. Do they have some special significance?"

. "Heavy metal band," Ishida chuckled "Foreign band, American I think. Popular with kids five, ten years ago. Don't hear them much anymore."

"It's an American heavy metal band, sir." Miyoshi hoped he didn't sound condescending.

"Who was the work for?" Yamamoto said.

"Hold on. I got the receipt." Ishida wiped his greasy hands on his pants and opened a metal file cabinet, finding the receipt in seconds.

Yamamoto looked at the form.

"Masaru Nakajima," Yamamoto said. "A regular customer of yours?"

"Nope. Never saw him before."

"Why'd he choose you?"

"Don't know." Ishida said. "Custom decal jobs like mine aren't all that common in Osaka. Word of mouth, probably."

"What shape was the bike in when he brought it in?"

"Fine."

"No damage? Scratches?"

"Nothing special," Ishida said. "Usual wear and tear, you know. Couple of scratches. Guy just said: 'Gimme a Guns 'N Roses logo.' Bike was red to begin with so I recommended he either choose another logo or repaint his whole bike. Offered him a deal on a whole paint over plus the logo. Said fine. So I did it."

"It may have been spotted in some other incident, sir," Miyoshi said, hoping he wasn't overstepping his authority. Yamamoto nodded.

"No way for me to know," Ishida said. "I just paint bikes."

Yamamoto looked at the receipt again. "1-14-21 Green Heights Mansion, Room 303 Daikoku-cho. That's not far. We can leave the car here and take the subway. Let's go have a talk with this Nakajima." He turned to Ishida. "Thanks," he told him.

"Sure," Ishida said, and turned back to his Harley.

Yamamoto headed down into the bottomless bowels of the Japanese subway system, with Officer Miyoshi trotting a few steps behind like a faithful dog. Down two flights of stairs to the ticket vending machines, then down another to the platform. The Yotsubashi Subway was a minor line and, outside of rush hours, practically deserted.

Yamamoto had always enjoyed problem solving. He was thinking now about the two murders that had happened in his city in less than a week, one a beautiful woman and the other an old man.

The death of the old man seemed straightforward enough. Some punk out joyriding probably got careless. Late at night, racing down the street, maybe with a pal, saw the old man too late to swerve and avoid him. Could be the old man was deaf, didn't hear them coming.

The time of the murder bothered him. What was the old man doing out in the street that late at night anyway. The hobo they interviewed at the scene said the rider just got on his bike and raced off. That ruled out theft. Maybe it was an accident after all. But leaving the scene of an accident. Did the killer care for human life so little? Just went home, took a warm bath and went to bed? Not out of the question, Yamamoto thought, what with the way criminals were punished, or not punished, these days. Another Prime Minister had just gotten off with a suspended sentence for accepting bribes. Company presidents dealt openly with gang leaders. The anti-gang law enacted a few years ago was a joke. Yamamoto shook his head in frustration and wonder.

"Something, sir?" Miyoshi said.

Yamamoto was staring, unseeing, at one of the signboards on the station wall reminding people not to run along the platforms. What of the police? Corruption was not new but the tone of corruption was changing. Things used to be like the old American gangster movies Yamamoto had loved as a child, cops paid off by whore houses and gambling dens but basically good people. But now Japan's gangs were into importing drugs and weapons, automobile theft, virtual slavery of Southeast Asian women. Would the younger officers like Miyoshi think *Everyone else does it so why not me?* The notion scared him.

The apartment buildings were taller, newer, cleaner in Daikoku-cho than in Dohbutsuenmae. Some people joked that it was the United Nations of Osaka. Bar hostesses from the Philippines lived there because it was close to the clubs they worked at. Foreign teachers lived there because it was near their language schools. Japanese salarymen and their families lived there because it was affordable.

The actual number of crimes in Daikoku-cho was not statistically high but the presence of foreigners gave it a reputation, among Japanese, as *scary*.

The building in which Masaru Nakajima, Suspected Motorcycle-riding Murderer, lived was a 10-story cement structure, walls lined with cracks from the countless minor earthquakes shaking the city each year. His name was on one of the mail boxes. The apartment number under his name read 303. Yasushi Yamamoto and Kenji Miyoshi, Police Officers, walked past the elevator and began climbing up the stairs to the 3rd floor.

Japanese police officers did not usually walk around with revolvers drawn, ready to gun down desperadoes. That was because Japanese citizens did not usually walk around carrying loaded guns. Japanese had not carried swords since warlord Hideyoshi Toyotomi took them all away in the sixteenth century to make plows.

Yamamoto pushed the doorbell of Nakajima's apartment and waited. No answer. He knocked once, then again. Finally a squeaky "Yes?" from the intercom

"This is the Osaka Prefectural police," Yamamoto said. "Mr. Nakajima?"

A pause. "Just a moment." Another pause. "Yes?"

"Could you open the door, Mr. Nakajima?"

"I'm just getting out of the shower. Come on in and I'll be right out."

It is perhaps one of the faults of the Japanese law enforcement system, a result of the low violent crime rate, that police officers are not more wary of suspected murderers inviting them to let themselves in, in a country where no one lets himself in. A police officer the year before had acceded to a request by a convicted killer, in transit from one jail to another, for a knife with which he could peel his own fruit. The killer immediately waved the knife menacingly at the naïve cop, and fled. He remained free for four days. This same insouciance allowed Detective Yamamoto and Officer Miyoshi to walk unarmed, and unsuspecting, into the lion's den.

It was not a matter of intelligence. Japanese police were highly trained and drilled to respond to a variety of circumstances. Murderers wielding shot guns was just not in any of the seminars. Yamamoto and Miyoshi were no more expecting to be shot at than they were expecting to meet Mothra The Monster. When they entered apartment 303 of Green Heights Mansion, they could perhaps be forgiven for not anticipating the events that followed. Yamamoto said *"Ojamashimasu"* as was the polite thing to do upon entering a home, and bent over to take off his shoes. This spared his life and gave Masaru Nakajima, Suspected Murderer, a clear shot at Junnichi Miyoshi, Soon-To-Die Police Officer. Yamamoto heard a BOOM and instinctively dropped to the floor. He heard an OOOFF as buck shot entered the chest, and blood and air exited Officer Miyoshi's body. He felt Miyoshi's body fall on top of him. He did not see Nakajima but heard him scream something incomprehensible before jumping over the two prostrate officers and heading down the hall.

Yamamoto rolled out from under the young policeman, careful to keep the boy's head from striking the floor. He ran into the apartment, shoes on, and found the phone, from where he dialed Osaka Prefectural Headquarters in Temmabashi, ordering up an ambulance. Miyoshi was gurgling up foamy red spit, wheezing in big gasps of air. His eyes were looking straight up until Yamamoto squatted down beside him, at which point he started blinking rapidly. Yamamoto surveyed the carnage that had been a young, healthy body and felt more useless than he had in his entire life. The hole in Miyoshi's chest was the size of a baseball. So much blood had already soaked his clothes that Yamamoto wondered how much more there could be. He tucked his legs under his knees and rested the young officer's head in his lap.

"You'll be fine," he said.

Miyoshi's chest heaved; his right hand reached up momentarily, grasping at something, nothing, before dropping back to the floor. He looked up into Yamamoto's eyes, said, "Sumimasen," he said—*I beg your pardon*—and was gone.

"I beg your pardon." Yamamoto said, closing his young comrade's eyes.

10

Foreign residents often complained of xenophobia.

Japanese hadn't felt comfortable with any outsiders, foreign or domestic since Shogun Ieyasu Tokugawa in the 17th century made it illegal to talk with anyone from another village. The lifetime employment system persisted in modern times. Workers changing jobs had a hard time gaining acceptance from their co-workers. *Why is he here? Can we trust him? Why did he leave his former company?* If you didn't go through hazing with all the rest of us, went common sentiment, *you will always be one of them.*

Foreigners compounded the problem. When a boy across the street got married you knew what gift to give and when—he was Japanese—but what to do with your upstairs neighbor from America or France or Algeria? You couldn't even remember her name, and there was the possibility of committing some Islamic or Christian sacrilege. It wasn't that most Japanese hated foreigners; they were baffled by them.

Enter Eric Thor, American Unknown Quantity, accorded full police powers in a country where even Japanese citizens were checked when they left the country, where the conviction rate for arrested suspects was 99%. Could he play the police game? Should he even be allowed to play?

"He's polite and hard working," Detective Kennichi Murakami reported to his mother as he shoveled rice into his mouth. "And he speaks Japanese pretty well."

"But can he eat sushi?" Murakami's mother asked.

"I don't know mother," he laughed. "I assume so."

"He's probably got AIDS."

"Mom, I am not going to sleep with him. He's my partner."

"Well." she said, unconvinced. "And why did you get stuck with him?"

"Probably because of the time I spent in the States, and my English fluency. No one has really told me but I think they just assumed Thor wouldn't be able to speak Japanese and they didn't want some crazy *gaijin* running around screaming 'Me American. You under arrest!' at people."

"I think our own police do just fine," Mrs. Murakami said. "What do we need more American GIs for?"

"He's not in the army, Mother," Kennichi explained. "He's a policeman, like me. He's from the Minneapolis Police Department and he's part of an exchange program set up to enhance international understanding and improve our respective police systems. He is going to be here for a year so you had better get used to me talking about him."

"Well," Mrs. Murakami said.

"Why don't you invite him over to dinner?" Kennichi's father had been silent throughout dinner, as he usually was.

"Fine with me," Kennichi said. Mrs. Murakami said nothing. "Is that all right with you, Mother?"

"Well." she said. "I don't know how to make any American dishes. I don't speak English, either."

A large pot in the center of the table was boiling water. A burner underneath was receiving gas through a hose that stretched to an outlet in one wall. Mrs. Murakami had thrown in cut cabbage, *shiitake* mushrooms, and other vegetables several minutes before. The thinly sliced beef she had just added was releasing fat froth, which she was busy ladling into a small bowl on the side.

"I already told you," Kennichi said. "His Japanese is fine. Why don't you make *sukiyaki*? Yours is the best, Mom."

"Well," she said. "Is he married?"

"No. That was one of the conditions of participating in the program."

"Must be lonely," his father said. "All alone like that."

"I suppose so," Kennichi said. "He hasn't been here that long, though."

"Away from his family and friends, strange food. Can't be easy."

"So what do you say, Mother?"

"I guess it's all right. And my *sukiyaki* is rather good, isn't it?" Mrs. Murakami said, warming to the idea despite herself. "Can he use chopsticks?"

"Yes, Mother."

*

Captain Kume sat under the *kotatsu* with his wife Sachiko. He was five feet six inches tall and weighed 120 pounds. His black hair was parted on the side and well oiled. He had brown eyes, almost black, set in a smooth, youthful face, divided by a flat nose. His lips were narrow and pinched together in a way that made him look perpetually angry, belying a cool head and compassion his colleagues respected. He wore frameless glasses. He had worn his for years. His legs were tucked under him in traditional style, though most men nowadays had taken to crossing their legs, western style. He could maintain that position for hours if necessary. Captain Kume was a man at peace with himself because he knew himself and his mission in life. He was a leader of men. Not because he had wanted to be, but because it was his fate. Problems needed solving, things needed organizing, and people had always turned to Kume to take care of them. In his early years on the police force, when he was a peon like the rest, even his elders had surreptitiously asked his views on this matter or that. He took no special pride in this.

You would expect the household of such a man to be run with the precision of a Seiko watch and the discipline of a Zen monastery. You would be wrong. Kume's skill in managing people and events had always been his ability to draw from those around and under him the best that they could achieve by convincing them it was what they wanted to do. He hadn't swept his wife off her feet with masculinity or wealth, nor had theirs been an arranged marriage. They both were members of a local tennis school and had begun dating quite innocently. He liked her sunny personality. She was attracted to his quiet strength. Even after twenty one years of marriage, Sachiko just felt like a better person when around her husband.

Their son, Tatsuya had one more year of high school left and was a model student. He was talking recently of going to medical school but wasn't sure. Kume never gave his preferences on the subject, though all in the family knew that he would support whatever choice the boy made.

Sachiko loved this also about her husband. Most friends and neighbors were pushing their children to attend "cram" schools—children went there immediately after school and studied until nine or ten in the evening. Children began attending as early as kindergarten, all for the purpose of getting into the best elementary school, junior and senior high schools and college—in order to get a job with a famous company. Kume wanted the best for his son as well, and helped him develop from an early age strong study skills, but did not believe happiness in life would be achieved by sacrificing his childhood for the sake of a higher test score. Kume believed happiness, and therefor success, lay in a balanced, rounded childhood, that included school, a variety of recreation. He and his son had played some sort of sport almost every weekend since Tatsuya was able to walk.

"How was your day?" Kume asked his wife of twenty-one years.

"Busy, busy," she said, filling her husband's glass with beer. "I had to fill in at the university for one of the other teachers who was off in Tokyo giving a concert. Then I had my usual afternoon classes and private lessons here." She blew a few strands of hair from her eyes. She looked, at that moment, exactly as she had twenty one years ago—or so Kume would have told anyone, had they asked.

"You're going to kill yourself if you aren't careful," Kume said. "Overworking like that."

"You'd like that," Sachiko said. "Then you would be free to chase after those pretty young girls at the precinct."

"How do you know I'm not chasing them now?"

"Poor me," Sachiko said. "My heartless husband comes home just long enough to eat and sleep while I slave away waiting for the love that never comes."

"Tsk. Tsk."

"The only solace I get is from my morning soap operas. Boo hoo."

"You weren't complaining last night about the love you were getting."

"Shhh! Tatsuya will hear."

"The only thing that boy hears when he is studying is the precision tuned computer called his brain as it stores ever more mathematical formulas, laws of physics and biological statistics. Though it is a good thing he was studying at his friend's house last night." Kume reached for a rice cracker and detoured to stroke one of his wife's breasts. "Even he would have heard the din you were making."

"You beast," she said, slapping him lightly on the face, leaving his hand in place on her breast. "I'm sure I don't know what you are talking about."

"Uh huh."

"Now leave me alone," she said. "I have dinner to make."

Kume watched his wife head for the kitchen. "What's for dinner tonight?"

"I thought we would have steak tonight. There was a sale at the market today on American beef."

"I should have invited our new detective from the US"

"How is he doing? You haven't said much about him?"

"I haven't seen him much. You know I've assigned him to the Madison murder with Detective Murakami. His Japanese is rather good. He is polite. He keeps his desk clean. He's outgoing. He's making an effort to get along with the other officers." Kume refilled his glass. "Those that give him a chance."

"Is he having problems because he is American."

"Everybody in my unit is a professional," Kume said. "But it's hard for some of them, particularly the older officers, to accept a foreigner into an institution so vital to Japan's well-being as the police."

"Like giving away military secrets?"

"In some people's minds, police *are* the military now. With no wars to fight, it is the police that protect the country from its enemies."

"Which to some means foreigners."

"Exactly. They see allowing foreigners to live and work here as unavoidable; a price to pay for economic freedom and military ties. Foreign companies can be monitored, controlled, closed if necessary and undesirables can be deported—all with no harm done to the inner workings of society. People cannot yet see that internationalization does not mean one country trying to defeat the rest of the world."

"Don't you think some people are just remembering the feeling of helplessness under The Military Occupation after the war?"

"No. This attitude is no different than it was before the war, even before Admiral Perry in 1853 came to Japan in his Black Ships and forced Japan to establish relations with the outside world. People see two choices: I dominate you or you dominate me. There is no middle ground. I remember reading some crazy story in one of the tabloids the other day claiming the US would impose trade sanctions if Japan didn't go along with the police exchange program. To be honest, I didn't know they even knew about it."

"I thought the exchange was the National Police Agency's idea," Sachiko said.

"It was," Kume said. "And they are funding the whole thing. But that doesn't mean anything to certain journalists and politicians who feed them stories. They see a conspiracy whenever there is a slow news day. Sensationalism sells."

"What are you going to do about the new boy? Thor, is it?"

"Absolutely nothing. He is going to be treated exactly the same, with the same respect and responsibilities, as any other law enforcement officer in my command. That means he'll have to make his own friends and pacify his own enemies. In my station, anyway, there will be no race barriers."

"This Thor is lucky to have you as his boss," Sachiko said.

"This is true."

*

The restaurant near the precinct was a drab, cement box. The tables were covered with fake linoleum, the chairs were bright red vinyl and the floor was grimy. Most of the tables had chairs upside down on them. The only other customer had a thin neck and a hairpiece that looked like an oil slick. Yamamoto imagined the customer was Officer Miyoshi's killer. He imagined wrapping his fingers around that neck and squeezing until the man stopped breathing or his head snapped off.

"One more," he yelled at the kitchen door. An old woman brought out a one-liter bottle of Asahi Super Dry beer, removing the empty one next to the bowl of soup called *ramen*, a kind of Chinese noodle soup the Japanese had imported hundreds of years before.

Yamamoto had never lost a partner before. Almost no policeman in Japan had lost a partner except from disease or old age. Yamamoto replayed the events of the day over and over, searching for an alternate ending. None came so he emptied his third bottle of the night.

"One more."

The only sound in the room was Oil Slick slurping up his *ramen* noodles.

Detective Thor walked into the restaurant, spotting Yamamoto and his bottle collection in one corner.

"Yamamoto-san," he called.

The Japanese detective turned towards the voice. "Thor-san. Come on over."

"Thanks," he said noticing Yamamoto's red cheeks. "What are you doing here when you could be getting a home-cooked meal?"

The American was friendly enough but Yamamoto wished he would mind his own fucking business when it came to people's home lives. "Did you just finish?" he asked.

"Yeah." Thor plopped down and looked around for a waitress. "A little help, please?" he called in Japanese.

"OK, OK," emanated from somewhere in back. The old woman padded over to their table.

"Could I see a menu?" Thor asked politely.

The old woman pointed to the banners on the wall covered with the names of today's dishes and their prices.

"Oops!" he said. "Yamamoto-san, can you give me a hand? My kanji reading is pretty weak. Are they the usual Chinese dishes?"

Yamamoto gazed over at the wall. "Yeah. Pot stickers, Spring Rolls, Ramen, Sweet and Sour Pork...stuff like that."

"OK. I'd like two orders of pot stickers, a bowl of ramen and some fried rice." He turned back to face a surprised Yamamoto. "And two more bottles of beer."

"I've already eaten," Yamamoto said.

"I know. I'm hungry."

"Do all Americans eat as much as you?" Yamamoto asked. "No wonder you are all so fat."

"Who's fat?" Thor said, patting his washboard stomach. "I love this stuff." He rubbed his hands together. "And besides, I have no girlfriends here who are going to complain about my garlic breath."

Thor was glad to see Yamamoto laugh.

"What about us poor guys at the precinct? I hope you don't fart like you eat? We'll all be killed."

"Americans don't fart."

Yamamoto's eyebrows shot up.

"Just kidding," Thor said.

"You Americans are pretty good at joking." Yamamoto laughed again while picking up one of the new bottles. "You should make a movie with Bruce Willis." Thor hoisted his glass with his right hand and held it ready to receive the beer. He placed his left hand lightly on the glass to show greater respect.

"Where are you staying now?" he asked the American.

"I've got a room in one of the police dormitories," Thor said. "I don't want any special favors or anything, but man, I barely have enough room to lie down and straighten my legs."

Thor picked up the bottle and motioned for Yamamoto to empty his glass.

"Are you planning to rent your own apartment eventually?"

"Sure, if I can find one I can afford that isn't three hours away, yeah."

"I know a couple of real-estate agents might be able to help. Just tell me where you want to live."

"Thanks." The old woman brought Thor's Spring Rolls. "Want some?"

"No thanks," Yamamoto said. "The Spring Rolls aren't very good here."

Thor halted with his first bite in mid-air. "Thanks for telling me."

"Just kidding," Yamamoto said. "They're not bad but I ate already."

"And I thought you were this nice, polite, serious Japanese law enforcement officer."

Yamamoto's face clouded slightly and he turned away.

"I lost my partner today."

Thor grimaced. He'd heard the news when he returned to the precinct. He hadn't known Officer Miyoshi was Yamamoto's partner.

"Man, I'm sorry."

"He was a good kid," Yamamoto said.

Thor nodded.

"My old partner got transferred out last year and they gave me Miyoshi. To break him in."

"I heard he was a nice guy."

"He was a kid," Yamamoto said, pouring himself some more beer. "He didn't know anything about anything. He was so awkward I felt like beating him half the time, but he was hard-working and serious about learning his job, unlike a lot of kids these days."

Thor noticed a two-inch cockroach scurry across the next table. "The risk of death comes with the territory." He didn't know what else to say.

"Not in Japan," Yamamoto looked angrily at Thor and then turned away. "I don't mean to show disrespect for your country, Thor-san, but murders just don't happen here that much, and when they do, they are usually one yakuza knocking off another, which suits me just fine. The biggest danger most people ever face is being barfed on in the subway late at night by a businessman returning home from too much partying." He took a long pull of his beer and poured some for the American. "People don't go around shooting each other here."

"Maybe you could talk about this with some of the other detectives, or maybe Captain Kume," Thor said.

"What for?" Yamamoto looked astonished. "My partner is dead, Thor-san. What can anyone say?" He was silent for a few moments and then chuckled. "And here I am pouring out my guts to a *gaijin*."

"Listen." Thor wanted to say something uplifting but couldn't think of a damn thing. "It wasn't your fault."

"You don't think so? I ducked at just the right moment."

"What are you talking about?"

"I was taking off my shoes when the guy unloaded on Miyoshi with a shotgun."

Thor recalled the one time he had seen a policeman die in action. He and his partner had been patrolling in South Minneapolis when they saw a kid leaning suspiciously into a late model Chrysler idling at a corner. The area was known for drug and gang activity, so it was standard procedure to investigate. They pulled up and ordered the kid to back away from the car. He and his partner, Bud Cort, got out and approached. The kid appeared to throw something into the car, which immediately sped away. Thor returned to the patrol car to contact dispatch as his partner pursued the kid on foot. As Thor prepared to chase the Chrysler, he heard gun shots. He found his partner on the ground, leaning against a tree. Cort was bleeding from the abdomen, but was alert. Go, he said, pointing in the direction the boy had run. While Thor was chasing the kid, Cort called dispatch with a detailed description of the kid. Thor searched in vain until other squad cars started showing up. The boy, 16 years old, found two days later. Officer Cort died on the operating table that night. Thor knew about losing a partner.

"Nothing you could have done," Thor said.

"We were pretty sure he was the guy who wasted the old man." Yamamoto said. A small tear appeared in the corner of Yamamoto's left eye. "I should have known."

"Known what? That this guy had somehow gotten a shotgun in a country that has fewer guns than a single New York block?"

"I should have known."

"You tell me how," Thor said. "You said yourself that these things don't happen in Japan. You might as well have expected the guy to zap you with a laser gun."

Yamamoto pushed back his chair and stood up. "I have to go."

"Home?"

"I'll see you." He put some money on the table and walked unsteadily out the door.

Thor paid the bill and left his dinner for the cockroaches.

11

Detective Yasushi Yamamoto stood on the step outside the restaurant, breathing the cold night air. Light-headed and swaying slightly, he watched his breath vaporize and disperse. Thor had been sympathetic, but how could he understand the weight of his responsibility in this matter. As Miyoshi's sempai, his elder, was he not responsible for his safety? Yet what had he done? Instead of waiting for the suspect, Nakajima, to finish his shower, he had alerted him and given him time to arm himself. Then he, the seasoned professional, had helpfully bent down and given the bastard a clear shot at his partner.

The hours since the shooting had been filled with routine procedure. After struggling from under Miyoshi's body, he had called for help. The apartment was soon swarming with officers, from Headquarters; from the nearest station, Osaka South; and from Yamamoto's Toyonaka Station. The coroner pronounced the corpse dead, the gaping hole in his chest making it an easy call, the crime scene squad photographed and fingerprinted; an ambulance and attendants removed the body.

After going home to bathe and change his clothes, Yamamoto wound up at the restaurant where Thor had found him among the bottles. He was still on the case, he assumed—no one had said otherwise—but without a partner. Anger swelled in him, displacing the guilt just a little. The search for Nakajima, which should have ended in the apartment, had only just begun. Apartment tenants had been questioned while Yamamoto was home but he was in no mood to go back to the station and face his colleagues. Besides, it was *his* partner lying in the morgue. *He* would find the killer. To hell with protocol.

He started off, his footsteps sounding brisk and purposeful on the pavement as he headed back to 1-14-21, Green Heights Mansion, Daikoku-cho.

*

He found the superintendent's apartment on the first floor of Nakajima's apartment and rang the doorbell.

"Yes?" a woman's voice over the intercom.

"Police," Yamamoto said.

"Yes?"

"I'd like to ask you some questions. About the murder today."

"Again? But we told the police everything we knew this afternoon."

"Please," Yamamoto said, with uncharacteristic pleading in his voice. He took out his police identification and held it in front of the door bell monitor. "I was here when it happened," Yamamoto said, trying to keep from slurring his words. "When Officer Miyoshi was killed. He was my partner."

"Just a moment, please," the woman said. "It's awfully late." Yamamoto heard slippers shuffle up to the door and stop. The chain jangled as she unlocked the door. "Yes?"

Yamamoto caught the woman's eyes on his cheeks and ears and wondered how red his face was.

"Yes," she said. "A terrible thing. I am very sorry your partner was killed. Our tenants don't usually do that."

"No, of course not," Yamamoto said. "Is your husband home, ma'am? I'd like to get some information about Mr. Nakajima."

"I'm sorry," the woman said. "He's out with friends tonight at a *karaoke* box in Umeda. I don't think he'll be back until late."

"Perhaps you can help me then. Can you tell me how long Nakajima lived here?"

"Just a couple of months. He moved here in November. Do you need the exact date?"

"No." Yamamoto scribbled in his note pad. "Did he have any friends in the building?"

"I don't know, really," the woman said. "I don't remember meeting him more than once or twice. Never saw him in passing, in the elevator, that kind of thing." Yamamoto noticed that she looked him right in the eyes, no shyness, no coquettish giggling, no feigned stupidity, like so many housewives. She was no Playboy centerfold but she had a confident strength that made her very attractive. Here was a woman who would stick by her man, Yamamoto thought, who wouldn't nag night after night when he returned home late from work. Here was a woman a man could grow old with. He envied her husband. "We don't really keep that close tabs on our tenants. We have quite a few foreign nationals in the neighborhood as you probably know."

Yamamoto was interested in her choice of the term "foreign national" instead of the more common, but slightly derogatory "foreigner" that most Japanese used. Yamamoto and she, both Japanese, were the only people in sight yet she was using a polite term to describe non-Japanese.

"Yes, I know."

"As I told you, the police already questioned my husband this afternoon. Some of the tenants too, though most were still at work. You are welcome to try them again if you think it will help. Some may be back now."

"I will," Yamamoto said. "Thank you for your time."

"I hope you catch the man who killed your partner, Detective Yamamoto."

"Thank you, ma'am."

Yamamoto took the elevator to the third floor and rang the doorbell of Apartment 300. Nothing. Ditto for 301. He moved over to 302. He could hear a stereo playing inside and people laughing. He rang the doorbell. No answer. He knocked on the door. Finally it opened. A beautiful girl in her late teens wearing tight blue jeans and a white T-shirt stood in the doorway holding a glass of beer.

"Yes?" she said, in English. Yamamoto was taken aback. She was not Japanese. He wished Detective Thor were here.

"Uh," he scrambled to remember his high school English or at least some line from a song by his beloved Beatles. "Japanese speak?"

"I can speak Japanese," she said in Japanese. "What do you want?"

"You Filipina?" he said, still in English.

The girl's manner immediately changed and her initial friendliness gave way to wariness. "Yes," still in Japanese. "Are you from the police?"

It occurred to Yamamoto that this beautiful young woman was likely a *Japayuki* hostess. After arriving from Thailand, Taiwan or The Philippines with promises of work as dancers or singers many women of South East Asia found the only dancing they were expected to do was around a *futon*, while the high salaries they were promised, along with their passports, ended up in the hands of the yakuza who recruited them. The lucky ones sometimes did end up as hostesses with impressive salaries. Either way, their visas were good for only three months. Those wishing to remain longer were eventually forced underground, living with a Japanese boyfriend or with a compatriot whose visa was still valid. This girl's expression said that either she or one of her friends inside was overstaying their official welcome. Yamamoto didn't care about illegal aliens tonight. He was searching the man who murdered his partner.

"Yes, I am," Yamamoto said, in Japanese.

The girl looked frightened. "My husband is Japanese."

"Do you live here?"

"No, I live in…I don't live here," the girl said. "I live someplace else."

"Look," Yamamoto said. "I'm not here to give you a hard time. Could you just tell me your name?"

"Kanazawa." A pause. " Maria Kanazawa."

"Look, Mrs. Kanazawa. I'm only here to ask about the guy who lived next door. Is Mr. or Mrs.," Yamamoto looked at the name plate next to the doorbell, "Sato here? It won't take long."

She turned and yelled into the apartment. "Sheri!" The two exchanged words that Yamamoto decided were not English. A short girl in pigtails walked slowly to the doorway. Yamamoto guessed she was no more than fifteen or sixteen, and very pregnant.

"Mrs. Sato," Yamamoto asked.

"Yes?"

"Is your husband here?"

"No." Her rising intonation made it sound like a question.

"When do you expect him in?"

"I don't know."

"Will he be home some time this evening?"

"Maybe."

Yamamoto pinched the bridge of his nose between his thumb and forefinger. The beer was beginning to wear off and he was getting a hangover. "Were you here this afternoon when the shooting occurred?"

"No." she shook her head vigorously.

Yamamoto glanced into the apartment and saw four or five Philippine men and women sitting around a *kotatsu*. The air was cloudy with smoke that didn't smell like tobacco. He doubted that the mother-to-be in front of him was married to anyone. Sato was either the name of a rich boyfriend renting this apartment for her, or a name leftover by the previous tenant.

"Mrs. Sato," he said. "About Nakajima, your neighbor..."

"An asshole." She used the word *aho*, which in Japanese, particularly in Osaka, was as strong an insult as there was.

"You knew him, then?"

She shrugged, then nodded. "I knew him."

"Did you see him often."

"Sometimes."

"Where? On a date? Did you go into his apartment?"

"Yeah."

"Which?"

"Both," she said. "But not anymore."

"Why not?"

She shrugged again. "He is just not a nice person."

"What do you mean? Did he harass you?"

"No."

"Then what was wrong with him?"

"He didn't pay—." Yamamoto saw Mrs. Kanazawa's friend grimace. "I have to go." She tried to close the door.

"What didn't he pay for, Mrs. Sato?"

"I don't know," she said, pushing against the door. "I made a mistake. I don't speak Japanese well." She headed back into the apartment. "I have to pee."

Yamamoto turned to Mrs. Kanazawa. "Look. I am not after you guys. I don't care whether you've been here for five years performing live sex shows for Buddhist monks on crack cocaine. A police officer was killed here this afternoon, my partner, and I'm trying to find the man who did it. I promise not to hassle you anymore if you and your friend help me out. But if you don't talk here I'm going to have to take you all down to the police station and I don't think you want that."

The nineteen year-old girl mulled over the question for a moment in silence. She looked hard at Detective Yamamoto, trying to decide what kind of man he was. Was he a pervert like the Japanese men she had to fight off every night at the club where she worked? *How old were you the first time you fucked, little one? Do you like the taste of cum? Have two men ever fuck you at once? How about tonight?*

Maria Kanazawa had never stolen anything or harmed anyone in her life. She made enough money pouring drinks, lighting cigarettes and fending off groping customers to support herself and her six brothers and sisters in The Philippines. All she wanted each day was to put in her time and go home. She had slept with exactly one customer and gotten pregnant. It was his idea to get married, which surprised her, and she took him up on it; she thought it was her ticket to a permanent visa. She never lied to him about feelings of affection but he didn't seem to care. If theirs was a marriage absent of love, at least it was honest. He was in his late thirties, rather old for marrying, and not very good looking. He wanted a wife to bear him a child, wash his clothes, and feed him. Seemed to her a fair trade. Maria started working a year after her daughter was born so she could resume sending money back home. Her husband was out almost every weekend. Marie wondered if he was golfing, as he claimed, or with a new girlfriend. It didn't really matter to her. He paid the bills and never beat her.

She was a legal resident of Japan and had committed no crime. She had what she wanted.

Her cousin, Sheri, however, was a different story. When she had heard from relatives about Maria's success in Japan she had come over as fast as she could borrow money for the airplane ticket. Maria had let her stay at her apartment in the beginning but couldn't find her a job; the club she worked at was legitimate and only took foreigners with proper visas. Sheri spent her first weeks out on her own and soon got hooked up with a club owner with a taste for adolescent girls. He paid the rent on her apartment and gave her money to live on. When she got pregnant he decided she wasn't so cute anymore and stopped coming around. She had to find some other way of paying rent. Friends she knew were smuggling a Philippine narcotic called Shabuh into Japan and looking for dealers. The money was good. She didn't have to leave the apartment; people came to her. As they had tonight.

If this Detective Yamamoto decided to search the place he would find her stash and Sheri would at the least be on the first plane back to the Philippines, which Maria decided wouldn't be such a bad thing for her. But she didn't know much about Japanese law or how they treated drug cases involving minors. Would they send her to jail? For that matter, would they send them all to jail just for being there? She had to make a decision quick about whether to trust this short, stocky cop. Something in his eyes said she could.

"All right," Maria said. "Listen, Sheri is afraid, that's all."

"I can see that."

"If I tell you what you want to know will you promise—please—not to tell anyone?"

"Mrs. Kanazawa," Yamamoto said. "If you can tell me anything that will help me track down this worm I will forget ever meeting you."

Maria ran her fingers from the front of her scalp to the back. "She sold him, um, something," she said, "and he didn't pay for it."

"Sex?"

"No." She gnawed her lip. "Shabuh."

Yamamoto knew of the substance. One of the new synthetic amphetamines, it gave an artificial euphoria by speeding up the heart rate and causing the body to manufacture large quantities of adrenaline. Most people just laughed a lot, stayed awake for twenty-four hours and crashed for a day or two. In others it caused anxiety and paranoia. If Nakajima were taking Shabuh, Yamamoto decided, it would explain a lot about his behavior.

"Do you know how many times she sold him the stuff?"

"No. Just that she gave him some about a week ago and he told her he would bring the money the next day. When he didn't, she went over to collect. He backed her up against the wall and said if she ever bothered him again he would kick her in the stomach."

"So she just gave up."

"What could she do? She doesn't have a visa." Maria said. "Oops!"

"I figured that already, don't worry about it." Yamamoto said. "Could you go and get her back out here, please? A few questions and I'll be on my way. Don't worry."

Maria went to knock on the bathroom door and spoke a few words to Sheri. She finally flushed the toilet and came back to the door. From the face up she looked every bit a confused fifteen year-old.

"Do you know what kind of work Nakajima did?"

"No. I only saw him a few times. The jerk."

"Did you ever see him leave for work in the morning? Pass him on the way to the elevator?"

She started to shrug again and stopped. "He had this really loud alarm clock that woke me up most mornings at 8:00."

"Any idea where he works? Nearby, maybe?"

"I have no idea. I always just went back to sleep."

"Did you ever notice any of his friends? People coming or going?"

"He was only here a couple of months. Like I said, I didn't know him. I just sold him stuff, you know."

"When did you start selling to him?"

Sheri looked over at Maria, who nodded slightly. "Last month some time. He heard us partying one time and came over. He was kind of skuzzy, you know. I was going to tell him to get lost but he said he recognized the smell of Shabuh and asked if I knew where he could buy some. I told him I could get it for him, which I did, and that was that. He paid the first three or four times so when last week he told me he didn't have the money but would bring it the next day I thought it was OK."

"Did he ever bring any friends?"

"No. He was always alone."

"Well, thanks," Yamamoto said. "I don't think I'll be back but if either of you remember anything I would really appreciate it if you would call." He gave them each a business card and headed towards the elevator.

Just before the elevator arrived he heard footsteps. He turned to see Mrs. Kanazawa coming towards him.

"Did you remember something?"

"No," she said. "I have to tell you something."

"Yes?"

"I do not sell drugs."

"I never said you—"

"You didn't have to. You all think it anyway. And I have never sold my body to anyone in Japan or anywhere else."

"I'm sorry, Mrs. Kanazawa," Yamamoto said. "I didn't mean to suggest—"

"I just wanted *you* to know that. I've got a messed up cousin, and maybe you don't see the best of my countrymen, and maybe it's not your fault, but it seems that the only type of people you want from the Philippines are whores, so that's all you see, but we are not all like that. I am not a whore or a pusher."

Yamamoto turned as the elevator opened. When he turned back, Maria Kanazawa was already gone.

12

They all stood in line, the men who had worked with him, along
with family members and friends. They were all dressed in black;
black suits with black ties for the men and black dresses with pearl
necklaces for the women. The young boys wore shorts with sus-
penders; the girls wore pretty sundresses. The line stretched one
hundred fifty feet or so down the street and around the corner, the
only movements besides the gradual shuffle being a cough or the
occasional gentle rap on an unruly child's head. People stepped up
one by one to the reception desk to sign the reception book and
present their envelopes stuffed with condolence money. The amount
of money varied by age and family and business relationship, but all
of the bills were old and worn, in keeping with tradition. To give
new bills would have indicated you had expected him to die. Those
coming from great distances were presented in return with different
cash envelopes to help defray the travel costs.

Japanese accepted death more easily than other races. There
was sadness, of course, but Japanese saw death as yet another of
life's inevitabilities. People got old, they died and the young
moved on. Funerals could even be fun, especially for those on the
fringes, providing a chance to see old friends and relatives not met
for many years. There was always a big lunch after the service

where people could share fond memories of the dearly departed, and unlike in some western countries, the festive atmosphere was rarely forced. Mourners cried their hearts out at the funeral itself, then spent lunch time drinking beer and sake, recalling the shared good times. *Grandpa sure loved to tie one on, didn't he? Oh yes, remember the time he fell asleep on the train, ending up in Otsu? Spent the night! Gosh, what a character.*

The first week's funeral was attended by anyone with business or personal contact. Services were reenacted for four successive weeks, with the attendants gradually decreasing in number until only the immediate family remained. The one-year anniversary would bring everyone back together for a less depressing service and even more lively luncheon.

That was how funerals usually were. But Kenji Miyoshi had been only 23 years old. Both his parents were still alive, even his grandparents were still alive. People were not prepared for his death. His death did not fit into the usual path of inevitability. Officer Miyoshi had no children, was not married, had only a girlfriend whom he had dated since high school and who was now sitting next to his mother, crying softly into her third hand-kerchief of the day.

The drone of the Buddhist priest's chant played in the background like mood music. *Namanda namanda namanda.* Inside, guests approached the Buddhist altar, covered with chrysanthemums surrounding a picture of Miyoshi wearing his police uniform. One by one they took a pinch of incense, held it to their foreheads, and deposited it into the urn full of similar embers, repeating the step three times before holding their hands together in silent prayer. They bowed toward the bereaved family, who bowed back, and moved on to find a seat.

Kenji Miyoshi lay in a box under the flowers. After the service, while the guests were eating lunch, his family would take the body

to the crematorium. Later they would pick out the bones that had-
n't burned and put them in a box. A stone would be erected in a
small plot of land within a couple of weeks. Relatives would stop
by occasionally, placing Miyoshi's favorite sake, a piece of fruit,
perhaps lighting a cigarette for him, and leaving it at the base of
the gravestone.

Kenji Miyoshi was gone.

13

Detective Eric Thor liked women.

He had no color preference. White, black, yellow, blondes, brunettes, redheads were all fine. Talking, dating, playing tennis— it was all fine with him Women were fun to be around. He had dated often before coming to Japan.

Yuki Nishimura was a woman, Thor was quite sure. She had the requisite number of curves. Her jeans left no room in front or back for anything but a shapely woman. She smelled like a girl, too, from several yards away. She most definitely behaved like the kind of woman the Japanese referred to as *burikko*. *Burikko* were flirts. Regardless of what they did behind closed doors, they were overtly sensual, coquettish, in a way that traditional Japanese society frowned upon. Open flirting of the kind American women engaged in, at least in the eyes of Japanese, the kind where a look across a crowded bar could say, "Hey big boy, is that a California Roll in your pocket or are you just happy to see me?" was not acceptable in The Land Of The Demure Woman. As James Bond's Japanese counterpart in Goldfinger had said: "In Japan, 007, the man always comes first." Traditionally, women were supposed to be passive in matters of romance. The man made a clumsy move; the woman chastely rejected him. He tried and failed a second time. If he was courageous, or drunk enough, to press his case, an interested woman might submit, with further, increasingly feeble protestations. During the sexual act, it was considered seductive for the woman to become aroused reluctantly, demonstrating that only the overpowering virility of her partner caused her to behave in such a wanton manner. *Burikko* were different. *Burikko* acted childishly one moment, provocatively the next. They were bad girls; at least other girls thought so. At least that's what Thor had read and heard in college. Surfing the internet before coming to Japan he had found dozens of "Everything You Need To Know Before Travelling To Japan" websites. Several of these sites claimed that Japanese women had changed in the 1990s and beginning of the twenty first century, particularly women in metropolitan areas like Tokyo and Osaka. Today's women, they said, were *all* of low moral character, and deserving of the epithet "Yellow Cab," meaning you could call them anytime for a ride. They claimed that foreign men were especially attractive to such women. But these same sites also offered to link you up with these women, for a fee, next time you visited Japan, sounding suspiciously like escort services, so Thor wasn't sure what to believe.

Being far from home, alone, unattached and involuntarily celibate, Thor found himself wanting to believe the latter. Images of himself walking into a Tokyo bar and being immediately accosted by hordes of nubile women had been occupying more of his idle time of late. Problem was, he did not, of late, have enough idle time to get away and test his theory.

The woman standing in the doorway of Select Heights Mansion, Apartment 210, stood about five feet tall, weighed about ninety-eight pounds, by Thor's estimation. He hoped she would accost him in a Tokyo bar someday. She had long, jet-black hair. Her face reminded him of Lucy Liu from the TV show *Ally McBeal*. He mused that perhaps she reminded him of Lucy Liu because he had seen that show on TV last night, only they called it *Ally, My Love*, and all the actors spoke Japanese, not English. The front desk had told him his TV could be instructed to play the English track, filtering out the Japanese, but he could not punch the right combination of buttons and finally gave up. On the English track, not the show. Even in Japanese, he could follow the basic story arc—it was a rerun he had seen. And he had a thing for Lucy Liu. The woman he was now staring at was Japanese, not Chinese American like Lucy Liu, but Thor didn't care. She had that same look Lucy Liu had when she wanted to torment one of the men on *Ally*. She was tormenting Thor now.

Murakami spoke first, "We're with the Osaka Prefectural Police. Tsuyoshi Tanaka, owner of *Mr. Dandy*, said you and Lisa Madison sometimes worked together. We found your name and address in Lisa's address book. May we ask you some questions?"

"All right, " Yuki Nishimura said, speaking not to Detective Murakami, but gazing up oh-so respectfully at the tall, handsome American detective. "Sir."

"Would you say that you and Lisa were friends?" Murakami said. "Outside of work?"

"Yes." Her eyes wandered up and down Thor's tall frame.

"How close a friend?" Thor said. He felt like a Christmas turkey ready for plucking.

"She was my best friend," she said. "Are you a detective, too?" She gazed at Thor as if he had just dismounted a white horse, eyes opened wide.

"Yes," he croaked.

"How long, Ms. Nishimura?" Murakami asked. He appeared immune to her spell.

"About two years," she said, still to Thor. "And you work for the Osaka police and everything?"

"Yes, I do." Thor said too loudly. "Yes." He cleared his throat. "I am here on a one year exchange program. Working with Detective Murakami here."

"Did you bring your wife with you?" Yuki said.

"Uh, I'm not married." Thor wanted to take out his handkerchief and wipe his upper lip.

Murakami was trying to remember if his male friends at Berkeley had been such weaklings with women. He couldn't remember. Perhaps Americans felt their women were not as attractive as those in Japan.

Murakami coughed. "Excuse me, ma'am," he said to Yuki Nishimura. "Do you think I could have a glass of water?"

"Oh, of course," she said. "How rude of me. Let me get you both some tea."

After she had left the room Murakami pulled Thor off to one side. "Have you never seen an attractive woman before?" He said in English. "You're staring at her like she's a piece of meat."

"Me?" Thor said. "*She's* the one who's staring. Man, I've never met a woman who was so openly sexual before. At least not without several beers inside her. "Those eyes of hers are hypnotic."

"You need to spend an hour or two at a Soapland," Murakami said.

"What the hell is that?"

"Legalized prostitution. They look like tiny hotels, but furnishings are limited to a large Jacuzzi, maybe a shower, and a cot. You ask for a bath and a massage at the reception area. You get a handjob, blowjob, a fuck—depends on how much you pay up front. Used to be called Turkish Baths until the Turkish Government lodged a formal protest with the Japanese government."

"Is that true?"

"Yeah, Turkey threatened to withdraw their ambassador. Happened about ten years ago."

"No," Thor said. "About the baths. Are they really legal?"

"Oh," Murakami said. "Technically, no."

"Technically? In what sense?"

"Well, in the sense of them being legal. They are in fact illegal, but laws against what they do are about as strictly enforced as hitchhiking in the US."

"Wow."

"You should go, Thor-sand," Murakami said. "The state you are in now, you're no good to me."

"And I won't get in trouble for this?"

"Not unless you take a picture of yourself in action and send it to the *Yomiuri Daily News*. For now can you please try to behave in a dignified manor?"

"I wasn't *doing* anything!"

"Let's not forget why we are here," Murakami said.

"Yeah, yeah." Thor did a couple of deep knee bends, stretched his shoulders, and took several deep breaths. He forced the image of Lisa Madison's near decapitated body into his mind, making it easier and easier to forget about his sex life.

Yuki came back in with a loaded tray.

"Did you know her ex-husband?" Murakami said.

"Kimura-san?" she said "No."

"When did you see her last?" Thor asked.

"Two or three weeks ago." She noticed the change in Thor's temperature immediately. The American was no longer interested. "We went out together after work."

"How about the night she was killed? Sunday night."

"I was at my parents house." Thor couldn't identify exactly what had changed, but Yuki Nishimura was now as sexual as a used tissue.

"Go there often?" Thor said.

"Once a month or so." Short, clipped answers. She wasn't cooperating any more than she had to.

"So you went out with Lisa two or three weeks ago."

"Yeah, I guess."

"By yourselves?"

"No. We went out with a couple of friends."

"Women friends?"

"Two guys."

"Could you tell us their names, please?"

"They aren't going to like this." She shook her head like a child rejecting lima beans. "Do I have to?"

"Yes," Murakami said. "You do."

"All right," she sighed deeply to convey her unhappiness with the imposition. "I was with Larry Baker and Lisa's date was a guy named Guy Halpern."

"Had you ever met Halpern before?" The American asked.

"Yeah. Why?" The *burikko* was gone, replaced by a woman not sure where things were headed.

"Could you tell me when, please?"

"Lisa went out with him once in a while."

"How often?" Thor asked. "Once a month? Twice a year?"

"Once in a while, you know? I didn't keep track." She pretended to study something on the far wall. "Why don't you go talk to her ex-husband? Maybe he killed her. He wanted Megan, you know?"

Yuki was obviously uncomfortable on the subject of Lisa's dating habits. Thor made a mental note to continue on that path later.

"Mr. Kimura may or may not have had a motive," Murakami spoke up, "but he does have an alibi during the time his ex-wife was killed. The superintendent of his fiancée's apartment building has a record of when he entered and left the building. He was there the night Ms. Madison was killed."

"He's getting married again?" She looked surprised.

"That's what he said," Murakami said. "Why?"

"No reason."

"Tell me more about this sometime boyfriend of hers, Guy Halpern," Thor said.

"I told you. They just dated sometimes." She began to straighten things around the apartment. "He didn't talk about his private life, he was just a date, a good time."

"What did you think of him?"

Silence.

"Ms. Nishimura?"

"He was kind of creepy."

"Lisa must have found some redeeming feature in him, don't you think?" Murakami said.

"I don't know. I just don't know, I tell you."

"Look," Thor said. "You were her best friend, weren't you? She must have talked about her love life. Who she liked and why. That kind of thing."

"I guess." Now she was straightening cushions on he sofa.

"So?" Thor got up to follow her. "Her mother said he was not a winner; you said he was a creep. What was he to Lisa? Money? Drugs? Was she hooking? What?"

"Hooking?" She was incredulous. "Are you kidding?"

"You tell me."

Yuki held her cup of Japanese tea to her lips with both hands and stared off into the distance. "Shabuh."

"What?" Thor didn't understand.

"It's a narcotic," Murakami said. "Produced in The Philippines. Very popular in South East Asia and gradually making its way into Japan."

"Are you saying Ms. Madison was buying drugs from this Guy Halpern?" Thor said.

"I don't know," Yuki said.

"Will you stop with the 'I don't know, I don't know'. You just said—"

"I said I don't know and I don't." She was visibly upset. "We were friends but there was a lot we didn't talk about. All I know is that Guy deals Shabuh and whenever we were all together he was always hitting on me to find customers for him."

"Just you? Not Lisa?" Thor said.

"Not while I was there. It always made me wonder, though."

"That maybe she was already dealing for him or using?"

Yuki shook her head. "She wasn't using. She didn't even like other people drinking in the house because she didn't want Megan to see. Even when we went out she didn't drink that much herself. I'm sure she wasn't using."

"But couldn't she have been selling?" Thor said.

"I don't know," Yuki said. "Just what I told you."

"Does this Guy Halpern have any kind of legitimate occupation?" Murakami said.

"He sells hippie jewelry and fake bags on the bridge down in Dohtombori."

"Hippie jewelry?" Thor said.

"You know. Hand made silver earrings and rings. Beads. And fake Chanel hand bags from Thailand. He lays out a big sheet, sets out his boxes and looks bored."

"He makes a living doing this?" Thor's immotile eyebrows threatened to rise a millimeter.

"I guess," she said.

"But he can't get a proper visa doing this," Murakami said.

"He's enrolled in a Japanese language school. Class gets out at 2:30 and he's off to his spot by the river the rest of the afternoon.

Sometimes he hits one of the craft fairs at the temples in Kyoto or Nara."

"Do you know the name of the school he goes to?" Murakami said.

Yuki thought for a moment, then shook her head. "No idea."

"Did you like Lisa?" That from the American.

"I already told you we were best friends. Of course I liked Lisa. There were things I didn't know about her and some things that bothered me, but we had fun together. I don't poke my nose into things that aren't my business."

"What kind of things?"

"Like Guy, for instance."

"Anything else?"

"She was a nice person but she's dead. Can't we just let it go? I don't know anything useful."

"Did she ever talk about owing people money?" Thor said.

"No."

"Stealing anything from someone?"

"No."

"Don't you wonder why she was killed so violently? You read the papers, right?"

"How would I know?" she said. "You keep asking me things that I don't know about. *I* didn't kill her. Why don't you just go and ask..." Yuki put her hand to her mouth.

"Ask who?"

"No." Her eyes went from Thor, over to Murakami and back again, all in a heartbeat.

"Who?"

"Just ask...someone else."

"Like who?"

"Like her other friends. Like Guy Halpern. Or Peter Randall. Ask them."

Thor bent over until he made eye contact. "Was she seriously involved with either of them?"

"I don't know, I told you!"

"I thought you were best friends."

"We were friends, OK? We worked together, OK? We went out, we had a good time, sometimes I baby-sat Megan. I didn't live with her."

"Who would want to kill Lisa, Ms. Nishimura?"

"How should I know? That's your job." She looked at her watch and feigned surprise. "Gosh! I really have to get going. If you are both finished..."

Thor would have none of it. "Did she have any enemies?" Fights with anyone recently?"

"No."

"Boyfriends you haven't mentioned? A customer from the coffee shop, perhaps?"

Silence.

"Who?" Thor raised his voice.

"All right," Murakami said. "Who was the secret boyfriend?"

"I'll get fired."

"If he is a customer of your shop we promise not to tell your boss where we got the name."

Yuki laughed. "That would be a nice trick. It was the boss she was sleeping with."

"Mr. Tanaka?" both officers said at once.

Yuki nodded.

"The owner?" Thor said. "Lisa was dating that fat pig?"

"She was."

14

Tsuyoshi Tanaka did not live in Osaka City.

His coffee shop/bar and his business hotel and his hostess club were in Osaka but he lived in *the* fashionable suburb of Ashiya. He lived in a house that had cost over a million dollars when he bought it in 1985 but would easily fetch double that today, real estate bust or no. A similar structure in San Francisco would bring about five hundred thousand dollars; perhaps a third of that in Sioux Falls. Ashiya was the Beverly Hills of Kansai Prefecture and Japanese dreamed of living there the way Americans dreamed of winning Powerball. Houses were average-sized by American standards and most yards were less than a one-fifth an acre. Driveways were crammed with foreign cars, mostly Mercedes and BMWs, with the occasional Jaguar thrown in.

Tanaka was part of the nouveau riche, Japan's answer to the Texan wildcatters of the late 19th and early 20th century. Land was Japan's petroleum. People fortunate enough to have title to land in the vicinity of downtown Osaka after World War II reconstruction began were millionaires many times over today. Tanaka's father had tended rice fields in Umeda, in the center of present day downtown Osaka, in the early 1950s. When a neighbor gave away a huge tract of land to the government on condition they place a central train station there, the surrounding land skyrocketed in value and the elder Tanaka's fortune was sealed. He built a coffee shop and a few parking garages and lived off them, renting out the vacant lots to farmers for enough to cover taxes, biding his time until deciding what to do with his terra firma mine. By the time the younger Tanaka took over the family business, love hotels, renting rooms by the hour, were coming into vogue and it was easy to get construction financing. With one cash cow firmly in hand, Tanaka Jr. noticed that business entertainment expense accounts were rising with the wealth of Corporate Japan. He anticipated correctly that bars staffed by modern-day geisha were the wave of the future. *Mr. Dandy's* value had long since diminished but the old man had liked it. Even after the elder Tanaka retired his son had kept it going. Besides, it was a good tax write-off. Tanaka stopped insuring the place when his father had died the year before, despite what he had told Detectives Thor and Murakami. It wasn't worth the premiums.

The Tanaka estate was on a fairly large plot, by Japanese standards, a square surrounded by a wall, as most homes in that price range were. The house was a 3-story concrete structure. There were rose bushes on each side of the entrance. Murakami mentally calculated how many thousands of years it would take him to save enough money just to buy the garage, even with a 99-year mortgage now offered by Japanese banks.

Thor thought the place felt like a prison. Or a fort. There was a state-of-the-art video intercom on the door, mounted cameras inside the compound. Murakami pushed the button and bent over to present his face for inspection.

"Detectives Murakami and Thor from Osaka Prefectural Police. We are here to see Mr. Tanaka."

"Just a moment," came the reply.

The door opened and an elderly maid bowed, inviting them to walk towards the house. A Japanese rock garden lay tastefully hidden on the south side. As they reached the entrance the officers paused to let the maid pass.

They both stepped in. The maid brought them to a waiting room overlooking the rock garden. "Sorry about before," Thor said to Murakami. "With Nishimura."

"What?" Murakami said. The drive from Nishimura's apartment had been mostly silent. "Oh, the girl."

"I'm usually more in control than that."

"Forget about it," Murakami said.

"No, really. If we're going to work together, we've got to trust each other. You can't trust me, my judgement, if you think I'm going get horny for every girl we talk to."

"I understand," Murakami said. "Foreign men find Japanese women particularly appealing."

"No, it's not that." Thor's laugh surprised the Japanese detective.

"You do *not* find Japanese women attractive?"

"No. Yes! They *are* attractive, but that's not what got to me." Thor massaged his face with his hands. "Forget it. I'm just tired. I'll be OK."

The door opened. The maid brought tea.

"Doesn't this stuff keep you awake?" he asked Murakami when the maid had left.

"Tea? No. Does caffeine bother you that much?"

"This much in one day does."

"I thought you Americans couldn't function without your coffee."

"Not this one."

The door opened again and an attractive woman in her late 30's stepped into the room. She was tall for a Japanese, slim and graceful like a model.

"Please," she said when Thor started to stand. "My husband is in the bath now. He takes his quite early. I'm Mrs. Tanaka."

"I'm Detective Murakami," Murakami said. "This is my partner, Detective Thor."

"Indeed?" Mrs. Tanaka said. "And does your Detective Thor speak Japanese?" She addressed Murakami, but looked at Thor as she spoke.

"He does," Thor said. "I'll be working with the Osaka Police for the next year."

"Amazing," Mrs. Tanaka said. She was wearing black stockings and a knee-length peach-colored skirt with a matching jacket. A gold chain with a one-ounce American gold Eagle was hanging around her neck, over a white silk blouse. Her hair was wrapped in a bun and pinned back. "I'm glad to see that Japan is finally internationalizing, if belatedly. Are you enjoying your stay here, Detective Thor?"

"Very much, ma'am. It's a beautiful country." Thor wasn't sure he truly believed that, having spent most of his time downtown. It seemed the appropriate thing to say.

"And you are here about the murder of the Madison girl, I suppose."

"That's right."

"You know then?"

"Ma'am?" Thor said.

"About the two of them."

"What do you mean?" Thor said, knowing already the answer.

Mrs. Tanaka looked at Thor pityingly, as though he had not yet heard of the birds and the bees. "You must know that the two were having an affair," Mrs. Tanaka said., stating rather than asking. "My husband and the Madison girl."

Thor looked at Mrs. Tanaka and nodded. "Yes, we knew."

Mrs. Tanaka nodded, satisfied. "He didn't kill her. You can be sure of that."

"Excuse me," Murakami said. "May I ask how long you knew about the two of them?"

"Lisa and him? Oh, a year or so, I suppose."

In a country so dedicated to matrimonial infidelity as Japan, Murakami knew better than to be surprised by Mrs. Tanaka's knowledge of her husband's perfidiousness. He did find it odd that she chose to announce it to two police detectives investigating the murder of her spouse's girlfriend. "Men are that way in Japan," she said to Thor with a doleful laugh. "I don't suppose such things happen in America. There is not much one can do about it, though, and men are usually careful to keep the business to themselves. I think the fact that she was white-skinned, if you will forgive me Detective Thor, was what attracted him to her. A diversion. I'm sure it would have ended soon on it's own. They always do. Unfortunately, Ms. Madison died before that could happen. It must look terrible for my husband."

"Did you know her, Mrs. Tanaka?" Murakami said.

"Yes, I saw her a couple of times at *Mr. Dandy.*"

"What did you think of her?" Thor said. "Before you discovered the affair?"

"An interesting question. I'm sure most men thought she was a beautiful woman, if that is what you mean. I never spoke with her except on the rare occasion I stopped by *Mr. Dandy.*"

"Did Lisa know that you knew about them?" Thor said.

"I don't believe so."

"Did your husband know? That you knew?"

"No." A short, firm head shake. "And I would appreciate your not telling him either. Some secrets are best kept."

"How did you feel when you heard about Ms. Madison's death?" Thor asked.

"I didn't think much about it," Mrs. Tanaka said, "to be quite honest. She was nothing to me. Though I suppose it will inconvenience my husband to have to go out and find a new one."

"Find a new what?" Tsuyoshi Tanaka asked from the doorway.

"Find a new plate glass window for *Mr. Dandy* to match the old one," Mrs. Tanaka answered, not missing a beat. "It was rather unique, was it not?"

"Oh that," Tanaka said. He looked warily at the detectives, decided to smile. "Our two friends here have heard all about that." He guffawed, inviting others to join. "Too much, I'm afraid." He looked at Murakami. "Detective's Murakami and..." He slapped his forehead.

"Thor," Murakami said.

"Yes, of course. Excuse me, Detective Thor. I am horrible at remembering foreign names."

Thor was struck at the difference between the Tanaka they had met in the police station and the man standing before them now. This man, in his crisply ironed *yukata* robe and *haori* top looked and spoke like a Japanese Orson Welles. The man they had interviewed at the police headquarters had all the charm of a rabid dog. Thor wondered if Tanaka was putting on airs for his wife. Or had the routine at the police station been the act?

"I'm sorry we interrupted your bath, Mr. Tanaka," Murakami said, "but we'd like to ask you a few more questions concerning the Madison murder."

"You didn't interrupt my bath and I would be happy to answer any and all of your questions," Tanaka said. "Besides, I wasn't the most cooperative of people last time we met. I was upset. You understand."

"What made you change your mind?" Murakami asked. Thor kept his eyes on Tanaka but wondered about his partner's reaction to Tanaka's olive branch. In his short experience with Japanese, he sensed that people were eager to let bygones be bygones, no matter how blameworthy the other party. Thor would have said something like "No, no, it was nothing" or "Perfectly understandable. Forget about it. You were under a lot of stress" in an effort put Tanaka at ease.

"I reflected on my actions and realized I was completely in the wrong." That, anyway, sounded typically Japanese, Thor decided.

"If you will excuse me, gentlemen," Mrs. Tanaka stood. "I must help the maid prepare dinner. It was a pleasure meeting you both." She smiled and left the room.

Tanaka sat on the sofa vacated by his wife and looked expectantly at the detectives.

"We would like to go over some of the information you gave us before," Murakami said.

"Is there a problem?"

"No. Just routine. You understand."

"I see."

"Mr. Tanaka,," Murakami said, "How long did you say you had known Lisa Madison?"

"She worked for me a year and a half."

"Could you tell us how you first met her?"

"When she applied for the job," Tanaka said. "I placed an ad in one of the part-time magazines, she came for an interview, and I hired her."

"What was your relationship with Lisa Madison?"

Tanaka looked surprised. "Why, I was her boss, of course."

"How much did you pay her?"

"Three hundred thousand yen a month." Thor did some quick mental arithmetic and figured that out to be about $2,800. Not much in the world's second most expensive city, especially for a mother and child.

"Do you remember sending her a fruit basket one time when she was sick?"

"No, I don't believe I do."

"Or picking up some groceries for her?"

Tanaka paused. "Maybe."

"Are you this caring with all of your employees, Mr. Tanaka?" Murakami said.

"All right, maybe I did send her the fruit and the food. Hey. She's a foreigner. I was just trying to make her stay here more pleasant."

"Which magazine was the ad in?"

"I don't know." He ran his hand over the top of his head, which looked like a Brillo Pad. "*Part Timer News,* I suppose. One of those."

"Why did you choose Lisa?"

"She looked like a hard working girl."

"And you weren't worried about hiring a foreigner?"

"No. Why should I be? I thought the customers would like her."

"Did she have previous experience working in a coffee shop?"

Tanaka snorted. "How much experience do you need to serve coffee and whisky?"

"Did Lisa take drugs?"

Tanaka was caught off guard. "What?"

"Did Ms. Madison, to your knowledge, use or sell illegal narcotics?"

"She wasn't on drugs."

"And she was not engaged in the sale of drugs?"

"No," Tanaka said. "Not at my shop. She wasn't like that."

"You are sure?"

"Yes."

"But how can you be so sure, Mr. Tanaka? Perhaps she was dealing outside of work," Murakami said. "After all, she was just one of your employees, right? You have dozens of employees, right? You couldn't know what she was doing twenty-four hours a day."

Tanaka reached down to the table in front of him and removed a cigarette from the silver box in the center. The lighter next it was the shape of the Empire State Building, the flame popping out of the top. He blew smoke rings up at the ceiling. "She wasn't on drugs."

"But how could you really know for sure?" Murakami said. "You weren't seeing Lisa Madison outside of work, were you, Mr. Tanaka?" Murakami looked as if that thought had just this moment occurred to him.

All expression went out of Tanaka's face. "No, of course not."

"Yet you did bring some groceries to her apartment when she was sick."

Tanaka sat silently, the only movement his foot tapping against the sofa.

"How much did you pay her?" Thor spoke for the first time.

Tanaka appeared not to have heard.

"Beyond her base salary? How much extra were you giving her?" Thor said.

"What?"

Back to his normal self, Thor thought, ignoring the foreigner.

"Perhaps we had better continue this questioning back at the station," Murakami said, rising.

"Hold it!" Tanaka said. "What's going on here." He smiled, trying to look reasonable. "I've answered your questions twice already. This isn't really necessary, is it?"

"It will be if we arrest you."

"For what? Giving you guys a hard time?"

"Murder, perhaps?"

"I didn't kill Lisa."

"Then why are you lying to us?"

"I'm not."

"Were you sleeping with Lisa Madison?" Thor said.

Tanaka started to shake his head, then stopped. "Yeah. I was."

Murakami sat down. "Then why didn't you tell us that in the beginning?"

"Why do you think?" He turned to confirm that the door was closed.

"Because you thought it would lead us to suspect you in Ms. Madison murder."

"You would have, wouldn't you?"

"Well, Mr. Tanaka," Murakami said. "You are certainly a suspect now, so how about giving us some straight answers?"

"All right, all right. Where do I start?"

"Where did you really meet Lisa?"

"At a language school."

"You were studying English?" Thor said.

"For a while. Nothing wrong with that."

"And Lisa was your teacher."

"Yes."

"How long were you a student there?"

"Three months or so."

"Would you mind telling us why you chose to study English?" Thor said.

Tanaka puckered his mouth in another Japanese equivalent of a shrug. "I wanted to learn to speak. I have a few foreign girls at my hostess club in Kita-ku. We were beginning to get more foreign customers and, you know, I just wanted to be able to speak with them. Make the club look better, higher class."

"Yet you quit studying after three months."

"After Lisa started working for me I told her I wanted to keep her as my teacher."

"Private lessons," Thor said.

"Yeah." Tanaka didn't pick up on Thor's irony.

"And the lessons were at her apartment?" Murakami said.

"Yeah. Or at *Mr. Dandy* after it closed."

"You were, I assume, paying Lisa extra for these private lessons. Or were they included in her regular job duties?"

"Well," Tanaka said. "This is how it was. I started out paying her 10,000 yen for ninety minutes of lessons a week." About $90, Thor estimated. A dollar a minute.

"Were you sleeping with her from the beginning?"

"No. She was working for me about a month or so before the first time."

"And then how much did her lessons cost?" Thor said.

"Nothing," Tanaka said, emphatic in his denial. "After we started sleeping together she wouldn't take my money anymore. Except for working at the shop."

"Did she continue to teach you English?"

"Sometimes."

"But no extra money?"

"No."

"She just slept with you because you are such a classy guy," Thor said.

Tanaka remained calm, but his brows furrowed. "You ought to be careful what you say to people, Detective Thor."

Thor smiled. "Is that a threat, Mr. Tanaka?"

"Of course not." Tanaka smiled.

"Mr. Tanaka," Murakami said. "What was the daughter, Megan, doing while you were, um, together?"

"When she was teaching me English, Megan was always there. We never fucked at the apartment. Either we went to a love hotel or did it at the shop."

"You have a bed at the shop?" Thor said.

"No."

"Oh."

Tanaka pulled his robe tighter around him, looked down at his feet. "I loved her."

"You loved her." Thor said.

"We are not like you in America, Detective Thor." Tanaka tried to sound professorial. "Our marriages are arranged, often loveless from the beginning. We stay married our whole life. Partners are chosen because of business or political ties. Love is not part of the deal A *gaijin* like you wouldn't understand."

"Your wife was chosen for you?" Thor said. He had read several articles bemoaning the rising divorce rate in Japan, particularly among the middle-aged. He decided there was no point in mentioning that now.

"Of course," he said. "She was chosen by my parents. I provide a house for her and the children and more money than even most Americans have. How and where I choose to find love is my business."

"Nice story."

"*Ujimushi yaroh,*" Tanaka said in a low voice. *You maggot.*

Murakami ignored the taunt. Thor didn't know what it meant. "You didn't seem too broken up over her death the other day," Thor said. "If I remember correctly, you were more worried about paying for shop repairs."

"I was under a lot of stress. You understand."

"I still don't understand why you employed her at your shop." Murakami said. "Couldn't she be your lover while working at the school?"

"We didn't start sleeping together until after she started working for me. I told you that."

"Did she ask you for the job? At the coffee shop?"

"She told me she was looking for a higher paying job. Said her school wasn't paying her enough to live on."

"So you offered her work at your coffee shop."

"Actually, I wanted her to work at my hostess club, *Don*. She had the looks and could have made double what I was paying her at *Mr. Dandy*."

"Why'd she turn that down?"

"Said it wasn't her style."

"So you offered her the job at *Mr. Dandy*."

"I told her I could use someone at a coffee shop I owned and if she ever needed a job to give me a call. She asked to start right away, and did."

"How much do you pay the other girl on the night shift, Yuki Nishimura?"

"Two hundred fifty thousand a month."

"Why the different pay scales?"

"Yuki is single. Lisa had a kid."

A snarling sound drifted in from the verandah outside. The men turned to watch two cats, frozen and ready for combat. Tanaka got up and rapped on the window. When neither cat moved, he opened the sliding door and said, *"Scat"*

Murakami said, "When was the last time you saw Lisa, Mr. Tanaka?"

Tanaka kept gazing out into the yard, keeping the door open. "Saturday night."

"At *Mr. Dandy*?"

"Yes."

"Did you and she go out after she finished work?"

"I wanted to, but she said no. Said she had something to do at home."

"And you left."

"Yeah."

"Did you see her on Sunday? The night she was killed?"

"I told you. I was at my club in Kita-ku."

"As a matter of fact, we checked with your staff about that and your manager said you left there before midnight. Lisa Madison was killed around 2:00 AM."

"That moron," Tanaka muttered to himself.

"What was that?" Murakami said.

"Nothing."

"So where were you between midnight and two on the morning of January 13th, Mr. Tanaka?"

"I don't remember."

Murakami chuckled. "I don't think you understand, Mr. Tanaka. You have admitted sleeping with the deceased, you knew where and when she worked and you had easy access to the murder scene. Right now you are our best bet unless you supply us with a better alibi than 'I don't remember'."

Tanaka was silent.

"Let's say you had a fight," Murakami suggested helpfully. "Lisa told you she didn't want to see you anymore. She was tired of you. You wanted to talk it over on Saturday, change her mind, but she wasn't interested. You lost control, flew into a rage, and started hacking away. Before you knew it she was bleeding all over your nice hardwood floor. Had to cover your tracks, so you trashed the entire shop. Made it look like some lunatic did it. Then you pitched the murder weapon in the Yodo River. What was it you used to kill her?"

"You got nothing."

"We got you, Mr. Tanaka. A filthy, fat, punch-permed gangster-type, the kind the Prime Minister is telling us to rid society of. What we lack in physical evidence we can make up for with news coverage. The public will eat it up."

"I did not kill Lisa."

"Prove it."

Tanaka was looking around like a caged animal. "Look, I can't tell you where I was, but I promise I wasn't at *Mr. Dandy*."

"No good. Give us a name or an address or we'll take you in right now."

"I can't!"

"Why not?"

"Listen," Tanaka licked his lips nervously. "If I told you where I really was and it got out I'd be through. You might as well shoot me right here."

"I'm getting tired of waiting, Mr. Tanaka."

Tanaka leaned closer to the two detectives. "Banana Club." He spit it out like a mouthful of spoiled fish.

"*Shit!*" Murakami threw up his hands.

"What?" Thor said. "What's this Banana Club?"

Murakami stood up and shouldered on his overcoat.

"What is it?" Thor laughed, "A gay bar or something?"

"That's exactly what it is," his partner said. "The most exclusive club of its kind in Osaka. The hostesses consist of true transsexuals, and what we Japanese call 'new half", which means guys who've got new breasts, plus their original equipment still attached down below. Clientele include ball players, politicians, anyone with fat wallets and a yen for a walk on the wild side. The utmost secrecy is assured. And I supposed," Murakami said to Tanaka, "you have dozens of witnesses, Mr. Tanaka."

"The staff can vouch for me." He looked morose. "I'll be ruined if this gets out."

"We have to check." Murakami did not appear sympathetic.

"Please don't." Tanaka was whimpering.

"You had better hope we do, Mr. Tanaka," Murakami said. "And that at least one person there backs your story."

*

The road back to Osaka was bogged down with rush hour traffic. Thor wondered when Japan would reach a point where auto sales had to be curbed for lack of road and parking space. He felt like getting out and walking.

"There goes our best suspect," Murakami said.

"If his alibi checks out."

"It'll check. Hanging out at gay bars is not something a straight guy in his position would make up."

"Not even to save his ass?"

"Not in Japan."

"I thought Japan was more cool about such things than we are in the States," Thor said. "I've seen gay singers and comedians on TV. Even cross dressers."

"Yeah, but that's show business. It's like putting on a costume. Even if it's real, it's not real. Like when pro-wrestlers bleed; they really are bleeding, but they didn't really get as beat up as we are led to believe."

"You're saying the gays on TV are not really gay?"

"Oh, they're gay. It's just that, because we, the viewing audience, only see them on TV, not in our offices or at our schools or on the streets, they don't *feel* real to us. Gay neighbors and business colleagues are something else. They never came out of the closet like American gays did. When AIDS hit Japan they went even farther underground. Tanaka is going to lose a lot of business if it gets out that he likes boys as well as girls."

"Will it get out?" Thor said.

Murakami shook his head. "No. If his alibi checks I don't care who he fucks."

"So we're down one suspect."

Murakami nodded.

They rode in silence a few more minutes as traffic inched along. Thor wondered how often cars ran out of gas on these roads.

"How's the police dorm working out for you?" Murakami said.

"Shoot, I forgot to tell you," Thor smacked his forehead with the palm of his hand. "I got my own place yesterday. Yamamoto knew this real estate agent that was so eager to please he was ready to show me the Imperial Palace. And I thought it was hard for foreigners to find their own places."

"It can be, but not when you have a friend in the police. It's harder in Tokyo than here anyway."

"Well, I don't know what Yamamoto has on this guy but he couldn't have been more helpful. I told him my budget, desired commute time, and he whips out this book with floor plans, age of the buildings on his list and how many minutes to major points in Osaka." Thor shook his head. "He was great."

"What did you do about the key money?" Key money was the legalized bribe one had to pay to get landlords to rent one an apartment. In addition to a normal deposit—often six month's worth—an additional two or three months went straight into the landlord's pocket, never to return.

"I put down six month's rent. I get five back when I leave as long as the apartment is undamaged," Thor said. "What do you think?"

"How big is the apartment?"

"Two rooms, plus a small kitchen, bath/laundry room and a tiny verandah. He said sixty square meters, which I guess is about six hundred fifty square feet. Small, but I can lie completely flat and don't have to fight other cops in the dorm for the shower anymore."

"Not bad. But don't lose that contract. Terms have a way of changing as time passes. 'Unavoidable' rent increases during the lease, extra key money demands; landlords get pretty creative. If yours gives you a problem, let me know."

"Thanks."

The light at the intersection ahead flashed yellow; Murakami decided not to run it. The pedestrian light hadn't changed yet but a high school kid was about to charge across anyway until he saw the black and white approaching, at which point he stopped dead in his tracks and inspected his navel.

"Had any guests yet?" Murakami asked.

"You mean women?"

"Or are you like Tanaka? That's OK with me if you are, I just—"

"No. Just women for me," Thor said.

"Really?"

"Fuck you."

With traffic crawling along, Murakami said, "Say, do you know what you should say instead of that?"

"Instead of what?"

"Instead of 'Fuck you.' When speaking Japanese, I mean."

"Hold it, I know." Thor rubbed the scar above his eyebrow with his index finger. "Got it. *Baka yaroh!*" Translated exactly it meant *You fool!* but the emotion was stronger. Japanese were not into scatological or sexual expletives, at least when speaking in their own language.

"That's not bad, but everyone knows that one."

"How about *Aho!*" What Osaka residents said instead of *Baka yaroh*, which was popular in Tokyo and most of the rest of Japan.

"Too Osaka dialect. People in Tokyo will think you are a hick."

"I give up."

"Try '*Hottoite yo.*' It kind of means 'Leave me alone' and is usually employed seriously, like when someone is hassling you. You know, like 'Get out of here!'" But you can also say it as a joke."

"*Hottoite yo!*"

"Yeah, that's it."

"What a teacher," Thor said. "Thanks."

"Sure."

They rode a few more feet in silence. "What have you been doing for dinner now that you have your own place?"

"McDonald's, mostly. Or some place on the way home," Thor said. "I haven't had much time to shop for pots and pans."

"My mother says I should invite you over for dinner."

"I'd love to, thanks."

"I didn't invite you," Murakami said. "I just told you what my mother suggested."

"*Hottoite yo!*"

"Pretty good. But with more feeling."

"Fuck you." Thor was laughing.

"You are such a low class foreigner." Murakami sniffed. "Besides, my mother isn't much of a cook."

"I doubt that," Thor said. "I heard Japanese women were born to cook."

"That's the Chinese."

"In any case, I would be honored to meet your family and I'm sure I will love your mother's cooking."

"OK. How about Sunday night?"

"Sounds great."

"By the way," Murakami said. "Do you Americans eat everything with your bare hands?"

"*Hottoite yo!*"

"You are learning, grasshopper." When Thor did a double take, he added, "I used to watch *Kung Fu* reruns in the dorm at Berkeley."

15

Shinsaibashi was Osaka's answer to the hustle and bustle of Hong Kong, the shopping Mecca of Asia. It ran about a mile from Namba Station north to Honmachi, and was completely covered except at intersections. Its hundreds of shops were open from ten to eight, seven days a week, and sold everything from freshly roasted green tea to Big Macs to silk wallets. The bridge under which the Dohtombori River flowed, and the adjacent bars and restaurants, were favorite gathering places for young and old. The Kirin Plaza was where Kate Capshaw met Michael Douglas in the movie *Black Rain*. On Saturdays, Sundays and holidays the stream of people flowing over the bridge and off into the distance looked like a river of laser-guided Ping-Pong balls.

Detectives Thor and Murakami found Guy Halpern standing behind his sheet at the north end of the bridge, sitting, looking bored, on a wooden crate. Halpern was wearing Levi 501s, New Balance tennis shoes, a red flannel shirt and a blue down parka. On the little finger of his right hand was a gold ring in the form of a lion's head. The parka was open and his gut was hanging over his jeans. As the two detectives approached a young woman stopped to look over the merchandise.

"Isn't it nice?" Halpern said to her, in Japanese.

"How much?" she asked, pointing to a pair of earrings.

"Six thousand, five hundred yen," Halpern said. About $60.

"Expensive!" the woman yelped, scurrying away.

"Not much luck today?" Thor asked. Murakami stopped at a stall next door which offered "genuine imitation glass rings."

"Hey, sport," Halpern said. "How about a Hunting World bag? Or a Chanel bag for your wife?"

Thor disliked him immediately. Halpern was the kind of guy who called everyone "sport" and insisted on attaching suffixes to people's names. If Halpern had met the American detective before, he might say, "Hey, it's the Thor-meister, or Thor-dude."

"How much?"

"For you, 8,000 yen."

"Nice guy." Thor picked up one of the bags. Sloppy stitching and design indicated it was a knock off, probably from Thailand. "How did you get this space? Don't you need a license or something?"

"What are you, a cop?" Halpern tried to laugh good-naturedly, but his eyes watched Thor intently, like a caged animal.

"Yeah," Thor laughed. "And I came over here from Minneapolis to bust you for creating a public nuisance."

"Shucks. Nabbed by the long arm of the law."

Halpern was a big guy, six two or three, about 240 pounds. He'd played football, or maybe he'd wrestled, and he hadn't always had the flab. His shoulder-length blond hair was tied back in a ponytail.

"No, really. I'm just interested," Thor said. "How is it you get this prime spot when there are plenty of red-blooded Japanese hustlers about?"

"Easy. I arrived one morning at about 6:15 and asked a *yakuza* who seemed in charge 'Can I have a space, please?' He said, 'Yes' and I said, 'Oh' and he said, 'What?' and I said, 'Oh.'

"And finally he said, 'Fine, I'll show you your spot. Here it is.' And he brought me here. Later, this kindly old lady came along and asked for 5,000 yen, which I gave her, knowing it was going back to the *yakuza*."

"And that was that?" Thor said.

"For that month, yeah," Halpern said. "Each month the old lady comes back and I pay and nobody bothers me."

"And you make enough to live on?"

"I'm a student here," said Guy Halpern around a shit-eating grin. The bra straps of high school cheerleaders had dissolved under that grin ten years and forty pounds ago. "I go to *Japan Language College*. I'm not allowed to work full-time, but this helps. I also have some savings I draw on from time to time."

"Neat."

"So what's your story?" Halpern said. "You don't look like the usual American tourist. I'm on Candid Camera, right?"

"What's an American tourist look like?"

"You know. Jeans or chinos, maybe sweats if they're senior citizens, camera hanging from neck, maybe a kid or two in tow. A friendly but lost look on their faces. Sticker shock when they look in the stores. You, on the other hand, you're wearing a jacket and tie. You work here?"

"I told you," Thor said with a smile. "I'm a cop." Halpern laughed. "And I'm here investigating a murder."

"Well I'm clean. I ain't never been to Minneapolis." Halpern was counting the few bills in his cardboard cash box. He looked up at Thor. "You really a cop?"

"I really am."

"Like I said, I've been here all afternoon."

"No, this one happened a few days ago," Thor said. "Girl named Lisa Madison."

Halpern froze in mid count.

"Do you know her?" Thor asked.

"What is this?" Halpern said. "You with the American Consulate or something?"

"I told you, I'm a cop."

"Yeah, working a beat here in Japan. Right."

"Yeah," Thor said. He gave the strap on the fake Hunting World bag a quick snap, ripping out some of the stitching. "Oh. Sorry."

"Hey," Halpern started to rise but changed his mind. "Be careful with that stuff, will you?"

Thor handed the bag to Halpern.

"Pretty neat, huh? Me being a cop and all."

"And you're investigating Lisa's murder."

"I am."

"Then I guess you know she and I were seeing each other."

"That's what I heard."

"So you aren't here by accident."

"No."

"Then why didn't you just tell me that in the beginning?"

"Sorry." Thor shrugged. "I was interested to know how you got this spot. Figured you would be more open if you didn't know I was a cop."

"Shit," Halpern said. "I wondered when you'd get around to me." Halpern put down his box and looked around. "Well, I didn't kill her."

"Oh?"

"I didn't."

"Who said you did?" Thor said, amiably. "I'm just trying to get as much information as I can about Lisa, the people she hung out with. You know. Just doing what cops do. That's all."

"How does this work, then?" Halpern said. "The Japanese cops call you in special just for this?"

"No. I'm here on an exchange program. One year."

"An observer?"

"No. Full police powers." Thor showed Halpern his ID card.

"How's your Japanese?"

"Not bad."

Halpern looked Thor over again. "So what do you want to know?"

"How about starting with where you were on the night Lisa Madison was killed?"

"What night was that?" Halpern said.

"The night of January 12th, morning of the 13th."

"No. Like what night was that? Monday, Friday? What day?"

"Between 10:00 PM Sunday night and Monday morning around 2:00 AM."

"Well, let's see," Halpern said, stroking an imaginary goatee. "I guess I was busy."

Thor looked down at the greenish-brown river and thought about throwing Halpern in. "That's real helpful, *Guy*." Thor put extra emphasis on Halpern's first name, making it sound derogatory. "But can you be a little more specific?"

"What day was that again?"

"Last Monday morning, early."

"I remember!" Halpern snapped his fingers. "Right across there." He pointed at a tall building on the other side of the river. "The Boar and Fife. British style pub. Third floor. I was there."

"On a Sunday night?" Thor said.

"Don't start work Mondays till late afternoon."

"What time did you get there?"

"Don't know. About seven. Eight, maybe."

"And you left when?"

"When the place closed. 3:00AM."

"You were there the whole time?"

"Damned straight," Halpern said.

"Doing what?"

"What do you think I was doing, Sherlock? The usual. Drinking. Playing darts. Talking to the ladies."

"You didn't leave at all during that time?"

"Nope."

"Think anyone there can vouch for you?"

"Ghandi the bartender can. My table was right next to the counter."

"Ghandi?"

"That's what everyone calls him. Some Indian guy. I don't know his real name."

"Anybody else?"

"Who else do you need? I didn't go with anybody, if that's what you mean." Halpern got up to attend a potential customer. She walked away when Halpern approached.

"Do you ever actually sell anything?" Thor said.

"Sure. All the time when I don't have cops scaring everybody off." He sat down again. "You want witnesses, right? I was pretty smashed."

"But you think the bartender saw you."

"I know he did. He's the one kept feeding me brewskies all night."

Murakami said, "I'll go check," and jogged over the bridge.

"Who's he?" Halpern said.

"My partner."

"Pretty sneaky of you guys."

Thor was getting tired of sparring.

"How well did you know Lisa, Guy?"

"We went out a few times."

"Were you sleeping together?"

Halpern blinked. "Huh?"

"You know," Thor said. "When you both take off your clothes and rub against each other?"

"You're a riot," Halpern said. "What do you think, I gave her an overdose of American white meat?"

"I'd like to know," Thor said. "And you're going to tell me."

"OK, fine. Yeah, we did it a few times. Though I get the feeling you knew that already too."

"Did you know she was also sleeping with her boss?"

"No." Halpern considered this for a moment. "Not surprised, though. You saw what she looked like."

Thor recalled the nearly decapitated body he had seen. "Yeah, I saw her."

"Man, what a piece." Halpern shook his head. "With a face and body like that it's a wonder she wasn't hooking full time."

"She was hooking?"

"Naw, I just mean she could have. Shit. If I looked like her I'd just sit down, put a collection plate next to me, and spread my legs."

Thor tried, and failed, to picture one thing the Lisa Madison described to him by her ex-husband might have found attractive in Guy Halpern. "How'd you meet?"

"At the Boar and Fife." Halpern removed a tray of rings and put it under the table, replacing it with one containing bracelets. "Maybe these will move better today," he said to Thor. "Lisa plays darts. Man, what a partier she was. One night she was whipping some *salaryman's* ass and I was next in line. My turn came up and I beat her, by two points. After the game we had a few beers."

"You sleep with her that night?"

"What do you want, home movies? But yeah, as a matter of fact I did. That happens more over here than back home. Maybe it's because nobody seems to have AIDS here. You find someone you like, you get to it." Halpern sighed, reminiscing. "Just like the old days back home."

"You knew she was divorced?"

"I knew."

"Did you ever meet her daughter, Megan?"

"Sure. I picked Lisa up at her apartment a few times. Played with the kid while Lisa was getting ready or till the baby-sitter got there."

"Ever think of getting married?"

"Yeah. Right." Halpern guffawed. "I'm not what you'd call the marrying kind."

"She ever mention any enemies to you?" Thor said.

"No."

"Problems she was having at work or with friends?"

"She wasn't into spilling her guts, you know? She always wanted to get to where we were going as soon as possible and didn't like talking too much along the way. That's one thing I liked about her," Halpern said. "None of this touchy-feely, what-do you-really-think-about-me crap. That and the way she fucked."

"Pretty good, was she?"

"An absolute fucking animal," Halpern said, warming to the subject. "If I didn't get her off three times a night she practically beat me up."

"When was the last time you saw her?"

Halpern became more cautious. "Couple of weeks ago."

"Did she say anything about a letter she had received?"

"A letter? No."

"Did you call her after that last time together? Or she you?"

"No. I been busy."

"Do you know anyone named Peter Randall?"

"Nope."

"A Japanese friend named Minoru?"

"Now you're asking a tough one. Japanese don't use first names much, even among friends. I probably know some dude named Minoru—there aren't that many first names here—but I can't think of anyone now."

"You're sure."

"Sure as I can be. Like I said."

"She seem upset, afraid, worried about anything when you saw her that last time? Money problems? Maybe some neighbor harassing her? Trouble with her ex-husband?"

"Shit, I don't know. We just fucked."

"No one pressuring her to do something she didn't want to do?" Thor suggested.

"Like what?"

"Like sell drugs, for example?"

Halpern stood, looking for customers. "I wouldn't know anything about that."

"Gosh, *Guy*, but I think you would," Thor said. "Hard to see you making enough to live on hawking this crap."

"That bitch Yuki told you that, didn't she?"

"Did I mention anyone named Yuki?" Thor said.

"Forget it."

Thor saw Murakami walking back across the bridge. In the distance, a giant mechanical crab perched over a restaurant door extended and retracted its claws. "Story checks out," Murakami said.

"The bartender remembers him?" Thor said. "He's sure it was Halpern?"

"Says he was drinking non-stop until they kicked him out at 3:00."

"Gosh, guys." Halpern bent down to get another tray and smiled. "Sorry to ruin your day. C'mon back someday when you need some fancy jewelry for your women."

Thor squatted down and placed his face two inches from Halpern's. "I have to go now, *Guy*." He grabbed Halpern's shoulder. "But I'll be back real soon. I like you, you see, and I'm dying to hear more about your pharmaceutical business." Thor threw Halpern back onto a pile of freshly minted imitation Gucci bags.

16

The woman in bed with Eric Thor was naked, as was he himself. Her breasts were large for a Japanese woman—she must have been Japanese because her hair was black—Thor guessed C cup. Thor hadn't yet seen them but knew this to be true. He also knew that the left one was slightly larger than the right one. She was left-handed.

Thor's penis was engorged and as hard as his pistol back in Minneapolis. He wondered absently what happened to the rest of his body when so much blood was occupied in his penis—which part of his body did the blood come from. Might the blood deficiency cause him to faint?

He looked down at the woman's hip where his hand rested, sliding it down to her exquisite rear end, so soft and smooth. She shook her head back and forth, drawing Thor's attention to the string of pearls around her neck, causing his erection to flag slightly. *Turn around*, he thought, *face me so I can enter you.* Entering her from behind didn't occur to him.

She moaned and shifted slightly on the futon, one of her legs brushing against his penis, then she was still. Why wouldn't she just turn around, Thor wondered?

She mumbled something.

"What?" he said.

She reached back suddenly and grabbed his penis, rubbing the tip with her thumb, squeezing it in a way both pleasurable and unbearable, and began moving her hand slowly up and down, up and down. Thor closed his eyes and prayed he wouldn't ejaculate. Not yet.

"I'm sorry, I didn't hear you?" He spoke to the back of her head. "What are you trying to tell me?"

She stopped moving for a few seconds, in response to his words, then resumed her caressing.

"Hey. You keep rubbing me like that and I'm going to lose it before we even get started." He tried to mask his desperation with a chuckle. "Why don't you let me do something for you?" Her moaning was building in intensity. Thor had to shift as she yanked his penis towards her vagina. Her first stab was wide to the left, glancing off her one leg. He could feel sticky wetness oozing out of her patch, running between her legs, seeping under his legs, ass, and elbow like spilled honey. She released his penis and pushed him back, her clenched fist coming perilously close to the family jewels.

"Whoa!" he said. "You're going to damage the goods."

Thor reached around to touch her breast again, to turn her towards him. Her long, single braid flowed down her neck, over the collarbone, through her impressive cleavage; when she breathed, the hairs, now blond, twinkled in the moonlight. Gazing at her hair made Thor harder.

She was still trying to ram him into her, still missing, her moaning building to a wrothy howl.

"Are you OK?" he asked. "I don't think you're supposed to make those kinds of sounds."

Thor endeavored once again to turn her body towards him but her skin was slick and his hand slid off her shoulder blade. Thor held up his hand in the moonlight. Blood dripped down his fingers, past his forearm, plop, plopping, on the bed below.

"Are you always this color?" He felt he should ask.

"Shhh!" she said.

Thor wanted to pull away but she was holding his penis again like a vice. He knew it would break off if he made a sudden move.

"I'm not like the rest," Thor said. "I want to know you. Stop hiding from me!"

He tried again to pull her towards him but his hands couldn't find purchase anywhere on her slippery body.

"Look at me!" Thor yelled. She continued to face away from him, blood flowing now from between her legs, her hair, cascading down her neck like a small stream. "Will you please just look at me! Just turn around, will you? Just look me in the face and turn off the alarm clock. The alarm clock turn off the alarm turn your face around turn off the alarm..."

Thor's eyes popped open in the darkness and he reached automatically for his alarm clock, pushing the appropriate button. The bell kept ringing.

"The phone," he muttered to himself. He struggled out of his futon and staggered over to the phone, knocking over an empty can of Asahi Super Dry.

"*Moshi moshi,*" he said. "Hello?"

There was a click, followed by faint static. "Hello?"

"Eric? Eric?"

"Yes? Who is this?"

"Eric? lo?"

"Hello?"

"Helloello? Its Bill Enqebretsssss"

"Bill?" Thor said. "The connection's not good. Hang up and call me back." He hung up and waited for his once-and-future MPD partner, Bill Engebretson, to try a different line with AT&T

or whomever fucked up the first try. When the phone didn't ring right away he turned on the one light that came with his new apartment and found his bathrobe on the floor next to his futon. He was looking for the slippers he had bought yesterday when the phone finally rang.

"Hello, Bill?" No echo this time.

"Eric? Shit! What the hell was that?"

"Dunno. Bad connection, I guess." Thor reached over to his 3-foot high refrigerator and pulled out a carton of Kirin-Tropicana 100% Blended Juice. "It's OK now. What the fuck are you calling at—" he looked at the clock next to his bed, "2:05 AM?" He pried the carton open only to discover that it wasn't supposed to be pried open; there was a pull-off plastic cap on one side. He yanked it off and took a swig.

"Only 11:05AM here in Minneapolis," Engebretson said. "Not my problem if you guys can't keep time over there."

"Thanks."

"Hope I didn't interrupt a fun dream."

Thor's dream girl flashed back into his mind. "No." The image of her bloody, sexy, moonlit silhouette was still hauntingly fresh in his mind. "I never remember my dreams." He wished that were true.

"You get that fax I sent you?" Thor said.

"I got it," Engebretson said. "What the hell you think I'm calling you for?"

Thor looked for a pen and paper, found a yellow pad in a still-unpacked box next to the phone. "What have you got?"

"Seeing as we got nothing better to do than run background checks for the Tokyo Police Department—"

"Osaka."

"Osaka. Whatever," Engebretson said. "I hope you appreciate this."

"Anybody give you a hard time?"

"Running a criminal record check? Naw. Tina in records is into those Japanese cartoons."

"*Anime.*"

"Yeah, whatever," Engebretson said. "Told her you could get her anything she wants, half price."

Thor looked at the handle of his phone. "Listen, you Neanderthal. Anything I get here's going to be in Japanese, no English dubbing or subtitles. What's she gonna do with that?"

"Hey. Your problem, not mine."

"You'll make a fine captain someday."

"Damned straight," he said. "And I told Hibberd in Vice you could get him a Nikon on the cheap."

"But they cost more here than in Minneapolis!"

"So? Pick one up at *Ritz Camera* when you get back, I don't give a fuck," Engebretson said. "You want what I found out or not?"

"I'm afraid to ask. Any more strings attached?"

"Naw, I just made all that up." Thor could hear papers shuffling. "Here's what I got on a Dolores Madison of Tampa, Florida. Maiden name Dolores Homer, married to one James Madison, they had one child, Lisa."

"Arrests?"

"Dolores Madison is not wanted in the State of Florida, the State of New York or any other of the fifty states or District of Columbia. There are no outstanding federal warrants either."

"Oh well."

"She was ticketed for speeding in Colonie, New York in 1978 and last year in Plant City, Florida for running a red light. Paid both fines."

"Nothing else, huh?"

"Oh yeah," Engebretson said. "I almost forgot. She sliced up twenty-seven people at the Mall of America two weeks ago with a Gillette Sensor For Women. Then she blew up the building and drove to McDonald's for a Big Mac. Made all the papers."

Thor was doodling stick men on his note pad. "Anything on her divorce?"

"She's divorced?"

"That's what she told us."

"News to me," Engebretson said. "You want I should check on that, too? What with all our murderers, pushers and gangs getting religion these days I got nothing else to do."

"You love this," Thor said. "I can see you now, telling everyone at the precinct you're on some international case, hunting ninjas."

"Hah! At least I work for a living. You're over there hanging out with geisha girls waiting on you hand and foot, admit it."

"You got me." Thor gazed out the window. "I miss you, you asshole."

Engebretson's swivel chair creaked over thousands of miles of fiber optic cable. "So how is everything going over there anyway, Eric? They treating you all right?"

"It's all right," Thor said.

"Just all right? The way you were yacking before you left, this was going to be the greatest assignment since peanut butter and jelly sandwiches."

Thor sifted through the mixed metaphors. "Did you ever consider trying for your elementary school equivalency degree?"

"Yeah, yeah. So how do your *Japanese law enforcement brethren*," Engebretson tried to sound highly educated, "like having a real cop showing 'em how to do things?"

"Some of the guys have been all right. Some aren't too happy about it." Thor decided against mentioning the anonymous notes he had recently found on his desk inviting him in no uncertain terms to return to the US. "The guys do their jobs. A different set of rules, that's all. You know how it is. I'll be all right."

"But nobody's invited you ice fishing yet? Is that what you're saying?"

"Could be because there's no ice here, but yeah," Thor said. "As a matter of fact, though, I am having dinner at my partner's parents' house tomorrow night."

"He lives with his parents? Sounds like a Mamma's boy."

"They just do that here. Different customs. You know. Saves money, I guess. Apartments are pretty expensive."

"So how is this new partner of yours? You getting along?"

"You sound jealous."

"Fuck you," Engebretson chuckled. "So? How is he?"

"He's a good guy, I think. A bit full of himself, maybe, but I suppose I would be too if I was Japanese and had a BA in Psychology from Berkeley. He knows what he's doing." Thor scratched out one of the stick men he had made and began drawing three-dimensional cubes. "He's good."

"And he doesn't mind having an American as his partner?"

"I guess we get along pretty well. He's trying. Anyway, he's a good cop." Thor saw that his clock now read 2:18. "Well listen, partner. I think we've spent enough of the Mayor's money today. Besides, I need my beauty sleep. Say 'hi' to everybody for me, will you?"

"You got it," Engebretson said. "You watch yourself, you hear? Or I might have to come over there and knock some heads together."

The image of a slightly overweight, six foot six inch Dane rampaging in the streets of Osaka brightened Thor's mood. "Yeah. You, too, partner. Talk to you soon."

Thor took one last swig of juice and put the carton away. Back in bed he lay in the darkness, arms behind his head, trying to remember his dream girl and figure out why she had visited.

17

Intruding smells wafted out from the kitchen where Mrs. Murakami was cooking, seeping under the door to the living room where Detective Murakami's father was explaining to Detective Thor why high school baseball was more exciting than professional baseball.

"There are two national tournaments at Koshien Stadium in Osaka, in spring and summer," the elder Murakami said. "They show every game on TV, from morning to evening." He refilled Thor's glass with beer. After putting the bottle down he waited patiently for Thor to notice that his own glass was empty. Japanese manners dictated that you keep a constant vigil on friends' beer glasses to ensure they were never empty. This meant by extension that you should not fill your own glass, lest you deprive your neighbor of doing it for you. Thor had read about this custom, but was not yet adept at it. He took a sip of his newly filled glass. Mr. Murakami's glass remained empty.

Thor had read of the tournament. Mr. Murakami immediately replenished the beer in Thor's glass. When he made, reluctantly, to fill his own glass, Thor belatedly caught on.

"Oh!" he said. "Excuse me, Mr. Murakami. Allow me." Thor had given up trying to remember if the paper label on the bottle was supposed to be facing up or down while the beer was being poured. He hoped it didn't matter overly much.

"Oh, thank you, Thor-san," Mr. Murakami held up his glass to receive the beer. "Most people join in a betting pool—I'm talking about the Koshien High School Baseball Tournament—and you can always find crowds gathered around some big TV at an electronics store. It lasts several days."

"Who goes to the games?" Thor said. "On weekdays." Thor checked his partner's glass, found it was still full, and put the bottle down on the table.

"Students, mostly, since they are on vacation. But you can find lots of suits and ties there, too." Mr. Murakami emptied his glass, emitting a satisfied, "Ahhhh!"

"What's the big attraction?" Thor pounced on the bottle. Empty.

"Mom!" Mr. Murakami said to his wife of twenty-five years. "Another beer!"

Thor estimated they had gone through seven or eight of the one liter bottles.

Mrs. Murakami brought a tray of Japanese appetizers along with a fresh bottle, taking away the old. Mr. Murakami grabbed it, poised to replenish Thor's glass. "Go ahead," he said. Thor guzzled what remained, holding out his glass with both hands, as he had read was the polite thing to do with one's elders.

"Those kids play like there is no tomorrow," Mr. Murakami said reverentially. "Head first slides, diving for fly balls. It's great!"

"You mean the pros don't do that?" Thor asked. He picked up a stalk of asparagus wrapped in a thin slice of meat.

"Your major leaguers in the US play like that all the time, but our guys are just a bunch of lazy bums."

"That's surprising. I thought Japanese were always gung-ho for the team," Thor said.

"Pros here play baseball almost 12 months a year," Mr. Murakami said. "The regular season goes from April to October. After the Japan Series—like your World Series—they begin fall practice and play various all-star exhibitions. After New Years they go indoors and pitch and throw and run to keep in shape. Then spring training arrives and it's time for the regular season again."

"Sounds rough."

"The companies that own these teams—department stores, car companies, newspaper companies, food companies—like to get their money's worth," Kennichi joined the conversation. "When they're not actually playing baseball, ownership has the players on game shows, doing exhibitions, anything to generate revenue. Pros here don't make what Americans do, but they still make a lot more than the average person. The companies feel they have a right to keep their employees working full-time."

"Do players ever get cut?"

"The weaker ones do," Kennichi said. "But after a guy has been around for four or five years, especially if he's been up with the parent club, it becomes harder to fire him. Almost embarrassing from a PR standpoint. It's as if the teams have an obligation to keep him employed."

"What happens when he just can't hit or pitch anymore?"

"On the weaker teams he may keep playing, since the team wouldn't win anyway, and can't afford anyone better, so it doesn't matter. Fans get attached to him and love him no matter the stats. Stronger teams can put him on the bench, bring him out in the later innings or as a pinch hitter."

"Even if he can't hit anymore?"

"Even if he can't hit anymore." Kennichi made eye contact with Thor and then looked over at his father's glass. Thor got the hint and grabbed the bottle. "Sometimes they arrange a trade to a weaker team, allowing the guy to keep his pride. But you will occasionally see older players out there with .220 batting averages."

"I would think gratitude would make the guys play harder." Thor stabbed a scallop wrapped in bacon, covered with Hollandaise sauce.

"They are grateful," Kennichi said. "Just burned out. After a while it gets to be simply a job for them. They practice hard and work all year, but it's hard for them to get too interested in bruising their bodies bellyflopping in left field for a ball they might not get to anyway. There's little danger of someone taking their place so why risk the injury?"

"But the high schoolers aren't jaded yet. Is that what you're saying?"

"Yeah."

"In the spring," Mr. Murakami said, "I'll get us some tickets and the three of us will go."

"I would like that." Thor said.

Mrs. Murakami came in and announced dinner. "We're having *sukiyaki* if that is all right," she said to her American guest.

"I've been looking forward to this, Mrs. Murakami," Thor said. "Kennichi says you won first prize in a national cooking competition."

"Eh?" she said.

"He's joking, Mom," Kennichi said. "American humor."

Mrs. Murakami blushed, smiled and then busied herself with seasoning the giant frying pan full of sliced beef and assorted raw vegetables. She poured a little soy sauce, added some sugar and checked the taste.

"It's ready," she said. "Would you prefer a fork and knife, Detective Thor?"

"Mom!" Kennichi said. "I told you already he can use chopsticks just fine."

"Actually," Thor said. "I'm rather clumsy with the things, but I'll do my best. Thank you for offering."

"All right," she said, sending a scolding look at her impudent son. "Help yourself."

Having said that, she started piling meat into Thor's bowl of scrambled raw egg.

"*Itadakimasu.*" Thor intoned the traditional dinner preamble and plucked a slice of meat. "This is delicious."

"No, no," Mrs. Murakami shook her head happily. "Were the appetizers all right?"

"I'm sorry," Thor said, mouth full. "I forgot to tell you how delicious they were."

"No, no," she said. Japanese liked to say, "No, no" whenever complimented.

"Your husband and son are lucky men."

"My goodness!" she said. "I envy American wives if all men are as polite as you." She pointed at her husband. "He doesn't appreciate me at all. Poor me!"

"Sure we appreciate you, Mother," Kennichi said. "You do great laundry."

"Ha!" she said.

Thor had not eaten since late morning. He could feel the alcohol beginning to affect him, hoped it didn't show. His eyes moved to his beer glass, which Mr. Murakami took as a signal that he wanted more beer.

"Bottoms up," Kennichi's father said.

"Oh leave him alone," Mrs. Murakami said. "He has work tomorrow."

"*I* have work tomorrow, too. He can drink."

"But you drink like this every night." She snatched Thor's glass away before Mr. Murakami could. "Would you like some water? Or juice?"

"Water would be fine, thank you."

"Humph!" Mr. Murakami said. He got up and fetched a clean glass, filled it with beer and handed it to Thor.

"Kennichi tells me you are living alone," Mrs. Murakami said.

"Yes. But the place I have now is very nice."

"Does it have a washing machine?"

"No. But there is a Laundromat nearby. I'm using that till I can get a washing machine." Thor ate more sukiyaki, hoping it would soak up some of the beer.

"Terrible," she clucked. "They don't even provide you with a furnished apartment."

"No. It's fine, really. I had the choice of living in a police dormitory. I just felt I needed a bit more space. I'm fine, really."

"Nonsense. From now on you just give your dirty clothes to Kennichi and I'll wash them."

"That's very kind," Thor said. "But I can't—"

"And why don't you have dinner here every Saturday?"

"No, really, I—"

"Good," she said. "Now that's decided." She added more meat and vegetables to the giant pan.

The room was beginning a slow spin while Thor's stomach started to toss and turn.

"Excuse me," he said in his most cheerful voice. "I wonder if I might use your toilet."

"Are you all right?" Mrs. Murakami looked concerned. "It's right over here."

"I'm fine," he croaked. "I'll be fine." Thor closed the door and reached the toilet bowl just as asparagus, scallops, sliced beef and vegetables, marinated in beer, escaped the maelstrom within. The performance wasn't lost on Mrs. Murakami.

"Now look what you've done," she said to her husband.

18

Detective Murakami was gratified to see that American police officers were capable of hangovers.

Thor's prior immunity to jet lag and sleep deprivation had left the Japanese detective wondering. But here it was Monday morning and the American walked in looking like he had gangrene of the head.

"How do you feel?" Murakami asked in a cheerful voice.

"Fuck off." Thor said this in English. "No Japanese today. No Japanese." He collapsed in his chair. "No English either. No speaking. Let's just sit here in silence."

"My mother was pretty worried about you."

"Have I met your mother?" Thor placed his head gingerly on his desk.

"You should have heard her scold my father after you left. 'You old fool,' she said. 'What will he think of Japanese people now?'"

"You're father can drink more beer than the 82nd Airborne."

"He does like his beer." Murakami rummaged around in his desk until he found a spare bottle of *Regain*. "Here. Try this." He gave Thor a gentle nudge.

"Leave me alone."

"It will make you fell better."

"What's in it?"

"You don't want to know. But it will settle your stomach and keep you going until the end of the day."

Thor downed the entire 100 milliliters in one gulp. "Gagh! Tastes like cough medicine."

"Not feeling well, Detective Thor?" Captain Kume had materialized in front of Thor's desk. His white shirt was freshly ironed, his tie neatly knotted. His dark blue suit was immaculate and sharply creased. He held a sheaf of papers in his left hand.

"Yes, sir." Thor sat up when he saw who it was. "No sir, I'm fine."

Kume looked at his new American officer for a moment. He had heard nothing about drinking problems.

"Getting settled into your new apartment, are you?" Kume said.

"Yes, sir. It's very nice, sir."

"Eating well?" Kume kept his attention on Thor's eyes.

"Yes, sir. Fine." Thor didn't want to talk about food.

"Restaurant food isn't awfully healthy," Kume said. "So much grease and fat. Bad for the stomach. Can you cook?"

"A little, sir." *Please change the subject.*

"What you need is a good home-cooked meal."

"Yes, sir." What would happen to relations between the US and Japan if he threw up on Captain Kume, Thor wondered.

"You'll have to join my family for sukiyaki when you get completely settled in. Perfect food for cold winters. Do you like hot sake?"

"Um, excuse me, sir," Thor said, rising gingerly. "I have to go to the men's room for a moment."

"Certainly." Kume watched Thor dash away.

"It's my fault, sir," Murakami said. "He had dinner at my house last night and my father likes his beer and, well, you know how it is."

"Oh, that explains it." Kume chuckled, satisfied that his American detective was not an alcoholic, then turned back to business. "Here is a copy of the coroner's official report. It confirms Lisa Madison died of a puncture wound to the heart caused by a sharp instrument, at least twelve inches in length, type unknown."

"Too long for a house knife or scissors," Murakami said.

"Yes."

"So it was premeditated. Someone brought along a special weapon specifically for the job."

"Not too many people walk around with knives like that anymore," Kume said.

"We're checking the hardware and building supplies companies."

"Good."

Thor came back from the bathroom. He was still pale but looked like he might pull through.

"Feeling better?" Kume said.

"Yes, sir."

"Good. I was just going over the coroner's final report with Detective Murakami," Kume said. "It looks more and more like a premeditated murder."

Kume handed the report to Thor.

"Maybe the killer is a butcher," Thor said. "Or flower arrangement teacher. Someone who would have access to that kind of knife without arousing suspicion."

"Could be. What do you make of the sliced throat after the stab through the heart?"

"An amateur might not have known the first thrust was fatal."

"We are forgetting one important thing." Thor rummaged around in his briefcase for the fax from Jansen and InterBank. "The missing ATM card and money. Lisa was loaded."

Murakami looked doubtful. "So Lisa Madison was killed for three million yen?"

"Why not?"

"It's just not enough. I can see some hard luck bum knocking someone over the head if they were walking down the street with a bag of money. But this crime was just too involved. Why go to the trouble of bringing a giant knife to do something a regular knife could have done. And if the assailant was after the money, why waste time trashing the shop, increasing the risk of a witness happening by, before leaving?"

Thor mentally converted three million yen to US currency. About $28,000. "That's a lot of money."

Murakami shook his head. "No. Not for a murder. Not here in Japan. Not for so much trouble. Lisa's nearly decapitated head bothers me. It's like it was a sign, a message. Too much trouble for a random murder."

"Maybe Tanaka's into some loan sharks for a lot of money. Or some gang wants him to sell his place."

"We're looking at Tanaka's financial records now," Murakami said. "Nothing yet to indicate he's hard up for money."

Thor wished he could go back home and sleep. There was something about the case that he was missing, buzzing in his head since the odd dream he had a couple nights before. Like a name on the tip of your tongue, or an errand you were supposed to do. There was something obvious that he was just not getting. His hangover was not helping.

A female officer ran over to Thor's desk. "Telephone, sir. A foreign woman on Line 3. I'm sorry, I could not catch her name."

Thor picked up his phone and punched button #3. "Detective Thor. Yes...I see...When?...We'll be right over." He hung up.

"Something?" Kume said.

"Maybe our first piece of good luck," Thor said, putting on his coat and scarf. "Someone called while Mrs. Madison was shopping for food next door and spoke with Megan.

"Let's go," Murakami said.

*

Megan smiled at Thor as soon as he entered the apartment and gave him a big smile, which he returned despite a splitting headache. Thor assumed she did not yet know about her mother's death. She looked at Detective Murakami with simple curiosity.

"This is Detective Murakami," Thor said. "He's my partner."

"I thought Detective Yamamoto was your partner," Megan said.

Thor scratched the back of his head. "I work with him too sometimes. Detective Murakami is my full-time partner."

"I see," Megan said. "Nice to meet you Detective Murakami."

"Nice to meet you, Megan," Murakami said.

"Mom's not here," she said. "Grammy said Mommy had to go on a trip for a while."

"I see," Thor said.

"I have to tell you," Mrs. Madison said, "I'm not too crazy about your questioning her. I mean, I know I called you and all, but then I got to thinking about it and I don't know if this is such a good idea. She is pretty darn young."

"I'm five, Grammy," Megan said. "And I like Detective Thor."

"I know you are, dear," Mrs. Madison. "You're a big girl." To Thor she said, "I explained to Megan that the person who called her is a bad person you police are looking for."

"I can help, I can help," Megan said. "We have to put bad people in jail. That's where they belong." Megan crossed her arms, hoping to look serious and strong.

"You did the right thing in calling us, Mrs. Madison. We need to know about the caller," Thor said. "You're a good girl, Megan."

"That's what Mommy always tells me." She started to put her thumb in her mouth, but glanced quickly at her grandmother and put both hands in her lap. Mrs. Madison didn't appear to notice.

"Why don't we just start talking and see what happens," Thor said.

"Can I stay?" Mrs. Madison asked.

"Of course. "Thor sat on the floor, cross-legged. It felt good to sit down. Blood didn't have to travel so far to reach his pounding head.

"Did someone call you today, Megan?" Thor asked.

"Yup," Megan answered. "It was a woman. A *bad* woman."

"You said it was this morning, Mrs. Madison, is that right?"

"Yes, that's right," Mrs. Madison said. "I had just gone next door to get groceries for lunch. I needed too many things for Megan to carry, I thought I'd just run over and be back in a few minutes. It couldn't have been more than ten minutes."

"Megan." Thor looked directly at Megan, trying to convey both friendliness and urgency. "I need you to do me a favor. I need you think back to this morning and try to remember what the caller, the bad woman, said to you. Do you think you can do that?"

"I think so." Megan didn't look as confident as she had a moment ago.

"Good girl," he said. "Now, the caller was a woman, right?"

"Yes, I think so. I couldn't hear it too good, though. She sounded far away, kind of like when Mommy has the radio on. I could hear it, but it was hard."

"Masking her voice," Murakami said to Thor.

"Or maybe a cellular phone." Thor said.

"OK." Back to Megan. "Did you recognize the woman's voice? Have you heard her voice before? Maybe talking to Mommy?"

"I don't know." Megan shook her head.

"What language did she use? Did she speak in English or Japanese."

"Japanese," she said. Happy to know the answer.

"What did she say first? Do you remember?"

"First she asked me if I knew where Mommy's *hanko* was."

"Mrs. Madison," Murakami said. "A *hanko* is a personal stamp we Japanese use on official documents instead of signatures. You push it into a case containing a waxy ink, then press it onto a letter or some other official document. Everyone has one, usually more than one."

"Yes, Lisa tried to explain it all to me one time. Said it was as valuable as a Social Security number, that if stolen, a thief could buy a car, rent an apartment, all in the name of the owner of the *hanko*."

Thor looked inquiringly at his partner. "It happens," Murakami said.

"What did you tell her, Megan?" Thor said. "The bad woman"

"I said, '*Shiranai.*' I didn't know."

"Is that true. *Do* you know where you mother keeps her *hanko?*"

"No."

"I've got it." Mrs. Madison reached into her purse and brought a small black case the size of a large man's thumb. "I looked for this after Lisa…after Lisa went on her trip." She patted Megan's head.

"The money," Thor said. "Could the caller, or whomever was behind the call, have used the *hanko* to get at the money in Lisa's account?"

"Maybe," Murakami said. "It would depend on the bank, and the branch. For one thing, it would depend on whether Lisa opened the account with that *hanko* or another one she might have; Japanese usually have one for every day use, and another, larger one, for more serious occasions, such as buying a house or forming a company. Or she might have just opened the account with her signature, which would mean any *hanko* would be useless. Also, most banks, especially a global bank like InterBank, are likely to have records including a picture ID, either within arm's reach, or scanned into a network computer system. Anyone else coming in, especially a Japanese posing as a blond, wouldn't have much luck. Finally, if she happened to go to the branch Lisa uses most often, and there are only two or three InterBank branches in the Kansai District, they would know Lisa on sight. Pretty risky in any case."

"But why?" Mrs. Madison said. "Lisa doesn't have any money. Well, not much anyway."

"Mrs. Madison," Thor said. "Your daughter has over $200,000 at InterBank."

Mrs. Madison's jaw dropped. "You must be mistaken. Lisa barely had enough money to pay her bills. Where would she get two hundred thousand dollars?"

"That is something we would like to know," Thor said. "All we do know is that in the past six months Lisa deposited the Yen equivalent of about $9500 on ten different occasions."

"Impossible," Lisa's mother said. "Could someone else have deposited it for her? Maybe she never knew. Maybe somebody was using her account without her knowledge."

"Everything was done through the ATM at the branch in Shinsaibashi, which means the person had to have Lisa's ATM card. The account manager knew her, knows her," Thor corrected himself for Megan, "quite well, Says that Lisa is quite a sophisticated investor in foreign currencies."

"Are you OK, Grammy," Megan said as her Grandmother sat down with her back against the wall. "You look funny."

"Grammy's fine, honey. Why don't you be a dear and get me a glass of water."

"OK." Megan padded off.

Thor said, "Do you have any idea where Lisa could have gotten that kind of money?"

Mrs. Madison looked up at Thor. "I have no idea." She began to sob. "I just don't understand any of this. What does it all mean?"

"We were hoping you could tell us."

"It makes no sense to me."

Murakami offered Mrs. Madison his handkerchief. "Had Lisa mentioned anything about her plans to buy something? A house, perhaps? Back in the U.S? Did she say anything about moving back to the US? Anything like that?"

"No. She always insisted that there was nothing for her back home. I'd ask her about money, about how expensive it was living in Japan for a single mother, and she just said not to worry. That it wasn't easy, but that she would manage."

Megan came back in with a glass of water. "What's the matter, Grammy?"

"Grammy's fine, dear. I'm just a little tired." Mrs. Madison took a deep breath and tried to smile at Megan. "Maybe you should go and play while I take a nap."

"Don't you want to hear about the letter?"

"What letter?" Thor said.

"In the *phone* call," she said, unhappy at being left out of the conversation for the past few minutes, and impatient that the adults didn't immediately know what she was talking about. "I thought you wanted to hear about the *phone* call."

"Of course we do." Thor readjusted his body to face directly at Megan again. "Did the caller ask you about some letter, Megan?"

"Yes," Megan said, happy at being the center of attention. "She asked if I remembered the letter Mommy got."

"What letter did she mean? Do you know?"

"She said it was in a pink envelope."

Murakami began rifling through the desk.

"Do you know where the letter is, Megan?" Thor said.

Megan shook her head, didn't know.

"What did you tell the bad woman?"

"Mom always tells me not to talk to strangers."

"So you hung up?"

"No," Megan said as if talking to a simpleton. "I asked her what her name and phone number was so Mom could call her back. Mom says that's polite."

"You are absolutely right," Thor said. "And what did she say when you asked for her name and number?"

"She said it wasn't that important and to never mind. She said she'd call back again."

"And she hung up?"

"Yeah."

"Megan, have you started learning to read yet?"

"Yes, I can read *Peter Rabbit, Anpan Man, Babar*," she counted off on impossibly small fingers. "Mommy says I'm special."

"You are, Megan, you are," Thor said. "And that letter." Thor tried to keep tension out of his voice. "Do you remember seeing any pink letters that Mommy might have written?"

"She got one in the mail a while ago, I think."

"Did you see Mommy's face while she was reading it?" Murakami asked. "Did she look afraid?"

For the first time a small crease formed between her eyes. "Why would Mommy be afraid?"

Thor's eyes shot daggers at Murakami.

"Oh, you know how grown-ups are, dear," Mrs. Madison said. "Sometimes we get sad. No reason."

"Yeah, I guess," Megan said, no longer happy with this game. "Can I go out and play now?"

"Sure, honey, you go ahead. But don't go too far."

Megan went to the entrance *genkan* and bent over to put on her shoes. Thor thought of Detective Yamamoto escaping injury because he had chosen an opportune time to bend over to take off his shoes in another *genkan*.

"Don't stay out too long, dear."

"I won't."

"You've been a big help, Megan," Thor said. "Your Mommy's right; you are a special girl. Thanks for your help."

"Bye."

"I think she's beginning to suspect," Megan's grandmother said. "I'll have to tell her eventually, I know. About the funeral and all. It's going to be so hard on her." She looked dazed. The room was suddenly silent.

"Did Lisa say anything to you about a particularly troubling letter she had received, Mrs. Madison?"

"No. Nothing." She pressed her hands suddenly to the floor, preparing to stand. "I do wish they had more chairs here. Hard on the back and legs."

Murakami moved to help her stand.

"Thank you, Detective. I'm going to make some coffee. Would you gentlemen like some?"

"Yes, ma'am, thank you," Murakami said. He watched Mrs. Madison dab her eyes as she left the room.

"Do you mind if we look through the apartment again, Mrs. Madison?" Thor called into the kitchen. "That letter might be here."

"I suppose it's all right."

"We'll try not to make a mess," he said.

"What do you think?" Thor said in a low voice to Murakami.

"I don't know." The Japanese detective picked up a pile of papers in a cardboard box and started sifting through them. "A blackmail letter?"

"Sure sounds like one. But then murder doesn't make sense. Why kill the person you are trying milk?"

"Maybe he or she gave up," Murakami said. "The records show that Lisa hadn't withdrawn any large amounts in the past 6 months. Maybe the blackmailer got frustrated, decided to put Lisa down in frustration."

"That's put her *away*," Thor said.

"What?"

"*Away.* Maybe the blackmailer put her *away.* If you say '*Put her down'* it sounds like he set her down on a table."

"I remember watching some TV show where they talked about putting a sick budgie *down*. I'm sure that's what they said."

Thor stared at his partner. "Sounds like an episode of *Monty Python*. Americans don't use the word *budgie*, we call them parrots. And I'm not sure, but I think British use the expression 'put down' when talking about putting animals to sleep, killing them." Thor rubbed his eyes with the knuckles of his thumbs. "Jesus, I feel like a fucking English teacher."

"You're the one who brought it up," Murakami said. "Besides, who says your American English is more correct than the Queen's English."

"God help me, my head hurts," Thor said "Let's focus on what we're doing here. Theory one: blackmailer loses patience, kills Lisa, takes ATM card. Doesn't explain the damage to the shop."

Murakami, finished with the cardboard box, stood, scanning the room for a clue.

"Perhaps it was real anger after all," Murakami said. "The guy was so angry about his bad luck that he went crazy. Maybe he's just nuts."

"I'd still like to know where Lisa got her money."

"Tanaka? For being his mistress?"

"He was already paying her a pretty good salary."

"Not that good," Murakami said. "Maybe Lisa was blackmailing him?"

"What for? Their affair? His wife already knew."

"*He* didn't know that, though. Maybe Lisa didn't know either."

"No. An affair is not something a man like Tanaka would pay, or kill, to keep quiet. His bi-sexuality maybe, but not an affair."

"We're both forgetting one thing."

"What's that?"

"Megan. Regardless of whatever Lisa was with other people, all accounts paint her as a caring, loving mother. Would she risk Megan's safety for money? It wasn't like she was starving on what she was making."

Murakami moved to the closet. "Her ex-husband?"

"As a blackmailer? What motive? She turned down alimony. Why blackmail him?"

Thor shook his head once and wished he hadn't. "Jesus." His head still felt like an expanding balloon covered with metal spikes. "Maybe there's no connection between the killer and the blackmailer. Maybe there was no blackmailer and Lisa was turning tricks on the side. Maybe I'm going to go home and cut off my aching head. I wish we could find that fucking letter."

Thor started probing inside some folded futons. "Speaking of letters. What about that letter her ex got?"

"The one she wrote to Hiroshi?"

Mrs. Madison entered the room with a tray of cups. "I hope you gentlemen like your coffee black." They both thanked her.

"Mrs. Madison." Thor took a big gulp and imagined caffeine coursing through his veins, stamping out evil hangover cells. "Mr. Kimura got a letter from Lisa a couple of days before her murder."

"What about?"

"She needed to talk to him about something upsetting. It took several days before he got it. Some postal mix-up."

"How sad for him."

Thor paused for a few seconds before going on. "Speaking of your daughter's ex-husband, Mrs. Madison, you gave us the impression that you quite liked him."

"Yes. He was a nice boy."

"Mrs. Madison, Kimura says you are hoping to take Megan back to the US with you."

"He said that?"

"Well, he said something about you trying to keep him from getting custody of her."

"Oh that." Mrs. Madison waved her hand in dismissal. "After the—, after I heard about Lisa, I did call the consulate and asked about the procedures."

"What kind?"

"Well, when a mother is killed and the father doesn't want to keep the child."

"Did Mr. Kimura indicate that he was not interested in taking care of Megan?"

"Well, no, not in so many words. But they *were* divorced, so I just thought, well, what would happen to Megan?"

"Did you know that he tried to convince Lisa to give him custody following their divorce?"

"No. She never told me." Mrs. Madison lit a cigarette, exhaled the smoke as she spoke. "Besides, that was before I knew he was getting remarried."

"So you have no objections to him taking Megan?"

"Well, I guess there's no other choice, is there? We'll just have to see." She unfolded her handkerchief, looking for a dry patch. "I don't mean to be rude, gentlemen, but if you are through looking around, perhaps you could leave. I'd really like to be alone for a while.

The two detectives left the apartment with no letter and no new clues.

Detective Thor's head still pounded like a pile driver.

19

Japan was the most over-bureaucratized country since the Soviet Union folded. Japan was a country that liked to know what its populace was doing, where and with whom. Recently moved to a new neighborhood? Expect a visit from the police to introduce themselves and find out the basics on you. Don't forget to register at your new city office. Renting an apartment? You need to affix a personal stamp, which would itself have to be registered with the city office. Leaving the country with an expensive ring or watch? Register them at the airport before you go, along with your airline and expected date and port of return.

The upside of all this paperwork was that people could be located more easily in emergencies. Like when they murdered police officers with a shotgun. The rental agreement between Masaru Nakajima and ABC Real Estate, owner of Green Heights Mansion, listed Nakajima's last known employer, a 24-hour convenience store called Welcome, in Namba. ABC had dug into its files and faxed a copy to the Osaka Prefectural Police Headquarters in Temmabashi. Detective Yamamoto dialed the number for Welcome and asked if they had a Masaru Nakajima working there. The manager said Nakajima had stopped working

about a month ago, which was just about when he had moved
into his new apartment.

Yamamoto picked up his overcoat and left the station.

*

Yoshikazu Takeda was the manager of the Welcome store in
Namba next to the Hikushimaya Department store. He was in his
early 30s and had a mustache and unconvincing beard. He was
restocking shelves when Yamamoto arrived.

"Yes, sir, Masaru Nakajima worked here," he told Yamamoto.
"Left on December 19th, last year."

"By "left," do you mean fired?"

"Well, as a matter of fact, yes." Takeda spun a few whiskers
between thumb and index finger. Japanese were no happier with
firing than with being fired. "I had to."

"Could you describe the circumstances?"

Takeda looked around. "Come with me," he said, waving
Detective Yamamoto into a storage room big enough for a few
days supplies, two adults and little else. "I don't like to talk about
these things in front of the staff," he said. "You understand."

"Sure."

"I hired Nakajima last October to work the 11:00 PM to 7:00
AM shift four nights a week. His job was to work the cash register and keep the shelves full. As you can see," he said, swinging his
arm around and almost hitting Yamamoto, "we don't keep more
than a few days worth of goods on the premises. We restock
almost every night."

"So he had access to your safe."

"No." Takeda gave one sharp shake of his head. "Only I have
the combination to that, but there is a slot where night employees
are to slip any receipts in excess of fifty thousand yen."

"Why did you let him go?" Yamamoto was writing in a small notebook with 'Pooh Boy Happy Life' printed on the cover in English. English on books, T-shirts and bags made the items *kakkoii*,—cool—regardless of the meaning of the words.

"I was just coming to that," Takeda said. "After about three weeks I noticed inventories stopped matching up—I take inventory once a week—and began to get suspicious."

"And you suspected one of your employees rather than a shoplifter."

"Well," Takeda said. "We do have some shoplifting, especially since the foreigners started shopping here, but our store is so small that the staff can keep an eye on most things pretty easily."

"How did you know it was Nakajima?" Yamamoto asked.

"I didn't. Not at first, anyway." Takeda shifted a couple of boxes to create some temporary chairs. Both men sat. "I started taking inventory twice a week, during the morning when I'm the only one here. I got one girl who comes in at 1:00 PM. Then I just checked who was on alone when things went missing. We only have two late night workers so it was pretty easy to narrow things down."

"What kinds of things was he taking?"

Takeda sucked air through his teeth, held it, blew it out. "You name it." He reached into his pocket for a pack of cigarettes, shook one out and popped it into his mouth. "Wasn't any particular pattern, if that's what you mean."

Yamamoto looked up from his notebook. "I'd rather you didn't," he said.

Takeda's hand froze with lighter lit. "OK." He put his cigarettes away. "Now, where was I?"

"He took a lot of things?"

"Oh, yeah. Yeah, I tracked him for five days. To make sure, you know? He started out taking rice balls, sandwiches, stuff like that."

"Uh. Huh." Yamamoto continued to write.

"And then it was cans of soft drinks, bags of rice crackers, dried fish. And then it was magazines."

"Did he ever take any money?"

"No, that's the funny thing," Takeda said.

"Probably figured you wouldn't notice the stuff missing."

"Yeah. I guess so. He wasn't a real bright kid." Takeda stood up. "Say, why don't we go outside and get some air."

"OK," Yamamoto said.

Takeda lit up as soon as they were out the door. He blew a stream of smoke contentedly up to the sky and smiled at Yamamoto. "So why are you looking for him?"

"He ran down an old man he was buzzing in Nishi-ku."

"Terrible." Takeda clucked sympathetically. "Is the old guy going to be all right?"

"He's dead," Yamamoto said.

"Gosh. That's too bad." Takeda shook his head. "What's the world coming too?"

"He also shot and killed my partner."

"Gee, I, I am very sorry to hear that." Takeda looked into Yamamoto's eyes and saw only coal black marbles. The face frightened him.

"Would you happen to know if and where Nakajima got a job after leaving here?" The cop was back, the killer back in its cage.

"No, I'm sorry I don't," Takeda said. Suddenly he snapped his fingers. "But our head office should. We send reports of all employees at the beginning and end of their employment to the head office. Other companies sometimes call to check an employee's work history. I'll call right away," Takeda said, eager to please. "Your partner, huh?"

"Yes."

"Was he married or anything?"

Yamamoto took out his card. "You can reach me at this number. Please call me if you find out anything."

"I will," Takeda said, looking at the card. "I definitely will."

*

The boy walking into the squad room looked lost. He had come here without telling his girlfriend or his parents.

"Um. The woman at the reception area said I should talk to Detective Murakami," he said.

"That's me," Murakami said. "Have a seat."

"Maybe I better come back another time." The boy looked like he wanted to run.

"Would you like something to drink? A Coke? Tea?"

The boy scratched his nose. "Tea, I guess."

Murakami motioned to one of the female officers near him and off she went. "Now have a seat and tell me what this is all about."

The boy sat down and looked over at Detective Thor, busy trying to figure out the Japanese directions to his jammed English typewriter. Murakami followed the boy's line of sight. "He's one of my prisoners."

"*Baka yaroh!*" Thor said. *You asshole!*

The boy's eyes went wide. "He speaks Japanese," Murakami said. "So be careful."

"Actually," Thor said. "I'm with the CIA. I've been tracking an international terrorist for months. Turns out it's Detective Murakami here and I'm about to arrest him. Trouble is," he banged the typewriter, "this typewriter was built before the Meiji

Restoration and I can't get it to work." Thor looked to the boy for sympathy. "Can't arrest him until I type this report."

The boy watched the exchange slack jawed. If he understood the joke, he didn't show it.

"He's just kidding," Murakami said. The boy laughed politely.

"His name is Detective Thor and he is a policeman here. He's American."

The boys cheeks contracted to form an "O."

"Must be an illegitimate child of yours," Thor said to Murakami in English.

"Fuck you," Murakami said. Then back in Japanese: "So what can we do for you?"

"I came, um, I want to, I...."

"Take your time," Murakami said.

"I saw something."

"Oh, what?"

"At the coffee shop."

"What coffee shop?"

"You know." The boy's eyes looked ready to water. "The coffee shop. Where the American was killed."

Thor put down his typewriter directions.

"Calm down," Murakami said. "What about the coffee shop?"

The boy had long bangs, as was the fashion for boys his age. He seemed to be hiding behind them now. "I saw something."

"You saw the murder?"

"No. Not exactly," the boy said. "After."

"After the murder? You saw the murderer?"

"No."

Murakami slowly inhaled, exhaled. "What exactly did you see?"

"The car. And some broken glass." The boy was looking straight down at his Nike sneakers.

"Go ahead."

He mumbled something too low to hear, then "I heard glass break and saw somebody run out of the coffee shop and get into a car and drive away."

"What kind of car was it?"

Consternation on his face. "*Shiranai.*" He didn't know.

"Did you see what color it was?"

"No. I'm sorry."

"Was it a man or woman? Did you see that?"

"Couldn't tell."

"Where were you when this happened?"

The old clock on the wall ticked. The boy was silent.

"What's your name?" Murakami said.

"Do I have to tell you?"

"No," Thor said quickly.

Murakami said, "Now, wait a second…"

"It's Araki."

"OK, Araki-kun," Thor said. He used the honorific suffix "kun," rather than "san" to show friendliness, warmth, to the boy. "I want you to know something. First, you aren't in any trouble. Second, we just want to know everything you know because it might help us catch the killer." He figured the kid was about twenty. "You've got nothing to worry about."

"But I didn't see much." He sniffled.

"That's OK," Thor said. "Just tell us what you know. Whatever you remember is fine." His voice was soft and low now. Non-threatening and hypnotic. Murakami felt like confessing to something himself.

"I wasn't alone."

"You were with your girlfriend."

"Yes."

"Fooling around."

Araki's cheeks reddened. "Yes."

"And after it happened," Thor said, "the murder, I mean. You panicked and left."

"No." Araki looked up, first at Murakami, then Thor. "When I heard the crash I'd already...we were all, you know, finished. I got out of the car to see what happened but it was too far away to see much."

"Where were you parked?"

"Behind *Miho Ashida*. It's a woman's boutique on Route 104 just down the road from *Mr. Dandy*, about 100 yards, I guess. All I saw was someone run out of the place and get into a car."

"Then you went back to your car."

"Yeah. And we decided to follow the car. You know. Kind of like a game. I ran back to my car—it was already running 'cause it was so cold outside—and took off after the guy."

"You are sure it was a guy?" Murakami asked.

Araki shook his head impatiently. "I don't know. It could have been but I don't know. It could have been a woman."

"OK." Thor said. "And then?"

"So I lit out after the guy. He didn't know we were following him so it was pretty easy to catch up."

"Did you get close enough to see the license plate?"

"Yeah, I suppose, but that wasn't the point, you know? I just felt like playing around. How the hell was I supposed to know somebody was dead. I thought maybe another kid broke into the place for cash or something. Shit! How was I to know?" The boy wanted absolution.

"Sure," Thor said. "If I were you, I'd have done the same thing. Hell, I might have stayed right where I was. Is she pretty? Your girl friend?"

Araki was motionless, then nodded.

"You lucky dog," Thor said. Then to Murakami. "I'll have to get this kid's secret with women. I haven't had a date since I got here."

Araki's eyes shot up to scan the two detective's faces, though he kept his head down.

"Take dating lessons," Murakami said.

"Maybe he can take me with him on a double date sometime."

"We go up there every Sunday." Araki smiled proudly.

"Gee!" Thor said, full of admiration. "What kind of car did you say you saw?"

"I don't—," Araki started. "Yeah, I do. A Benz! It was a dark blue Benz!"

"You're sure."

"Well, yeah, I guess." the boy said, not at all sure anymore. "Or maybe a Nissan Cima. They look pretty much the same, you know."

"And it was dark blue, you say?"

"Yes." A firm nod.

"Good for you!" Thor said. "How far did you follow the car?"

Araki was feeling better. "A half mile or so."

"Why did you give up?"

"The guy sideswiped a guard rail—hit it pretty bad—and screeched to a stop. I had to jam on the breaks just to keep from rear-ending him. When he took off again I decided, to—, I mean my girl friend was kind of scared and I decided to call it quits."

"Was the driver going that fast?"

"No, I don't think so. We were both doing fifty or so."

Thor reminded himself that was 50 *kilometers* per hour. He figured that was 30 mph.

"The street pretty narrow, was it?"

"Yeah."

"You think he knew you were following him?"

"I don't know. But he slammed the rail just after I got up close, so maybe he was looking at me in the mirror or something. I don't know."

"How come it took you so long to make your way here?" Murakami asked. Japanese weren't much at getting involved in actual emergencies but were usually pretty good about reporting things after the fact.

"Promise me you won't tell anyone I was here, OK?"

"Well…" Murakami said.

"Give the kid a break," Thor said to Murakami in English. "It's a deal."

Araki directed his answer to the American. "Well, my girl friend is still in high school, see? And her parents don't know about us yet. She told her Mom she was staying late at a friend's, and, you know how it is…"

"So you've both kept this big secret between the two of you until now."

"Yeah."

"So why now?" Murakami persisted. "What made you change your mind?"

"I don't know." Araki craned his head in the way Japanese often to stretch kinks in their necks. They also tended to do it when nervous. "I found out what really happened the next day on TV and thought you'd be bringing the killer right in. Then yesterday I heard on the news you didn't even have any suspects yet. My girl friend said to stay out of it but I figured you guys needed some help. No offense, but shouldn't you guys have caught the guy already?"

Murakami said nothing.

"So you decided to give us a hand," Thor said.

"Yeah." Araki nodded happily.

"Thanks," Murakami said, trying not to sound glum.

20

Almost two weeks of investigation had given Detectives Murakami and Thor a rice bowl full of suspects with air-tight alibis and the dubious honor of becoming household names throughout Japan. The so-called morning shows, most a combination of *The Today Show* and *National Enquirer*, were fascinated not only with the fact that the murderer was still at large, but that the National Police Agency felt it necessary to employ American law enforcement officers to show them their business. And if this Eric Thor was the best that Uncle Sam could come up with, certain broadcasters opined, then the US was in steep decline. Two weeks and no arrests.

The case was taking on international implications. Some American columnists were openly dubious about Japan's commitment to bringing the killer of a non-Japanese to justice. Japanese tabloids countered with statistics showing that American cities were the most dangerous on earth. The US ambassador to Japan issued a statement commending everyone on their fine efforts and exhorting all parties involved not to let their emotions get the best of them.

Thor and Murakami just wished the whole thing would go away. They began fantasizing about the killer turning himself in at the station or committing ritualized suicide on the 10 o'clock news. So far they had an ex-husband, a boss-lover, a best friend and a sometime boyfriend—all with alibis that Houdini couldn't crack, and a dead woman who was either smart or stupid, a good mother or a druggie hooker, an intellectual lightweight or a genius. Thor felt like jumping into the polluted Dohtombori River and contracting hepatitis so he could get taken off the case.

*

The sign on the door said *Incredible English Academy*, which was located on the second floor of a run-down gray building behind a computer store on a side street just east of Umeda Station. Five curtained booths, two chairs per, one desk, one telephone, one secretary, one window and one entrance. Thor thought the only thing incredible about the place was that anybody would pay for English lessons there. Murakami picked up a textbook from a magazine rack and leafed through it.

The two officers had been there for about ten minutes when the buzzer went off. Teachers and students erupted from their cubbyholes. Students went straight to the hall for a smoke, the teachers to the tiny teachers' lounge for a moment of monolingual serenity.

When the secretary called Peter Randall over and whispered that the two gentlemen sitting by her desk wanted to talk to him he looked a little nervous. He was wearing beige corduroys, Hush Puppies, a white button-down and a wool knit tie. His sandy brown hair appeared to have been cut with hedge clippers but was clean. With his tortoise-shell glasses he looked to Detective Thor like a cousin of Microsoft's Bill Gates. The American detective wondered if they had found the right Peter Randall. As he listened to what the secretary had to say, his upper cheeks and ears turned bright red. Thor supposed it was embarrassing to have two police officers walk into your place of employment asking for you.

"Perhaps we should go somewhere else to talk," Thor suggested. "Ms. Takano here said you've got a one-hour break."

"OK," Randall said. "Fine."

"Is there a coffee shop or small restaurant around here we can go."

"Next building."

Thor and Murakami introduced themselves on the way and Thor explained for the umpteenth time what he was doing in Japan. He was beginning to think he should just make a flyer he could hand out everyone he met on the street.

The two detectives ordered coffee. Randall had orange juice.

"Peter," Thor said after their orders came. "We got your name out of Lisa Madison's address book."

"Yes," Randall said. He looked to Thor like a deer in the road staring into the lights of an oncoming car. Murakami wondered to himself what attraction this timid creature offered to the Madonna-like Lisa Madison.

"So, you knew Lisa Madison," Thor said, helpfully.

"Yes." Randall opened his mouth to speak, put the straw in instead and sucked in some juice.

"When was the last time you went out with her?"

Randall swallowed before answering, his Adam's apple bobbing under his collar. "A couple of months ago. I guess I must be one of your suspects, huh?"

"Just routine," Thor said.

"Well, I didn't do it," Randall blurted out. "OK?"

"No one said you did." Thor's face looked carved in stone. "We're just exploring all avenues." Randall broke eye contact and sipped some more juice, bending the straw to a better angle.

"Did you go out often?"

"It wasn't like that, OK?" Randall said. "I only met her a few times. I would have loved to have a real date with Lisa. For Christ's sake, if she had wanted to, I would have in a minute. Lisa was a very stimulating woman. No, I, what I'm trying to say is that she was intelligent." His cheeks grew red again.

"Where did you go on your last date?" Thor said.

"The kabuki theater in Namba," Randall said. *"Shuten Dohji.* Do you know it?"

"No," Thor said. Murakami nodded.

"It was very nice." He looked from one detective to the other for a glimmer of support, but found none.

"Did Lisa enjoy herself?"

"Yes. Lisa was a very cultured woman."

"Cultured," Thor repeated.

"Yes. She knew, or she *tried to,* understand what was going on up on stage. The choreographed movements, how the actors can convey so much with a just a tip of their head. When everything they're saying is in Japanese."

"She went to kabuki often?" Murakami asked.

"Well, no, it was her first time, but she—"

"Peter," Thor said. "Did Lisa ever take drugs in your presence?"

"Huh?"

"Illegal drugs. Did Lisa ever use them, or appear to be on them, when you were together?"

"No!" We just went to the kabuki theater. Like I said."

"Not just that night," Thor said. "On any of your other dates. Did she ever offer to sell you any illegal narcotics? Some Shabuh, perhaps?"

Randall looked like road-kill again. "You mean *Shabu Shabu?* The meat and vegetable dish?"

"No," Thor said. "Shabuh. It's a Philippine amphetamine."

"I, I've never heard of it. Is it some new kind of cocaine?"

"We have reason to believe that Lisa may have been dealing it, or using it herself. She never said anything about it to you? Never acted strangely? Drunk? Like that?"

"No. We only went out a few times. Once to the Gala Hall to see the Chicago Symphony. Um, once to see a 'Cats' revival. And once to a *Noh* play, but I can't remember the name of it right now. She and I used to work at the same school and got to talking between classes about theater and culture and stuff. One of my students gave me a couple of tickets to a kabuki show one time and I got up the courage to ask Lisa if she wanted to go. She said yes." Then quickly, "She was already divorced by then."

"Did you ever meet her daughter?" Murakami said.

"Megan? Yes. Lisa had a couple of parties for the teachers at her apartment. Beautiful child, and quite precocious, you know."

"Ever talk to her on the phone?"

"Lisa?"

"No, her daughter, Megan."

"No, I don't think so," Randall said. He put down his glass. "No, wait. She did answer the phone a couple of times when I called."

"You called often?"

"Sometimes." Wary again.

"But you only went out a few times."

"I don't know, I think Lisa needed a friend. Someone to talk to. She'd call me or sometimes I'd call up just to say hi."

"What did you talk about?" Thor said.

Randall picked up the bill and folded it in half. He creased the edge and folded it again. "What does anyone talk about on the phone?" He kept his eyes on the check. "Life. Her job. Nothing special. Whatever was on her mind. You know."

"When was the last time you spoke with her, Mr. Randall?" Murakami said.

"Lisa? I don't know. A few months ago?"

"Why not more recently?" Thor said. "Have a fight? Or was she just tired of you?"

Randall put down the folded check and looked from Murakami to Thor. He began to frown. "No. I told you, we didn't keep a schedule. When she wanted to talk, she'd call. Or sometimes I'd call. Sometimes it was twice a week, sometimes not for a long time."

"How about Megan? Talk to her recently?"

"Megan? Why would I call Megan?"

"You tell me," Thor said.

"I don't get it." Randall shook his head, didn't understand.

"How about letters?" Thor drove ahead. "Did you ever write to each other?"

"No."

"Where were you on the night Lisa was killed, Mr. Randall?" Murakami said.

"What night was that?"

"January 12th. Sunday. Monday morning until 3:00 AM."

Randall pulled an appointment diary the size of the New York City phone book out of his rucksack and flipped through the pages to January 12th. He nodded once and snapped the book closed. "Korea. I'd let my work visa expire and had to leave the country to get it renewed. Everybody goes to Korea because it's closest."

"And you were there on the 12th and 13th?" Thor asked.

"Yeah. From the 10th, actually. Here's my passport." He handed it to Murakami. "I had to fly over on Friday to drop off the papers and wait until Monday to pick them up. They make you stay over at least one night. One weeknight. I got back Monday afternoon."

Thor and Murakami exchanged looks of commiseration.

Murakami said, "Mr. Randall, did Lisa ever mention a man named Minoru?"

Randall's face looked surprised. "As a matter of fact, yes. She told me there were two people who she could always count on being there when she needed us. Me and some guy named 'Minoru'."

"Must have made you feel pretty good," Thor said.

"Yeah, so? Good friends are a special thing, Detective."

"I agree," Thor said. "What about Minoru?"

"One time we were sitting waiting for a concert to start—I don't remember which one—and first she said she didn't know what she would do without me. That sort of embarrassed me but I didn't say anything. Then she said something like, 'Besides Megan, you and Minoru are the only people I can depend on.' And I said, 'Who's Minoru?' Then the lights went down and the show started. I forgot about it after that and the subject never came up again."

"Did she happen to say what his last name was?" Thor asked.

"Nope. Just 'Minoru'. It was just the one time, like I said."

"I see," Murakami said.

"I see," Thor said.

Randall looked at his watch. "Do you think I can go now? I wanted to pick up a bite to eat before my next class. I don't have another break until I'm off at 9:00."

"Sure." Thor nodded absently.

Randall was halfway to the door when he stopped and turned back to the two detectives, looking directly into the eyes of one, then the other. "I know what you guys are thinking. You guys, you jock, captain-of-the-football-team types, you're are all the same." He walked back to the table, chest out, ready for battle. "You look at me and think how can Lisa be interested in a guy like me."

"Mr. Randall, we—"

"Big jocks like you see a woman like Lisa and can only think about one thing, about, you know, *fucking* her brains out." Randall spoke the expletive so forcefully that he sent out a spray of spit, wiping it self-consciously with the sleeve of his shirt. "You can't imagine that she might enjoy doing anything on a Saturday night besides going out with some big macho gorilla like you and having her clothes ripped off. Well, she chose *me*, not you, not someone like you, it was me, and we had fun together. We talked, we laughed and I didn't make her feel like a whore. You can investigate me all you want but the only thing you'll convict me of is treating Lisa Madison like a human being."

Randall left the officers with the folded check sitting in the middle of the table in front of them.

21

Thor did not enjoy the drive to Ashiya as much this time. The houses began to look the same. There were so many Mercedes he wondered if they were just paper cutouts placed in front of the garages.

The maid at the Tanaka's house gave them a warm *Irasshaimase* welcome and led them to the waiting room. Mrs. Tanaka smiled as she entered the room. "I was wondering when you two would come back."

"You were expecting us?" Thor said.

"Of course," Mrs. Tanaka laughed, as if Thor had asked whether women liked shopping. "Beautiful American woman is killed. Wife of woman's boss knows of ongoing affair. I am surprised you did not suspect me earlier?"

"We like to be careful," Murakami said.

"I understand." The maid reentered carrying a tray laden with three cups of coffee, a bowl of brown and white rock sugar cubes and a small pitcher of artificial cream as thick as paint. Conversation stopped while everyone stirred in his or her ingredients. "It's rather exciting, really."

"You knew about your husband's relationship with Lisa Madison, isn't that right?" Murakami said.

"Yes." Mrs. Tanaka smiled pleasantly at Murakami. "I've already told you that."

"Mrs. Tanaka," Thor said. "You must forgive my still weak Japanese—"

"Not at all, Detective Thor. Your Japanese is excellent."

"But, as you said, you did have a good motive."

"It certainly must look that way," Mrs. Tanaka said. "From what I have seen in all the American movies we get here in Japan, the distraught wife, fearful of losing her husband and means of support, gets desperate and removes the source of her problems; her husband's lover. Makes interesting viewing. Except for two small problems."

"What would they be?" Murakami said.

"Well, for one thing, straying husbands are hardly news to lonely housewives in Japan. If an occasional fling was all that important no one would ever get married. Besides, my husband could never get a divorce without my consent and I would never grant it." She smiled at Thor. "But I don't suppose that revelation alone would satisfy you, would it, Detective?"

She set down her coffee cup and folded her hands in her lap. "Lisa Madison was killed at *Mr. Dandy*, yes? On Sunday night. Therefore, I could not have killed her."

"Why is that?" Thor asked.

"Because I was in Tokyo that evening."

"I knew it," Murakami mumbled to himself.

"May I ask what business you had in Tokyo that evening, Mrs. Tanaka?" Thor asked.

"My father's seventy-seventh birthday. Detective Murakami can tell you such events are milestones in Japan, occasions for relatives to gather and show their respect to the aged. People rent out a small restaurant or hotel banquet room. Everyone makes toasts and talks about the guest of honor's childhood and lifelong accomplishments. They can be long and boring, but we Japanese like them."

"And you were in Tokyo the whole weekend?" Murakami said.

"The whole week, in fact," Mrs. Tanaka said. "I flew up on Tuesday morning and came back the following Monday."

"Was the entire country out of town for the weekend?" Thor muttered in English.

"I'm sorry." Mrs. Tanaka said.

"You understand that we have to check anyway." Murakami said.

"Oh course. When you called to say you were coming I wrote up my itinerary, including flight numbers and departure times."

"That's very kind of you."

"When was the party, exactly?" Thor said.

"Sunday night. I went up a few days early, as I said, for the chance to catch up with cousins I hadn't seen for years. The party consisted of about one hundred people, an American jazz trio, noise makers. Actually, I hadn't had that much fun in ages. I stayed at the Hotel New Okawa in Shinagawa. I've also written down my room number, if you'd like to call and check. They'll also have a record of the party and my being in attendance." She had her maid find the telephone number.

"Would you gentleman like some more coffee before leaving?"

*

As Murakami was driving, Thor made the call from his cellular phone. He identified himself to the young man, Mr. Ono, who answered the phone.

"How can I help you, Detective Thor?" Mr. Ono asked cordially and in perfect English.

"I need some information on one of your guests. A Mrs. Keiko Tanaka."

"Is she staying with us now?"

"No. We believe she checked in on January 7th." Thor read him Mrs. Tanaka's address.

"Just a moment, sir. Let me check." Thor heard the clacking of a computer keyboard. "Yes, Detective Thor. Mrs. Tanaka checked in on January 7th and left on Monday, January 13th."

"I see," Thor said. "I understand there was a party given for Mrs. Tanaka's father." Thor suddenly realized they had forgotten to get his name. "I'm sorry but I don't know his name."

"Yes. There was a formal party for Mr. Honda on Sunday evening."

"Would you happen to know if Mrs. Tanaka attended that party?"

"Yes, she did."

"How can you be so sure?"

"The party, as with all our parties here, was by invitation only. Each seat is reserved for a specific person. If that person does not show up, the waiter takes away the invitation and we keep a record to insure proper billing. According to our records, Mrs. Tanaka was issued an invitation for Mr. Honda's party and all guests were present."

"This may sound like a strange question, would you know if someone else attended the party in Mrs. Tanaka's place?"

"We personally escort each guest to his or her seat."

"Yes, but if someone told the waiter that she was Mrs. Tanaka, the waiter wouldn't know if she were the *real* Mrs. Tanaka or not, would he?"

"I see what you mean," Ono said. "Perhaps not, but at these kinds of functions, guests are usually seated next to family, so the other guests at the table would surely notice if, do you call them an 'impostor'? were sitting there."

"Yes, of course," Thor said. "Could you check the guest list at Mrs. Tanaka's table? Just to make sure?"

"Just a moment," Mr. Ono said. More keyboard clacking. "There were 6 people. Besides Mrs. Tanaka, there were three Hondas, one Fujiki , and one Horitani."

"How late did the party last?"

"The room was reserved until 9:00 PM."

Murakami reached over and tapped Thor on the knee. "Ask about breakfast."

"Do you have any way of checking on whether Mrs. Tanaka had breakfast at the hotel on the morning of January 13th?" Thor asked.

"Just a moment." More clacking. "Yes. Mrs. Tanaka signed for breakfast for two and paid for it when she paid her room bill."

Thor relayed the news to Murakami. He shrugged.

"Do you know what Mrs. Tanaka looks like, Mr. Ono?" Thor asked.

"We are a very large hotel, Detective Thor. Much as I would like to, I'm afraid it would be impossible to get to know every one our guests."

"Of course. Well, thank you for you help, Mr. Ono."

"Not at all." Ono hung up.

The two detectives drove in silence for a few minutes. Thor looked at the mountains rising above Kobe, still green in the cold winter. Someone had told him once that looking at green reduced eyestrain. He wondered if it would help job strain.

"Scratch off another suspect," Murakami said.

"Maybe there really was a stand-in at the party but all of her relatives were in on the scheme and pretended she was there."

"A Honda family plot to murder Lisa Madison?" Murakami said. "Pretty big stretch."

"Or maybe there are two Mrs. Tanaka's, one a clone from outer space."

"I'm asking Captain Kume for a new partner."

They passed through a section of highway with six-foot high walls on each side to contain traffic noise. The wall also cut off the view of the mountains. Thor looked down at his thumbs and twirled them.

"But seriously, folks," Thor said. "Did you notice that she understood my English?"

"When you said everyone was out of town for the weekend? Yeah. And she said, 'I'm sorry.'"

"What did you make of that?"

"So she speaks English. So?"

"I don't know. It just seemed funny," Thor said.

"Everybody studies English in secondary school here."

"I know. I guess I'm just grabbing at straws."

Thor closed his eyes and went over what they had learned. Mrs. Tanaka had checked into the hotel on Tuesday the 7th, and out the next Monday. She was seen in Tokyo on Sunday night, at least until 9:00 PM. She had breakfast in the hotel on Monday morning. If Lisa Madison was killed at 1:00 AM, Mrs. Tanaka would have had to—.

"Airline records," Murakami said at precisely the appropriate moment. "Might as well check."

"Can't hurt."

Thor called All Nippon Airways to check the details Mrs. Tanaka had given them. The operator confirmed that Keiko Tanaka had been booked on a flight to Tokyo on January 7th, with a return reservation on January 13th.

He called the two other domestic airlines that fly the Osaka-Tokyo route and asked if any other Keiko Tanakas had booked round-trip passage late on the night of January 12th, the night Lisa Madison was killed, returning on the morning of the 13th. Only the Kansai International Airport had 24-hour service from Osaka, so he didn't ask about the older Itami Airport. To cover the possibility of Mrs. Tanaka using an alias, he asked if *anybody* had departed and returned between those two times. No luck.

"Well," Murakami said. "We're getting a great list of people who *didn't* kill Lisa Madison."

"And people who were out of town that weekend," Thor said. "If we were cat burglars we could have made a fortune that night."

"Only nine million people in Kansai left to interview."

"How about that Minoru guy?" Thor asked.

"What about him? He called Lisa's apartment once that we know of, talked to Mrs. Madison, and she forgot to tell her daughter. Peter Randall recognized the name but had no last name for him."

"Could have been the person who called Megan the other day."

"Disguising his voice like a women's? That's really reaching. In any case, we've got no last name and there's no 'Minoru' in Lisa's address book."

"Maybe she wrote it as a last name, by mistake."

"Must be hundreds of names in that book."

"It's not like we have anything better to do," Thor said.

"Unfortunately that is correct."

Thor snapped his fingers. "Maybe we don't have to." He took Lisa's address book out of the glove compartment and dialed the phone again.

The clear, high voice at the other end of the line clearly still believed in Santa Claus, The Tooth Fairies and mothers that were still alive.

"Megan," Thor said. "This is Detective Eric Thor. Do you remember me?"

"Hi, Detective. What are you doing?"

"Right now I am riding in a police car. And I'm calling you from a portable telephone. Isn't that neat?"

"Those are called cellular telephones," Megan said matter-of-factly. "I saw one on 'What's New?' on cable."

"Gosh, you're pretty smart." Thor remembered watching Sesame Street at her age.

"I know." Megan giggled.

"Megan, is your grandmother there?"

"No, she's next door at the vegetable shop. Do you want her to call you?"

Thor considered a moment. "Say, Megan, I need your help with something important."

"Sure."

"I need to get in touch with a friend of your mother's. Maybe you know him."

"OK. I know all of mommy's friends. You can ask me about anybody. Go ahead."

"All right. His name is Minoru. Do you know him?"

"That's *easy*!" She stretched out the second word: EEEEEASY! "He's a nice guy. Mommy likes him a lot." Megan liked this game. "OK. Next."

"Megan, do you know Minoru's last name?" Thor held his breath.

"Okada. O-K-A-D-A. Okada. I can write it in *kanji*, too."

Thor rifled through the book's pages with his free hand and found Okada, no first name, along with a telephone number and address in Kyoto.

"Got it!" Thor said.

"Got what?" Megan said.

"Oh sorry, honey, I was talking to my partner."

"Detective Yamamoto?"

"No, it's Detective Murakami today. You remember him?"

"Of course."

"Look, Megan, I have to get off the phone now but you were a real big help."

"A real, big, big, help?"

"A real, big, big, Godzilla-sized help."

Megan laughed. "Neat!"

"You are a very special girl, Megan."

"That's what mommy always says."

"Well," Thor said. "She's right. Bye."

"Bye, Detective Thor," Megan said. "See you soon."

*

1-22-10 Yawatashi, Kyoto was just across the line separating Osaka and Kyoto Prefectures. There was a cable car outside the Keihan Train station going up Otokoyama Mountain. People flocked to the all-but-unpronounceable Iwashimizuhachimangu Temple on top during cherry blossom season and on New Year's Day. The Okada home was a tiny, two-story house with enough yard space for a small green net into which someone, presumably the father, could whack golf balls.

Japan did not suffer the jurisdictional problems US law enforcement agencies did, so location of the house in a different prefecture, Kyoto, was of no consequence to two members of the Osaka Prefectural Police. A short call to the Kyoto Prefectural police, asking for permission to interview someone in their

district, was all it took. Thor and Murakami let themselves
through the small gate, approached the door and pushed the
doorbell.

"Who is it?" a man's voice said through the intercom.

"Osaka police," Murakami said.

"Please let yourself in," the voice said. "It's unlocked."

Recalling the recent death of young Officer Miyoshi, the two
officers were wary.

"Uh," Murakami said. "Mr. Okada?"

"Yes."

"Mr. Minoru Okada?"

"Yes. May I help you?"

"Can you come to the door, please?"

"I'm sorry, I can't."

Thor motioned silently to Murakami that he was going around
the side of the house. Murakami continued standing to the side of
the door.

"Mr. Okada. We'd like to talk to you."

"About Lisa Madison?"

"Yes."

"I understand. That was a terrible tragedy. I'd be glad to help in
any way I can."

"That's good to hear, Mr. Okada," Murakami said. "We need
all the cooperation we can get on this."

"Have you got any suspects?"

"A few. But nothing concrete. A few leads."

"I hope you find the killer and bring him to justice, Detective.
What was your name?"

"Oh, I'm sorry. My name is Detective Murakami. Osaka
Prefectural Police." He shoved his identification up to the mini-
camera in the intercom.

Thor came back whispered in his partner's ear. "The wall on the left side is flush against the house," he whispered. "There's a big sliding glass window opening to the yard on the right but I couldn't get a good view inside. Curtain's closed."

"Is someone with you, Detective Murakami?"

"Yes. My partner, Detective Thor."

"A non-Japanese?"

"Yes. It's a long story."

"Well then please come in," the voice said. "I'll prepare tea."

The two officers looked at each other. "What do you think?" Thor whispered.

Murakami shrugged. "No one makes you come in without greeting the door," he whispered. "Are you alone, Mr. Okada?"

"Yes, I am."

"Perhaps you could let us in. We don't like to walk into people's houses uninvited."

"Can I help you?" The voice from behind caused Thor and Murakami to jump.

"Who are you?" Thor said.

"Who are *you*?" The woman was in her late forties.

"Police." Murakami showed her his ID. "Do you live here?"

"Yes, I do," the woman said. "Is something wrong?"

"Possibly," Murakami said. "We are looking for a Minoru Okada. Does he live here?"

"Yes. He's my son." The woman looked at the door. "You were just talking to him on the intercom."

"That's the thing, Mrs. Okada. He refuses to come to the door."

"Well of course he does. His wheelchair won't fit in the entrance way."

"Wheelchair?"

"My son was born with a deformed spine. He can't walk."

Inside the house Minoru Okada was pouring tea in the kitchen. There was a plaid blanket draped over his legs. Thor guessed he was about twenty. "Please come in, gentlemen."

"Mr. Okada?" Murakami said.

"Yes. Please forgive me for not meeting you at the door. Our house is not very handicapped-friendly."

Murakami was embarrassed. "We're sorry to bother you."

"Not at all. I don't get many visitors and I don't get out much." Okada wheeled onto a line of carpet running from the kitchen into the living room. He carried the tray of tea on his lap. "Please warm yourself under the *kotatsu*."

"Mr. Okada," Murakami began. "We got your name from Lisa Madison's address book."

"I do miss her."

"You knew her well, then?"

"Fairly well. She used to visit me sometimes."

"How did you first meet?"

"In the park," Mrs. Okada said. "My son and I were enjoying the cherry blossoms next to the temple at the top of the mountain last Spring. Lisa was there with her daughter playing badminton. The birdie somehow landed in Minoru's lap. Lisa came over to retrieve it and I invited her to share our picnic lunch."

"And she started coming to your house after that?" Thor asked.

"Yes," Minoru said. "She only came here once every couple of months or so but we spoke on the phone about once a week." Okada wheeled over to the TV, picked up a photograph and placed it on the tray in his lap. He rolled over to where Thor and Murakami were sitting and handed the picture to them. It showed Lisa standing behind Okada, making a peace sign. Japanese often flash them when having their picture taken, though for them it just means "Hi. Wish you were here!" She wore blue jeans and a white blouse. Her hair hung in a ponytail. The background showed other people sitting under cherry trees in full bloom. Megan was standing next to her mother, looking intently at the camera.

Thor studied the picture, hoping a clue would pop out and land on the table in front of him. None did.

"Did she happen to call you on January 11th?"

"Was that a Saturday?" He looked at the calendar on the wall. "Why yes, she did."

"Could you tell us how she sounded that day?" Murakami asked. "Did she sound upset? Angry? Afraid?"

"Yes, I remember that very well. She called me in the morning and was quite upset. She said she had gotten some kind of letter and was unsure what to do about it."

Thor looked up from his tea. "A letter?"

"Is that important?" Minoru asked.

"Someone called Lisa's apartment a couple of days ago and asked Megan about a letter," Thor said.

"Did she tell you what the letter said?" Murakami asked.

"Not exactly." Okada wheeled back to the kitchen and put the tray on the table. "I believe it contained some kind of threat, or an implied threat. That's what she thought it was, in any case. I told her she should call the police but she said she couldn't."

"Did she say who the letter was from?" Thor said.

"No, she didn't," Minoru said. "I asked her but she just said that things were happening, that she was afraid, and that she didn't know what to do."

"Did her problem have anything to do with drugs?"

Okada looked surprised. "No, I'm sure it didn't."

"What did she say on the phone? Did she say who was threatening her?"

"She wouldn't say."

"Anything about blackmail?" Murakami said.

"I told you, she didn't tell me."

"What *did* she tell you?"

"She was so upset she wasn't making much sense. She told me she was afraid. I pushed her to tell me more about it, I really did. She finally played it down, said she was just tired and for me not to worry."

"But you knew it was more than that."

"She wasn't the type to ramble. I'd never seen her so emotional, so flustered."

"Did she ever talk of owing someone money?"

"No."

Murakami said, "Do you know anyone who might have wanted to kill Lisa, Mr. Okada?"

"No. I'm sorry. I never met any of her other friends. The only time I ever saw her outside of this house was that first time in the park." Mrs. Okada came into the room and placed a shawl around her son's shoulders. "The killer must have been a very angry person."

Murakami nodded in silent agreement and sloshed around the last few drops of tea in his cup, watching the leaves settle in the bottom. "Thank you for your help, Mr. Okada." He began to climb out from under the *kotatsu*.

"Can I get you gentlemen some more tea?" Mrs. Okada said.

"No. Thank you," Murakami said. "We have to get going."

Minoru Okada followed the two men as close to the entrance as his wheelchair would allow. "Lisa was a virtuous person. I hope you find her killer."

"We do, too," Thor said.

22

The call from Yoshikazu Takeda, manager of Welcome Convenience Store, came in at 9:14 AM. The woman cop told Yamamoto the call was on line 3. He jabbed the correct button.

"Yes?" Yamamoto said

"This is Takeda of Welcome Convenience." He paused. "You visited my store the other day in connection with the Lisa Madison murder."

"I remember. What have you got?"

"You asked me to call if I got anything on Nakajima."

"Yes, yes. You got something from your head office?"

"Oh that, uh, no. But one of my staff saw him. I told them all to keep an eye out for him."

"Where?"

"You wouldn't believe it," Takeda said. "At another convenience store. He's working there."

"At a Welcome?"

"No. It was a Kazoku Mart in Chuo-ku. About twenty minutes from here."

"Is your staff sure it was him?"

"Yeah. One of my girls lives over there. She stopped in there yesterday, on her day off. It's right by the Honmachi Station, exit #6."

"Nakajima is working there? At a convenience store in Honmachi?"

"Yeah."

"Did he see your employee?"

"No. He was ringing up a sale and she was in one of the aisles. She saw him from the side and headed the other way. She slipped out while he was helping a customer."

"Thank you," Yamamoto said and hung up.

Yamamoto sat in silence for a few moments listening to his heartbeat. He looked across at Detective Murakami's empty desk. Thor was on the phone talking to someone in English. Yamamoto reached back and felt the gun against his back. He saw in his mind the torn body of Detective Miyoshi at Nakajima's apartment and the boy's family at the funeral. He imagined putting Nakajima's head in a food processor, of running over his body several times with a heavy truck. His hands were shaking. He looked up to see Thor, done with his phone call, looking at him.

"You OK?" Thor came over and sat down by his desk.

"Fine," Yamamoto said. He met Thor's eyes and stared back at him.

"I've found Nakajima," Yamamoto said without breaking eye contact. They both just sat.

"Have you?" Thor said. "That's good news."

"Yeah."

A tear formed in Yamamoto's left eye. "He killed my partner."

"I know."

"I would like to kill him, tear him in half with my hands."

"I know."

"He deserves to die."

Thor nodded.

Yamamoto scrunched his eyes shut. The normally imposing face now looked forlorn.

"In the US, if when a cop's partner is murdered, you hunt the killer down and shoot him," Yamamoto said. "I've seen it in movies, on TV."

"It happens," Thor said. "Not all that often, but it happens."

"I'm Japanese," Yamamoto said, as if that explained everything.

"I know."

Yamamoto reached into his pocket for a handkerchief and wiped his eyes. Still the men looked at each other.

"I'm supposed to contact the chief of detectives at HQ and ask for instructions."

"I see."

"Those things sometimes take time."

"And you think Nakajima might get away," Thor said.

Yamamoto looked down at his big knuckles and cracked a couple. "I could get in trouble if I don't follow regulations."

Thor looked at the short man who looked strong enough to pick up a New Beetle. He remembered the tenderness with which Yamamoto had spoken to Megan Madison.

"You know," Thor said, looking out the window. "I was just thinking. Captain Kume told me to use my free time to familiarize myself with the main points in Osaka. I was thinking of heading over to Honmachi, since I haven't been there yet. To check out the neighborhood."

He returned his gaze to Yamamoto.

"Just to look around, you understand. And I'll be damned if I didn't forget breakfast this morning. I was hoping there was some place around there for me to pick up a bite to eat. Maybe I'll get lucky and find a convenience store or something."

Yamamoto kept fumbling with his huge hands. "If he were to die, no one would care."

"I certainly wouldn't," Thor said. "But I don't suppose your bosses would appreciate it, though. Besides, think how it would look for me."

The Japanese officer looked up. "What do you mean?"

"You start killing suspects and everyone's going to call it the 'Dirty Harry' affect, imported by yours truly from the bad old US. People will see me coming and head for the hills. They'll start believing all those stories about crazy Americans and guns."

Yamamoto emitted a small laugh and looked down at his hands again. "I'm a good cop."

"I know you are."

"But it was my partner. I should bring Nakajima in."

"Yes, you should."

"I'm going to Honmachi."

"Great," Thor said, standing. "I'm starved."

*

They took the Midosuji Subway to Honmachi Station and went out exit #6. The Kazoku Mart was across the street. When they reached the store they looked in the window to see if Nakajima was at the register. He wasn't.

"I'll go around back to cover the service entrance," Thor said.

It was about ten o'clock in the morning. There weren't many customers. *Salarymen* were at work and students from nearby Soai High School were still in class. Yamamoto walked in and headed down the magazine aisle. He rounded the corner and headed toward the snack food section. Nakajima was taking bags of potato chips out of a carton and jamming them on the shelves.

"Excuse me," Yamamoto said. "Done with your shower?"

"Eh?" Nakajima looked at Yamamoto like he was drunk.

"Last time I saw you, you said you were taking a shower."

"What *are* you talking about, old man? You want something, buy it. Otherwise, get out of here."

Yamamoto didn't move. "And if I don't, what then? Have you got your shotgun with you today?"

Comprehension began creeping over Nakajima's face like a late sunrise. He backed away from the register. One end of the aisle was a dead end. Nakajima turned, feigning a dash for it before reaching inside his jeans jacket for a switchblade, clicking it open. He waved it menacingly at Yamamoto. When Yamamoto didn't move, Nakajima made his move, lunging straight at his chest. Yamamoto caught his knife hand and yanked him forward, turning the knife away as he did. He put his left hand behind the elbow of Nakajima's knife arm and bent the arm back. Nakajima squealed in pain. The knife clattered out of his hand and onto the floor. With one arm still twisting Nakajima's offending hand, Yamamoto reached into his pocket with his free hand and pulled out his handkerchief. He bent over and picked up the knife.

"You are a lucky man, you little worm." Yamamoto folded the knife, pushing the blade closed against his pant leg, wrapping it in his handkerchief and sticking it in his pocket. He pulled out a pair of handcuffs and slipped them on Nakajima's wrists.

"What's so lucky about this?" Nakajima asked.

"You're lucky your arresting officer is a good cop," Thor said standing in the doorway. "You're lucky to be alive right now."

*

Masaru Nakajima admitted almost immediately to killing Mr. Kishi, the cranky restaurant owner. Japanese were prone to many of the same ills befalling other societies around the world, including corruption, bad weather, and increasingly, murder. But when caught by police, its citizens were almost unique in their tendency to confess. Perhaps it was the Japanese belief in inevitability. Or maybe they just weren't good at lying. Whatever. Nakajima explained to police that he was high on Shabuh he had gotten from a neighbor and was angry when the old man had come out and pestered him. He also admitted killing Detective Miyoshi, but said he was sorry. The day the police came to his apartment, he said, he had panicked and didn't know what else to do. He apologized publicly to Miyoshi's family, asking them to forgive him. Miyoshi's father told reporters he believed movies imported from America were the real culprit.

Unfortunately for Detectives Thor and Murakami, Nakajima had not killed Lisa Madison. According to the work log at the Kazoku Mart in Honmachi, Nakajima worked the 11 to 7 shift on the night of January 12th. Witnesses confirmed his presence. That didn't help Nakajima much as the cops already had him on two other counts of murder, one of a police officer. He would not be seeing the outside of a jail before the next millennium. But the killer of Lisa Madison was still on the loose.

23

The murder of Lisa Madison had been carried out with fine attention to detail. First the killer chose a place and time when Lisa was sure to be alone. Second, the killer left neither fingerprints at the murder site nor any trace of a murder weapon. Third, the murderer was either someone that Lisa's friends would not suspect or had constructed an alibi so airtight as to be unbreakable. The police had no serviceable clues and were running very low on suspects. Rookie officers at the station were calling the rest of the names in Lisa's address book but no one was optimistic about it leading to anything. The one lead the police had, the letter wanted by the mystery caller to Megan, was not to be found.

Thor and Murakami went back to Lisa's apartment to see if there was an unturned stone in the middle of the kitchen with a big sign on it reading: *Clue Here!* They called ahead to make sure Mrs. Madison would be there.

"Oh, Detective Thor. Detective Murakami. Come in." Mrs. Madison was wearing blue jeans, a flannel shirt and cotton gloves. "You are early."

"Traffic was lighter than we expected," Thor said.

"I'm just doing some final cleaning before I leave." She scratched her nose with her wrist. Cardboard boxes were piled all over the room.

"Will you be going back to the US soon?" Murakami asked.

"Tomorrow. I've arranged for Lisa's body to be flown back and I would like to get home myself. It's been quite a lengthy ordeal."

"May I ask what has been decided concerning Megan?" Murakami said.

"Hiroshi came and picked her up this morning. A nanny will take care of her until the wedding. It was all a big misunderstanding, this custody business. He's promised that Megan can visit me during summer vacations. I'm sure she'll be fine. He'll even pay her air fare when she visits."

"Have you or Mr. Kimura told her about her mother yet?"

"I told her yesterday, after talking it over with Hiroshi." Mrs. Madison sat down and blew a strand of hair out of her face. "She's quite a little girl. She cried for the longest time, of course. She had been asking more and more often why Mommy was gone so long, I was running out of excuses. When I finally told her she kept saying, "I want my Mommy. I want my Mommy. The poor dear. She screamed until she was hoarse in the throat. I tried holding her but she hit me, ran off to one corner of the room, and just kept crying. She finally picked up the remote control and turned on the TV, staring but not really watching. I was getting worried she might be having some kind of, you know, seizure or something but didn't know what to do so I just sat next to her, holding her hand. She let me hold it but didn't squeeze back. Just stared at the TV. Finally she turned to me and said, 'Grammy, are you going to be OK?' Can you imagine that? Her nose all runny, eyes swollen and puffy; she's lost her Mommy and *she* was worried about *me*. She told me she would be all right because she had her daddy but that she was worried about me because I'm all alone. It was her idea to visit me during summers because she wants to make sure I'm OK. Have you ever heard of anything so sweet?"

"No." Thor said.

"So here I am packing up Lisa's things for no apparent reason. Hiroshi doesn't want them and I don't know what I'm going to do with them. It just seems that throwing them away would be wrong somehow. I don't know."

"About the letter…" Murakami said.

"Yes, of course." Mrs. Madison was all business again. "As you can see, I've pretty much packed everything. No sign of any pink letters or envelopes, I'm afraid. I just got done vacuuming and was going to scrub under the sink. Lisa told me once that her rental deposit might be forfeit if the apartment was dirty when she left. Why don't you look around and call me if you need anything? I'll be right here." She headed to the kitchen.

"Thanks very much." Thor said. He and Murakami walked from the living room to the bedroom. The only visible items besides the boxes were a folded futon, an empty closet with a dozen hangers in the bedroom, and a sofa and end table in the living room. Movable items were sitting in boxes in the middle of the floor. Thor pulled open the desk drawers: empty. He moved the desk; nothing behind or under it. Looking back in the other room, the closet was still empty. Where was that damn letter? Thor scratched his nose and winced as his nail pricked a pimple. Too much fried food, he decided. He pulled out a handkerchief to wipe the blood. Murakami jangled the hangers in the closet. Everything in the apartment was empty. Everything was packed. Everything had been rolled up, folded, thrown away or packed.

Everything, that is, except Lisa's poster.

Thor looked at the poster of Lisa Madison hanging over the desk like a silent witness. He stopped wiping his pimple and stared at the poster. Mrs. Madison noticed Thor staring at her nude, dead daughter and laughed nervously. "Call me morbid but it is a good picture of her. Kind of a final connection. I even talk to it sometimes. I was going to roll that up last and take it home with me."

Thor kept staring. "Detective Thor?" Mrs. Madison said. Her eyebrows arched.

Thor walked over to the poster and pushed his hand against it. It happened to land on one of Lisa's breasts but he didn't notice. He moved his hand up, down, then in a circle.

"Detective Thor?" Mrs. Madison raised her voice slightly.

Thor's hand stopped where Lisa's right foot was touching the floor. He tapped that spot with his fingertips once, twice, and pried out the bottom left and right tacks and one in the middle. Two envelopes fell to the floor. One pink and one white. Thor picked them up.

"How did you know?" Murakami said.

"I didn't."

The white envelope contained a single sheet of rough, hand-made paper known as *washi*. On it was written four lines of Japanese *hiragana* , the phonetic alphabet.

> *Wasuraruru*
> > *mi wo ba omowazu*
> *chikaite shi*
> > *hito no inochi no*
> *oshiku mo aru kana*

Thor handed it to his partner. He could read the words but didn't know the meaning.

"Very old," Murakami said. "It says something about 'forget me if you want, but the Gods won't forget the promise you made" or something like that. We don't use words like that anymore."

"What kind of promise?" Thor asked.

"Doesn't say." Murakami shook his head. "I was never into poetry much. What about the other one?" He nodded towards the pink envelope in Thor's hand.

The pink letter was written in English. Sort of. The letters were all capitalized and appeared to have been written with the aid of a Japanese-English dictionary. The message, however, was clear.

LISAMADISON
YOU FILTHY CAL GIRL NOT WANTED
DEATH LISA!!

The white envelope was postmarked December 22nd at Osaka's Main Post Office. The pink one was postmarked at Itami Airport on January 7th. Lisa Madison's address was written in Japanese on both envelopes.

*

Despite having only a single runway, Tokyo's Narita Airport processed more passengers on a daily basis than any other airport in the world. Some cities, like Atlanta, had a higher volume of flights, but almost every plane landing and taking off at Narita was a 757 or larger. One-hour domestic flights used 747s reconfigured to hold five hundred passengers. There were so many passengers that gates had subway-like turnstiles to process tickets. Tickets for the domestic flights could be bought under any name, no ID necessary.

People wishing to rent cars, however, had to supply a valid license at the time the car was picked up and dropped off. Customers had to fill out rental forms themselves, by hand, as evidence that someone else had not falsely done so. Either *hanko*—personal seals—or signatures were acceptable.

The police had the killer's handwriting on a letter mailed from Itami Airport. Itami Airport was closed when Lisa Madison was killed, which meant someone flying in and out that night would had to have used Kansai International. KIX, as the airport made on reclaimed land was known, didn't have overnight parking. A single passenger would either have to take a taxi or rent a car. If that car were damaged, there would be a record of the repairs and to whom they were charged.

Detectives Thor and Murakami had already checked flight records to identify passengers who had left Tokyo the night of Lisa Madison's murder and returned to Tokyo the following day. Since Mrs. Tanaka had witnesses placing her in Tokyo on the evening of the 12th and the morning of the 13th, it was natural for the two detectives to have tried to find how she could have flown out of Tokyo after the party and flown back from Osaka by morning. But they had also already checked car rental agencies for a record of a Keiko Tanaka renting a car on the night in question and found nothing.

The letter forced the detectives to reconsider Mrs. Tanaka as a suspect because it was mailed on the same day she said she had flown to Tokyo. They obtained a complete list of all people who had rented a car from any agency in Greater Kansai on the night of January 12th at Kansai International Airport.

Keiko Tanaka's name was not on any of the lists.

Nor were any of the names written in Lisa Madison's address book.

Yuki Nishimura's, however, was.

*

"May we come in Ms. Nishimura?" Detective Murakami said.

The woman inside looked to Detective Thor quite different from the one he had seen during his first visit. Gone was the sexy temptress, replaced by a scared, haggard girl. Her eye's were bloodshot, lined with dark circles.

"You don't look well, Ms. Nishimura."

"I haven't been feeling well." She touched her lips absently. "Lisa's death has been hard." She refused to look at either of the detectives. Her eyes darted around the room.

"You are upset by Lisa's death," Murakami said.

"Yes. Yes, of course."

"You say you were good friends."

"Yes."

Murakami took out a copy of the rental agreement that had been faxed over from Kansai Rent-A-Car in Toyonaka. Yuki's name was printed along the time, along with her Visa card number. Her signature shown at the bottom..

"Is this your signature, Ms. Nishimura?"

She didn't look at the paper. "I'm sorry."

"What are you sorry about, Ms. Nishimura?"

She squatted down on the floor, hugging her legs, burying her face in between. Her shoulders heaved as she sobbed.

"Why did you drop the car off at the airport, Ms. Nishimura?"

She began rocking back and forth and let herself fall back on her behind. She leaned against the wall and wiped her nose on the sleeve of her sweatshirt.

"The agency records say the car was scratched and dented on the side when you brought it in. They say you told them you lost control when someone drove too close while passing."

Tears were streaming down her face. Thor took out his handkerchief and handed it to her.

"Thanks," she said.

Murakami said, "We've checked the paint on the guard rail with the car's and they match."

She took a deep breath and let it out slowly. "I panicked. After I hit the guard rail I didn't know what to do." She spoke in a monotone. "I thought the guy behind me had seen me, maybe written down the license number. I was sure he would call the police. I couldn't hide the car because it was rented. I had to get away."

"So you flew to Tokyo."

"Yeah."

"To see Mrs. Tanaka."

Nishimura looked up at Murakami and started crying again.

"Yes."

"To pick up your pay."

"No. She paid me before. I just didn't know who else to turn to."

"So you flew up after dropping off the car."

"Yes. We had it all worked out so that I would do it while she was in Tokyo. There couldn't be any chance that she would be suspected. She had known about the birthday celebration for weeks."

"How did you know where she was staying."

"She told me. She said to call her after I did it."

"But you went to her hotel instead."

"I didn't know what else to do."

"You had breakfast together," Thor said.

"Yeah."

When Murakami looked at him inquisitively, Thor said, "The bill. The guy at the hotel told me Tanaka paid for breakfast for two the morning of the 13th."

"How much did Mrs. Tanaka pay you to kill Lisa Madison?"

"Five million yen." Almost fifty thousand dollars.

"But that wasn't enough," Thor said. "You knew about Lisa's money in the bank and thought, "What the hell?' and decided to sample a little of that, too."

"That's why Mrs. Tanaka hated Lisa so much, the money. She found out her husband was giving her all this money and it drove her crazy."

"So why did she choose you?" Thor said. "Or was it your idea?"

Nishimura shook her head. "Mrs. Tanaka started dropping by the shop a few months ago when she knew her husband wasn't there. It was usually early evening before the nighttime crowd arrived. She asked me how much her husband was paying me. When I told her she clucked about how underpaid I was. She asked if I was making enough to live on. I didn't know what to say. She was my boss's wife and I thought he was testing me or something. I told her I was getting by.

"Next time she came by she asked me how often Lisa worked there. When I told her she looked surprised. She wondered why Lisa was getting paid more than me for doing the same work. I told her it was probably because she was foreign, that kind of thing is pretty common. When she told me how much more, I told her she must be mistaken. She said no, she had seen her husband's records.

"After that she started telling me about how reckless her husband was with his money, how he was pilfering away the family money. She was worried that soon there would be nothing left for her and her children. Wasn't it odd, she said, that an American should get all that money while his Japanese wife had to depend on handouts. She joked how nice it would be if Lisa had some terrible accident. I caught on to what she was getting at. She eventually made me an offer. Said she would give me five million yen if Lisa were to have an accident that could absolutely not be traced to her. That's what she said, 'an accident.' She told me the dates she would be out of town and said any time during that period would be convenient."

"When did she pay you?" Murakami said.

"New Year's Eve. She came by, she said, to give me *otoshidama*, a New Year's Cash Gift. It was a big plastic bag with five bundles of one million yen. The bag also contained a big knife."

"Is that what you used to kill Lisa Madison?"

"Yes. At first she said only that she wanted Lisa to have an accident. But when she brought the money she said I must use that knife to kill Lisa."

"She told you to kill Lisa Madison. She used the word 'kill'?"

"Yes."

"Specifically with the knife that she brought you."

"Yes."

"Where is the knife now?" Thor said.

"In Osaka Bay." She almost smiled. "I threw it over the side of the bridge when I drove out to the airport."

"Did you write the threatening letters to Lisa?" Murakami said.

"What letters?"

"You didn't write any letters to Lisa? One some kind of poem and another calling her a whore?"

She shook her head. "No."

Murakami signaled the officers standing outside the apartment to come in. "You'll have to come with these officers to the station, Ms. Nishimura."

"I know."

She got up and headed for the door. She folded up Thor's handkerchief and handed it to him.

"Thank you," she said.

As the American and his Japanese partner exited the building, Thor saw a public garbage can on the corner. He walked over and threw away his handkerchief.

24

The snow was falling gently as Detectives Thor and Murakami entered the courtyard for the third time. Mrs. Keiko Tanaka was in the garden, reaching up to clip off the broken branch of a ginkgo tree.

"This branch is old anyway," Mrs. Tanaka said. "If it snaps from the cold it might fall into the garden and damage one of my shrubs."

"Mrs. Tanaka," Murakami said. "You flew to Tokyo on January 7th, is that right?"

"That's right." She kept snip, snipping away.

"Did you mail this letter from Itami Airport?" He showed her the envelope. She looked at it a long time before resuming her pruning.

"Yes," Mrs. Tanaka said.

"Did you pay Yuki Nishimura five million yen to kill Lisa Madison on the morning of January 13th?"

"Lisa certainly was a beautiful woman," Mrs. Tanaka said.

"Yes," Thor said. "Did you pay Ms. Nishimura to kill her and supply her with the murder weapon?"

"See that bush there, Detective Thor?" Mrs. Tanaka pointed with her pruning sheers. Some of its white flowers had fallen to the ground.

"That one?" Thor followed Mrs. Tanaka's shears. "Yes."

"Do you know its name?"

"I'm afraid I'm not into botany."

"We call it '*Kantsubaki*'," Murakami said to Thor.

"Very good, Detective!" Mrs. Tanaka said, pleased.

"Ah," Thor said.

Looking back at the American, she said, "I believe you call it a Camellia, in English. You know it?" Her cheeks were flushed. She had been drinking.

"I've heard of it," Thor said.

"It's quite famous in Japan," Mrs. Tanaka said. "Movies have been made, books written. For us it shows the fragility of beauty. It teaches us that the greater the beauty, the more tenuous the existence."

"The neck," Murakami said.

"What?" Thor said.

"That's why you told Nishimura to cut her neck, isn't it, Mrs. Tanaka?"

"You are clever, Detective," she said.

"You've lost me," Thor said. "What is this about why she cut her neck?"

"It's the flower," Murakami said. "*Kantsubaki* is an incredibly beautiful plant that blooms in the depths of winter, a time when everything else is already dead. When it dies, the petals don't turn brown or fall off one by one as with most flowers The head of the flower drops to the ground in one piece, petals fresh looking and attached. We Japanese love that image, of such immense beauty, perishing seemingly before its time."

"It was perfect, you know," Mrs. Tanaka said, as if describing a successful dinner party. "I'd just returned from *Mr. Dandy*—I don't remember why I was there—but I was sitting in the living room looking out at the garden when it struck me how similar the two were. The flower and Lisa. Two beautiful heads." Mrs. Tanaka snipped another branch. "I started to think about this woman and about my husband and all that money he was wasting on her. I had always been able to tolerate his other dalliances. Men will be men. But I could not stand by and watch while he gave away all of our money to that slut."

"How did you find out about the payments?" Thor asked.

"He began complaining about my shopping, something he never took much notice of before. When I asked him about it he just said business was down because of the weak economy. But he kept going out as he always had. I began to wonder.

"I looked through his books one evening while he was out. The fool! He just wrote "L" as if that could have any other meaning. I knew who Lisa was. All the other expenses and salaries had full names next to them. And there was "L" in the column for *Mr. Dandy* employees. The idiot. I asked him and he denied it, of course. One night I took a taxi, following him for hours. I saw them leave together and go to a hotel. I told him the next day I didn't think it wise of him to sleep with foreign women, what with the risk of AIDS and all. I have no wish to get AIDS. Do you know what he did? He just laughed and said not to worry because I was too old to sleep with anymore so I had nothing to worry about."

Mrs. Tanaka's hands were shaking as she put down her sheers and faced the detectives. "I'll have you know men still proposition me on occasion."

"Mrs. Tanaka—" Murakami said.

"She deserved to die. She deserved to die for taking my family's money simply because she was young and attractive and willing to sleep with my husband."

"Why did you send the first letter?" Murakami asked. "The one with the poem."

"Oh that," Mrs. Tanaka said. She breathed deeply, regaining control. "I don't know. With all my free time I sometimes get some rather silly ideas. I picked up this old book of poetry that's been in the house for years but I'd never looked at. This one entry caught my eye. Before I knew what I'd done, it was in the mail. After that, events seemed to carry themselves. Actually, the whole thing seems rather poetic to me. Don't you think?"

*

The story provided fodder for the media for almost two months.

The prosecutor meticulously painted a portrait of a distraught housewife, driven to murder by her loneliness. He explained, in inexorable detail, how she conceived her plan, enlisted the aid of Yuki Nishimura, and carried out her plan. While overtly sympathetic to her case, the prosecution made it clear that Mrs. Tanaka had been caught up by events.

Yuki Nishimura's treatment was not as charitable. She was a greedy tart who somehow preyed on Mrs. Tanaka's pain for personal gain. Nishimura herself had carried out the murder. She alone had profited monetarily. She had no prior conflict with the deceased. Lisa Madison's name and nationality were rarely mentioned during the trail. It was conjectured this was done to avoid promoting sympathy for the accused. The victim was, after all, just a foreigner, several foreign attendees at the trial were heard to remark.

The media suffered no such constraints. Snapshots of Lisa
Madison before her death ran daily with headlines such as
"Foreign Temptress Drives Wife To Kill" or "Hooker Breaks Up
Marriage—Pays Penalty." Not a hint of blame was laid at the
husband's feet. Morning shows scrambled to find Japanese-
speaking foreigners to provide insight into what caused Lisa
Madison to behave so wantonly. "Why was she interested in
Japanese men?" asked one TV announcer. The whole concept of
international marriages was raised and scrutinized. Could
Japanese men trust foreign wives? Even the more respected
papers couldn't resist postulating that the whole affair was a
symbol of the innate incompatibility of Americans and Japanese.

During testimony Mrs. Tanaka recounted how she got the idea
to kill Lisa Madison from looking at her garden. The part the
kantsubaki played as inspiration had housewives nodding tear-
fully in empathy.

Yuki Nishimura admitted renting a car from Kansai Rent-A-
Car, driving to *Mr. Dandy* and killing Lisa Madison with a garden
knife supplied by Mrs. Tanaka. After killing Lisa, Nishimura
decided, she said, to demolish the place to make it look like the
work of an irate customer. Police using metal detectors located the
knife in forty feet of water next to the airport bridge exactly where
Nishimura said it would be.

She had planned to drop off the car and return straight home.
Hitting the guardrail caused her to panic and she went to Kansai
International Airport instead. She just made the 3:29 flight to
Tokyo and reached the Hotel New Okawa at around 5:30, where
she had breakfast with Mrs. Tanaka. Upon the advice of Tanaka
she had stayed in Tokyo until later in the day.

The defendants' written confessions ensured a guilty verdict by
the three judges hearing the case, and unusually, for Japan, speedy
trial. Tanaka's defense lawyer made a perfunctory request for

leniency on the grounds that his client would never have instigated the crime had the foreigner, whom he termed a prostitute, not caused her temporary insanity. Mrs. Keiko Tanaka was eventually found guilty of conspiracy to commit murder and sentenced to twenty years in prison. Yuki Nishimura was found guilty of murder in the first degree and sentenced to life in prison.

The trial caused a strain in the relationship between Detective Thor and his fellow officers at the Toyonaka-North Precinct, including Murakami. Reporters called the station daily to get Thor's views and reaction to the unfolding events. Japanese do not like stars, illustrated by the maxim "The nail that sticks up will be hammered down." That Thor neither solicited nor enjoyed the celebrity was of no consequence. He was famous, and therefore, disliked. Thor tried to deflect as many of the questions as he could, suggesting they talk to his colleagues or stop calling altogether but to no avail. The chilly atmosphere of his early days turned to a deep freeze.

Detective Murakami was sympathetic, but not immune. He liked the American, admired him even. But as the trial drew to a close, the almost tangible pressure of hundreds of years of history to side with his colleagues, his countrymen, against the outsider, was almost too much to bear. He found himself begging off Thor's drink or dinner proposals, rendering halfhearted excuses of prior commitments or family obligations. His actions bothered him, but a recurring question plagued him: *What will you do after the American leaves?* In another few months Thor would be gone, but Murakami had to work with these same people for years, decades. If he strayed too far from the group center he might not be allowed back in.

Thor coped well, as far as Murakami could see. They both approached their work professionally. When Murakami begged off Thor's invitations, the American responded with a joke. "Hey, no problem. Leaves more girls for me" or a "Thank God! I didn't really want you along anyway." Still, Murakami wondered if it might be a front. Americans were hard to read.

On a Friday afternoon in early April, Thor walked to his partner's desk and sat down on one corner. "What do you say we have a beer after we're off in," he looked at his watch, "fifty minutes?"

"Gosh, I'd love to," Murakami said. "Got to finish up these reports." He held up a pile of papers. "You know how it is."

"How about later? I'll meet you somewhere?"

"Thanks. I've got other plans. Thanks for asking, though."

"New girlfriend?" Thor said.

"I wish." Murakami chuckled.

"Going out with some of the guys?"

"No." Murakami noted that Thor hadn't pushed it this much before. "There's a movie I really want to see tonight on Channel 4."

"Sounds fun. Which one?" Thor asked.

"What?"

"What's the name of the movie? Maybe I'll watch it myself."

"It's, uh," Murakami snapped his fingers a couple of times. "Damn, the title just slipped my mind. Some American action movie."

Thor pulled out a copy of the English *Daily Yomiuri* from his briefcase and opened to the TV listings. "Let's see. Nine o'clock? Channel 4, says, 'Japanese Movie: Yokiro'. Can't be that one."

Murakami pinched his nose between thumb and forefinger. "I guess it was another channel."

"Then let's check it out. Channel 6 has a Japanese soap opera, Channel 8 has a Samurai Drama and Channel 10 says, 'SMAP takes Manhattan.', Channel 19 has The Iron Chef, and Channel 36 has 'Novice Rice Farmers'. You sure it was tonight?"

Murakami looked at Thor. "OK. So what is your point?"

"Come on with me outside. I don't want to fuck up the perfect harmony in here." Thor strode for the door. Murakami gathered his case and coat, half wondering if Thor was planning to get violent.

Thor was outside pacing in the parking lot when Murakami caught up with him.

"You know what my point is. I feel like a girl who's been fucked on the first date and my boyfriend wakes up to find out I'm not so pretty after all. Only in my case my boyfriend was the entire National Police Agency. I served my purpose as pet *gaijin* and now you all just want me to hide in a box until my term runs out."

"No, Thor-san, it's not like that—"

"It's not?" Thor's eyebrows rose higher than Murakami had ever seen them. "There are cops in this precinct who don't even hear me when I speak. I'm serious. I speak and they don't answer unless you or Captain Kume are nearby. It's like Tanaka is coming in after hours giving them lessons. Others smile dumbly and nod at everything I say and then turn to their neighbor and start giggling as soon as I turn away. But that's cool. We've got assholes in the US too. I can put up with them. But I had this dumb idea you and I were—I know this will sound really wild to you—friends."

"We are, Thor-san—"

"Cut the 'Thor-san' bullshit, will you? I'm not hot for your body, I just thought you were different from the other *gaijin*-phobes around here. We *are* partners, right? At least on paper. Turns out you don't like foreigners any more than anyone else here, except you won't admit it. But I want to hear it from your mouth."

"Look, Thor-san," Murakami said in English, "I think you're overreacting."

"Overreacting? Am I imagining the looks, the laughing behind my back, the way nobody ever asks me for anything except the time so they can practice their English? I feel like a goddamn ghost."

"Not everyone. Yamamoto, he's not like that," Murakami said.

Thor massaged his temples. "No, you're right about Yamamoto. He's a standup guy."

"I think the other guys just don't want to bother you, that's all," Murakami said. "You're a pretty big name now and maybe they just feel asking you for help would be a burden on your time."

"A burden?" Thor said. "On my time? What else am I supposed to be doing here? Hell, it's my job. It's what I came here to do, to work with you guys, learn how you do things, further international fucking relations. I knew there would be some culture shock, some resistance, but not from the guys I worked with. Not the hate mail."

"What hate mail?"

"Notes. On my desk. 'Dirty Harry Go Home.' and 'We No Need Foreigner.'" Thor laughed sourly. "'US is Sucking Country.' I liked that one. The English is so bad in some I'm not even sure what they say."

Murakami ran his hand over the top of his hair. "You shouldn't take it personally. Don't you ever get any flack from the citizens of Minnesota?"

"These are from other cops."

"What?" Murakami looked incredulous, but suddenly remembered watching Thor pick up and read a note his first day. He remembered asking about it. When Thor said it was nothing, he thought no more about it.

"They're right on my desk when I get here in the morning, once, twice a week. No postmarks. Just open envelopes."

Murakami looked back at the entrance, wondering who the culprit, or culprits, were. He had a pretty good idea. "I didn't know that."

"Damn right you didn't."

"You never told me," Murakami said, weakly.

"What was the point? At first we were busy with the Madison case. I thought they'd get tired of it. Later I was, well, too embarrassed. It'd have been like running to Mom to make the big boys stop picking on me. 'Murakami! Murakami! Make them leave me alone!'"

"Thor-san," Murakami said. "Eric. I swear I..." He stopped. "All right. I guess I have been avoiding you some, but I didn't know things were so bad. You've got to understand the pressure I'm under, too. I live here after all, you don't."

"Yeah. I know." Thor looked squarely at Murakami, who looked back for a few seconds before turning away.

"It's nothing you've done wrong, I promise you."

"Isn't it?" Thor really wanted to know. "Did they think I *liked* talking to all those damn reporters? The phone calls here? At my apartment? Guys following me around?"

"This trial wasn't easy for any of us, Eric. Everyone I've spoken to knows you worked your ass off, and maybe that is part of the problem. We Japanese have a kind of inferiority complex when it comes to foreigners, especially Americans. You recouped and defeated us in W.W.II when our leaders told us you would fold after Pearl Harbor. You regularly best us in international sporting events and now even our cherished economy is broken just as yours seems to expand limitlessly.

All this despite your inferior educational system and high tolerance for guns and crime. Japanese are a logical people, dependent on empirical models to guide us in our behavior, and you Americans do not fit any of the models we have erected for you.

You just shouldn't be as successful as you are. It's maddening. And for us, more than for people of other countries, terrifying."

"My helping solve a murder mystery prayed on those fears," Thor said. "Is that what you are saying?"

"I doubt most of them have thought about it in such depth, but, yes, that is what they are thinking. It doesn't make sense that someone from a country so chaotic, so unharmonious, can come to Japan and work so methodically."

"I thought you just said Japanese have an inferiority complex about the States."

"I know. It doesn't make any sense, but that's Japan. We like to think we are better than foreigners but deep down have this nagging feeling that maybe we are not. You confirm our worst fears."

"What's the solution, Dr. Freud, do I slack off?" Thor asked. "Be the lazy, disorganized American of your precious stereotypes?"

"Of course not." Murakami stared off into nowhere. "Japanese do not change easily, Thor-san," now he looked directly at his American partner, "because our people rarely stand up to chastise others for boorish behavior unless such behavior directly affects the bottom line of a business. Insult a customer and your boss will castigate you. But smoke on a train, sit in a seat marked for senior citizens, or call foreigners names, and people are apt to turn a blind eye. Interfering in other people's business is not done. If no one in authority stands up publicly to condemn such behavior, there is no impetus to change."

"I see," Thor said. "You're saying that, even when someone's an asshole, he'll never change because no one is going to stand up and tell him he is an asshole."

"Definitely not."

Thor gazed at a palm tree wrapped snuggly in burlap for the winter, leaves and all. They both sat silently, meditating on some of life's immutable particulars. Finally, Thor stood. "Well, I've got to get over to my ward office before it closes."

"Trouble?"

Thor shook his head. "My Alien Registration Card. In all the confusion surrounding the Madison murder, I never got around to getting one. I've been here the whole time on a tourist visa."

"Isn't it past the deadline?"

"No. I've got ninety days from arrival so I'm still OK." Thor picked up his briefcase. "That'd be rich. 'Cop Without Visa Deported in Disgrace.'" Thor chuckled. "See you on Monday."

"Yeah."

Murakami watched the American head for the subway entrance. When Thor had reached a spot roughly in the center, Murakami made a decision and stood. He raised his voice loud enough to carry back into the precinct.

"Detective Thor?" Murakami called, in Japanese.

"Yes, Detective Murakami." Thor was tired.

"You know," Murakami said. "My father said that, after seeing you barf all over our bathroom your first week here, you Americans must be a bunch of weak-livered babies who can't hold their liquor."

"Is that so?" Thor said.

"Yeah. But I told him it wasn't true."

"Did you now?"

"Yeah. I told him I met lots of good drinkers when I was at Berkeley. That none of them got sick like you."

"Thanks."

A couple of cops had come to see what the shouting was all about.

"So my father said that perhaps your weakness was due to defective family genes. Or maybe because you're all related to baboons."

"What did you say to that?"

"I told him I didn't think so. I told him that I'd never been prouder to serve with an officer in my whole career and that you must have just had a bad day," Murakami said. His cheeks were red but his voice strong. "We all do sometimes."

Thor kept looking at Murakami.

"So," Murakami said. "I suggested we try it again and see what happens, tonight, at my house. About 7:00."

"You said that?"

"I might have," Murakami said, in English. "What do you say, you big hairy, chaotic baboon?"

"All right, you slanty-eyed bastard." Thor laughed. "You're on."

25

Eric Thor, American Detective, sat in the living room of Kennichi Murakami, Japanese Detective. Seinosuke Murakami, Father, *Salaryman* and Rabid Fan Of High School Baseball, was still bathing, having returned home late from work. Eiko Murakami, Mother and Champion Cook, was busy in the kitchen wondering if the American would be able to eat tonight's special, a hot egg custard containing fish paste, eel and Lily roots.

"Who was she, really?" Thor asked. He hoisted the bottle of Asahi Super Dry and looked at Murakami inquiringly.

"Thanks." Murakami downed his full glass and held it out for a refill. "Who was who?"

"Lisa Madison."

Murakami held his tiny beer glass like a teacup, with both hands, and looked down at the bottom. "A woman?"

"You're saying all women are that fucked up?" Thor said.

"You think she was fucked up?" Murakami said.

"Her mother said she was an airhead. Her ex-husband said she was a genius. And his nickname for her, Tsubaki-chan, comes from Kantsubaki, meaning Camellia, which just happens to have been Mrs. Tanaka's inspiration for murdering her."

"Definitely odd."

"Plus," Thor continued, "she was sleeping with her boss for money and dating a drug dealer. In her spare time she went to kabuki and the symphony and called a paraplegic friend in Kyoto on weekends. All this and she managed to raise an adorable little girl. That's normal?"

Murakami speared a scallop wrapped in bacon. "Maybe they were all one and the same, like Captain Kume said."

"I know we all have different, sometimes conflicting, characteristics, but wasn't she taking the concept a bit far?"

Murakami cocked his head to the left. "In my experience in Japan and the US, I have noticed one great similarity between our cultures," he said. "Beauty for a woman can be a burden."

"You mean because everyone assumes they are nymphomaniac airheads?"

"Yeah, at least in the States, but more than that. I believe that plain-looking people have an advantage over good-looking people in both countries because they are born as blank slates. Society expects nothing from them because nobody cares. People look at a Plain Jane or a...what do you call the male counterpart?"

Thor hunched his shoulders.

"Whatever. Average people have the luxury to decide for themselves what they want to become. I don't mean just career-wise, but personality wise, and hobby-wise, too. They can be outgoing or introspective, into the arts or sports or both, and no one is going to tell them, 'Hey, why aren't you class president or head cheerleader or a fashion model?' Their personality growth depends on many external factors, of course, but also on their own soul."

"Then people like Lisa are destined to be messed up because of their good looks."

"Well, not destined, maybe. But I would say their personality options are more limited in some ways. Especially for women so sexually attractive as Lisa Madison and especially if they also happen to have real brains. I know American men have a tradition of not respecting beautiful women. For Japanese, the limits come from other women. Women here *hate* attractive women."

"They do in the US, too."

Murakami shook his head. "Not like here. Japanese women, especially housewives, can't *abide* attractive women who are successful in intellectual, traditionally male, fields. It's more than simple envy. A few years ago there was a Japanese newscaster who graduated from Princeton and came back to Japan speaking perfect English. She put in her years of spot reporting, and finally landed an anchor spot on a morning show kind of like your *Today Show*. She was intelligent, articulate, a gifted interviewer. And drop-dead gorgeous. She lasted about a month before getting the hook."

"Nobody wanted to see a pretty woman reporter?"

"The show had great ratings. Too good, in fact. The few men who watch TV in the morning were all watching her. And housewives, the largest block of viewers, were tuning in every morning, waiting, hoping for her to mess up, to flub an interview or drop an eyelash. Anything! But she never missed a step. Women viewers were *livid*. How *dare* this woman succeed where they could never hope to? Where did she get off knowing so much more than they themselves did *and* looking like a Japanese Jane Clayson? At 7:00 AM? Why wasn't she home having babies like they were, putting up with an uncaring husband? They began calling the station, complaining about her clothes, her tone of voice, her manners, whatever they could think of, threatening boycotts and pickets if she wasn't canned. The station finally caved in and gave her the hook."

"Maybe she had an attitude. Off camera issues."

"No. None of the gossip magazines reported anything like that. She was fine."

"But she got fired."

"She got moved. Now she does a nightly business show where the men can drool and the women are washing dishes and don't have to see her face anymore. She does her job, her morning replacement is homely and innocuous and harmony is preserved."

"But Lisa didn't have the option of changing news shows, is that what you're saying?"

"Exactly. She grew up beautiful with a once-beautiful, single mother who had failed to break out of the social stereotypes imposed on her. Maybe Mrs. Madison couldn't, or didn't want, to see that Lisa had more depth then she herself had. Lisa hid her intelligence to preserve the peace."

"What about her ex-husband? Kimura." Thor said. "He knew how smart she was, and loved her for it, but their marriage failed anyway."

"Maybe she had gotten so used to playing the part of a dumb blond that she couldn't totally give it up. Or perhaps the pressure of Kimura's expectations frightened her. Suddenly here was this man who demanded the opposite of what others had always expected: a personality. A brain. Maybe she panicked. I don't know."

"Or maybe their marriage just died of natural causes."

"Maybe so," Murakami said. "In any case, I think the Lisa that each of them knew was real, in its own way. She responded to different people according to what they had to offer her. Halpern replaced the high school quarterback-type she probably dated at one time; Randall satisfied her intellectual needs on a part-time basis, replacing her ex-husband."

"And Tanaka? I can't think of anything attractive about him."

Murakami gulped his full glass and waited for more. "That's tougher," he said. "Maybe Tanaka was Lisa's safety net, her insurance policy if she couldn't make it on her own after all. Putting up with him was like paying monthly insurance premiums."

"More like receiving them in her case," Thor said. "How do you explain the payments?"

"I don't know. She wasn't breaking any laws. Would you turn down ten thousand legal dollars a month?"

"I would if I had to sleep with someone as fat and ugly at Tanaka," Thor said.

"Would you? I'd at least think about it."

"Then maybe Minoru Okada was her penance for the rest of her sins."

"Now we're getting into religion." Murakami motioned for Thor to fill his glass again.

"Makes me glad I'm not a woman." Thor bit into a dried rice cracker the consistency of slate, nearly breaking a tooth. "Lucky my manly good looks never interfered with my development."

"Intelligence was too low," Murakami said. "Your brain was too small to be affected one way or the other."

Mrs. Murakami called from the kitchen, "Dinner!"

"But Dad's still in the bath," Murakami called back.

"He can join us when he's ready," she said. "Now come along while it's hot."

"Let's go," Murakami said to his partner.

"Hold it a second. Did your father really say I was a genetically deficient baboon?"

Murakami laughed. "No. He loved your 'freedom American mind'—his words, not mine—and wants to hear all about your high school baseball days."

"I didn't play baseball in high school," Thor said.

"That's OK," Murakami said. *"Pretend.* Keep *yourself* talking and *him* drinking and we might make it through the night without you painting our toilet again."

"Fuck you." Thor picked up a couple of beer bottles. "Then who said I have bad genes and look like a baboon?"

Murakami just smiled.

"I always knew you Japanese were a bunch of racists."

"You foreigners *are* pretty hairy, you have to admit."

"Ujimushi yaroh!" Thor said.

"Your Japanese swearing is getting better, though."

Mrs. Murakami emerged from the kitchen with a stern look on her face. "Kennichi, you're going to make your partner sick again and he won't be able to eat all this good *chawamushi* I've made."

"C'mon, partner." Murakami said, pulling Thor towards the kitchen. "Let's see how things taste this time."

About the Author

Robert Imrie has written hundreds of articles for Japanese newspapers and magazines on business, history and international relations. His book *Japan Money Matters* (Business World Books, 1992), is a popular business and history primer for American and European expatriates in Japan. In 1999 Imrie accompanied Minnesota Governor Jesse Ventura on his trade mission to Tokyo and Osaka.

A graduate of Union College in New York and Kansai University of Foreign Studies in Osaka, Imrie now lives in Saint Louis Park, Minnesota with his wife, the pianist Reiko Imrie.

Visit *www.fallenflower.com* for more information about this book and its author.